Yrsa and the Zeffen Hunter

Yrsa and the Zeffen Hunter

Tales of a Melder 1

Alex J Markson

This paperback edition 2023

First published by Parignon Press 2023

Copyright © Alex J Markson 2023

Alex J Markson asserts the moral right to be identified as the author of this work in accordance with the Copyright, Designs and Patents Act 1988

ISBN: 979 8 85 261418 6

This novel is entirely a work of fiction. The names, characters and events portrayed in it are the work of the author's imagination. Any resemblance to actual persons, living or dead, is entirely coincidental.

All rights reserved. No parts of this publication may be reproduced, stored in a retrieval system, or transmitted in any form or by any means, electronic, mechanical, photocopying, recording or otherwise, without the prior permission of the publishers.

* * * * * *

Website: www.alexjmarkson.com

A full glossary for the series featuring characters, places and other invented terms can be found on my website.

A larger version of the map can be found on my website.

Content warnings for my books can be found on my website.

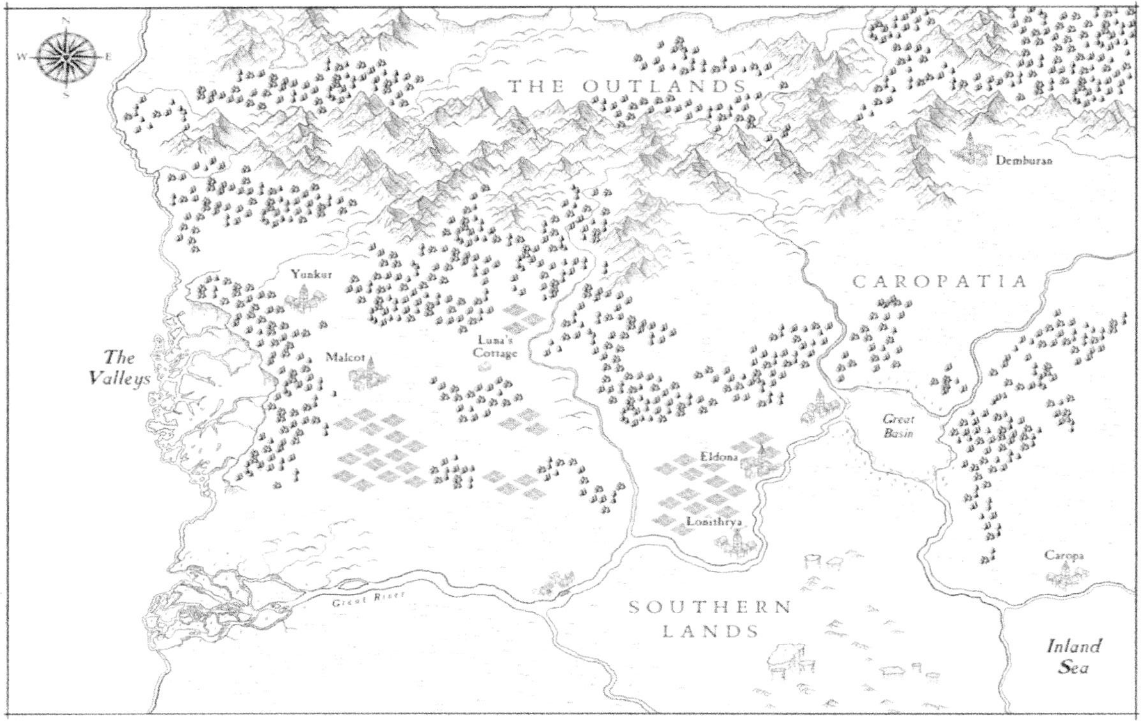

THE OUTLANDS
Demburan
CAROPATIA
Yunkur
Luna's Cottage
The Valleys
Malcot
Great Basin
Eldona
Lonithrya
Caropa
Great River
SOUTHERN LANDS
Inland Sea

Chapter 1

Snow had been falling through the night, but it was light and intermittent, the last breath of a hard winter. As Yrsa reached the brow of the hill above the village, the echoes of the last argument with her father were still floating in her head as she led her pony off the road towards the trees stretching out on either side. The road continued to Yunkur, but that wasn't her destination.

She stopped at the forest edge and looked out over the valley. It wasn't yet dawn, but the moonlight reflected off the snow-covered ground and the scene was surprisingly bright. Way below her, beyond the hill she'd climbed for a couple of hours, the settlement was clearly visible.

She could see all the houses she knew so well, the temple, the meeting house and, in the distance, the shimmering water in the bay. Nothing moved; everyone was asleep, waiting for the sun to rise and start their day.

Her pony shook its head and snorted, a cloud of steam appearing in the freezing air. Yrsa stepped nearer and stroked the mare's face.

"Well, Brimble," she said quietly. "That's the last time we'll see this view." The pony let out a gentle whinny and stamped a hoof.

"I know, you're cold. I am too, but we've got a fair walk before we find shelter. That'll warm us up."

She took one last look at her home and led her mare into the trees.

Yrsa had been planning her escape ever since she'd made the decision a few moons ago. The Valleys were not enough for her. She wanted more than a boring marriage to some older man. The voyages with her father as a girl had opened her eyes to the world outside. And after they'd stopped, much against her will, there was always something in the back of her mind encouraging her to leave.

Ando forced the decision. Ando. Another in a line of men her father had tried to marry her off to. He was a man of perhaps fifty, certainly twice her age, and a drunken idiot. Why would her father be so keen for her to marry him? He was wealthy. Her life would have been comfortable. That was what her father told her. He would not – or could not – understand her objections. They argued and argued, and Yrsa knew she had to get away before it was too late.

It hadn't been difficult to assemble everything she needed over the winter, as it all had to fit onto Brimble's broad back. But it had taken time to do it without giving herself away.

She hadn't planned to leave that night. But the argument with her father the previous evening had become more heated than usual, and she'd almost lost her composure when he'd brought her long-dead mother into the debate, trying to make her feel guilty. Asking her to marry Ando for her mother's sake, if not for his.

He'd never done that before, and she nearly said things she might have regretted later. She knew he would be hurt by her departure, but she didn't want to make it worse than it needed to be. So she kept her words to herself and decided it was time to go.

She'd paved the way for her escape over the previous weeks. It would have been easy to leave during daylight. People left the village all the time to go about their business. But when she didn't return, a host of them would have seen her, and been able to describe her heavily laden horse, where she was last seen, and which direction she was headed. That was no good. It would have to be at night. But that presented a problem.

The Valleys were peaceful now, had been for years. But the upper gates were still locked at night, and a watchman still sheltered in the old stone hut set to one side. Watchman was something of an exaggeration. The lads of the village took it in turns to spend the night in the hut. They were paid with some food and a flagon of ale to keep them warm. It was almost a rite of passage.

Yrsa had gathered information about the young men and when they were on duty. One – Ulrik – was a shy lad. Fit and strong, but somewhat friendless. She struck up conversation with him when they met in the village, and his bashful replies to her questions made her smile inwardly. He was perfect.

Knowing he was on duty one night, she slipped out of the house and made her way to the gate. Ulrik came out of the hut to see who was approaching.

"Yrsa," he stammered. "What are you doing here in the middle of the night?"

"I want to go through the gate."

He looked around, obviously at a loss as to what to do.

"But why?" he asked.

"To hunt."

"At this hour?"

"Oh, it will take time to get to the perfect place, and I want to be there before dawn."

"I'm not supposed to let anyone out."

Before he recovered his composure, she surprised him with a kiss and, even in the dark, she knew he was blushing. Pleased by this welcome turn of events, he opened the gate for her.

"Don't tell anyone," she whispered as she went through. "I'm preparing a surprise for my father."

Her words were true, in a way, and he looked around and nodded conspiratorially. She walked to the forest, spending a few hours resting in a small glade where she'd hidden a few coneys the day before. She made a point of dropping a couple off at Ulrik's house on her return, giving him a wink. She repeated the exercise three or four times, and he was hooked.

As Yrsa led Brimble through the sparse undergrowth, she smiled at the memory. As luck would have it, Ulrik had been on duty that night. Poor lad; he'd have some explaining to do when her father found out what had happened.

The reminder of her father brought an end to her amusement. She was sad to leave him, but his unthinking stubbornness left her with little choice. His idea of how her life would unfold differed too much from her own. She wanted to see the world. All he wanted was to see her married off and to a used husband at that.

The sun was climbing in the sky, its light penetrating the green canopy. She was within the managed area of the woods, where the undergrowth was regularly trimmed back, and trees cut for their wood. As they moved on, the going would get harder. She'd chosen to head away from the areas of the forest the village used regularly, and she didn't know them as well. She needed to find the path she'd scouted weeks before.

It snowed from time to time, but not enough to hinder their progress. When the sun was at its highest, she stopped by a stream to let Brimble rest and drink. Grabbing some sausage from her supplies, she sat on a fallen tree.

There was nothing like a little snow to suck all the sound from the world. There was no breeze. The flakes were falling straight down, floating so long in the air it appeared they were reluctant to join the others already covering the ground.

Normally, you'd hear the trees moving, their branches creaking in the wind. The undergrowth would be filled with delicate sounds;

animals and insects moving around, searching for food or a mate. But the snow hid it all. There was just silence.

"Right, girl," Yrsa said to Brimble, "let's go."

Their first destination was a hunter's cabin she knew well. They were dotted throughout the forest, commonly owned and maintained, and anyone could use them. If you visited in the good seasons, you chopped a few logs to leave behind for the use of those in winter or fixed anything that needed mending. In recent years, as the Valleys had prospered, fewer people hunted in winter, and some of the outlying cabins had fallen into disrepair.

She'd used them many times; at first with her father or brothers. As a child, she'd loved these trips. The hunting was exciting, and she proved to be good at it, soon exceeding her brothers' skills and matching her father's, although he would never admit it.

But she loved being in the forest, in the wild. There was a peace, a feeling of freedom, especially for a girl. She found herself drawn to something she couldn't define. A sense of belonging, something hidden she could feel but not see. Her father had shaken his head when she began to go alone, but he'd taught her well and didn't try to stop her. He knew she could look after herself.

The first cabin was an easy day's walk, even with the light snow, and they spent a comfortable, if cold, night there. In the following days, they travelled on, the snow coming and going, but never heavy, staying in cabins she'd used before.

But the fourth night found them in one she'd only located on her scouting trips in the autumn. It was clear it hadn't been used for some time; the Valley people didn't come this far anymore. Tomorrow, she would venture into unknown territory.

They set off at first light, everything covered in a white blanket and Yrsa worried she might not find the path she'd marked weeks earlier. But eventually, she came to a clearing and spotted three feathers sticking out from a tree trunk. Although the snow hid it, the path ran through this clearing.

It wasn't wide or level, but at first, it was easy to follow. As they went, the snow fell more heavily and a gentle breeze appeared, blowing the flakes into Yrsa's face. She pulled the hood of her cloak further forward and lowered her head, concentrating on the ground in front of her. Looking back to check on Brimble, the mare was stolidly following, her shaggy mane decorated with snowflakes. Every so often, she snorted and shook her head, sending a white shower to join the falling snow.

They followed the path for more than half the day but found nothing. The cabins were normally less than a day's walk apart, but she had no idea where the next one would be. If it existed at all. As the wind grew stronger, the snow swirled around, and the visibility dropped.

She stopped, deciding what to do. In this white-out, it would be easy to walk right past the cabin, even if it was only ten paces away. But it would be risky to try and build a shelter in the open, particularly with Brimble. So, she pushed on.

The snow was getting deeper and slowed her progress, each step becoming harder. She took the risk of leaving the path and walking under the tree cover, where the snow hadn't penetrated as much, but had to keep a close eye on the path to make sure she was still parallel to it.

Grabbing another piece of sausage from her bag, she ate as they walked. She needed a rest but there was no time. The sun was beginning to set, and the little light left was being smothered by the ever-increasing snowfall. If they didn't find the cabin soon, she'd have to contrive some sort of shelter.

Just as she was looking around for a suitable tree to lean a few branches against, she spotted a lighter area ahead of them among the trees. A clearing. As they drew nearer, a darker shape appeared to one side. The trees around them petered out, and they found themselves facing a squat structure made of stone and wood. A cabin.

Chapter 2

Yrsa led Brimble towards the sheltered side where the doors would be. The snow was now knee-deep, but finding the cabin gave her new energy, and as they turned the corner, they were free of the wind. The door was ajar.

She dropped the mare's reins and pulled the cloak from her head to look around, but the heavy snow reduced visibility and she could only see a few of the nearest trees. There were no footprints other than their own, but the snow would cover any evidence quickly.

"We may have company," she murmured to Brimble. "Or some fool's left the door open."

Opening her cloak, she checked the knife at her hip and moved slowly to the door before pushing it open. The cabins only had a small window, usually shuttered, and it was dark inside. The stale remnant of old fires clung to the planks and stones, but she picked up a fresher smell: the scent of recent horse dung.

Yrsa cautiously stepped over the threshold and checked quickly behind the door, as her eyes adapted to the dark, allowing her to see the whole space. Nothing. Her shoulders relaxed as she headed to the shuttered window, the wooden floor creaking with every step. Placing her hand on the locking bar, she gave it a shake. It felt firm and solid, although she could feel draughts forcing their way through several gaps in the frame.

Looking around, everything seemed in order, untouched. But her senses told her someone had been there, and the fireplace showed signs of a recent fire, the ashes still soft and loose. But whoever had been there was there no more, and she needed to settle in for the night.

Returning to the doorway, she laughed as Brimble came into view. The mare was standing where Yrsa had left her, but covered in a heavy dusting of snow, occasionally flicking her head to clear her eyelashes. Her eyes were focussed on Yrsa, who felt her pony wasn't thinking anything complimentary. Grabbing the reins, she walked Brimble to the second door, unlatched it and led her inside.

This end of the cabin was separated from the rest by a few wooden poles, with a bare earth floor. It wasn't ideal, and in summer, horses would have been left outside. But not tonight.

Yrsa removed the panniers, laid them over the poles, and undid the harness. When she was free, Brimble shook herself briskly, covering Yrsa in a shower of wet snow.

"Cheeky," she said to her horse, patting her rump. The smell of horse dung was stronger here, though she could see none in the dim light.

Stepping up to the wooden floor, she carried the bags to the table and reached for some kindling. A fire was the first need. If it hadn't been snowing, she wouldn't have risked it, but the smoke would be lost in the storm. One end of the cabin was built of stone to allow a wide chimney, beneath which was a large, open fireplace. Grabbing some of the wood stacked against one wall, she was glad to find it dry and soon had a fire going. Now to take care of Brimble.

There were always cooking pots in the cabins. Those she found were old and battered, but when she picked up the largest, its base was still wet from recent use. Filling it with snow, she put it by the fire to melt, the first of many to fill the water trough in the pen. Food was going to be more difficult. She had a sack of oats with her, and poured some into the feed trough. While Brimble munched on them, she brushed her down, the horse's warmth beginning to draw the cold from her own body.

After caring for her horse, she cleared the snow at the entrance, closed and barred the doors, and finally sat down. The fire was burning well, and warmth began to reclaim the cold cabin. She removed her cloak and hung it near the fire to dry.

Finding anything to cook was out of the question tonight, so she retrieved some bread, sausage, and cheese from the baggage. Boiling water allowed her to make a hot drink flavoured with herbs and dried fruit, a concoction her stepmother had taught her.

Fed and watered – and a lot warmer – they settled down for the evening. Yrsa sat on the bench nearest the fire, took out her pipe and filled it with leaf and a generous sprinkle of temkin, another pleasure learned from her father's wife. As she inhaled the heady mixture, her tired body relaxed, and she felt comfortable for the first time that day. The snowstorm was raging outside, and the cabin was creaking and moving, but they were safe. It was going to be a long night.

* * *

It turned out to be a long night, a long day, and another long night. The storm was unusual this late in the winter, and there was nothing to do but sit it out. On the first morning, Yrsa pushed Brimble outside, hoping the mare would empty herself there, but she was having none of it. She stood by the door and refused to go any further. As soon as she was back in the pen, she let go and watched Yrsa blankly while she shovelled it all away.

"Monster," Yrsa called her. In the morning light, she was able to see traces of fresh dung left on the shovel. Someone had stayed in the cabin no more than a few days ago.

On the second morning, they woke to silence. Complete silence. Not a sound, except Brimble's gentle movements. The storm had blown itself out. She unbarred the shutters, and pulled one open, to be met by a wall of snow halfway up the window. Her heart sank. There was no way they were leaving anytime soon.

Outside the door, the snow was two or three feet deep, and that was the sheltered side of the cabin. Making her way to the corner, she looked out over a white world. The snow had drifted into astounding shapes, covering bushes and trees, as if sculpted by some unseen hand. The Gods had been enjoying themselves.

She'd have to wait and hope the snow thawed quickly. They were stuck for now, and her food would soon run out. She'd packed enough dry goods for a few days, thinking she could easily restock in any town or village they passed. But the storm would force her to use it up quickly. Besides, it was boring.

"Time to hunt," Yrsa said to no one in particular, though Brimble was watching her. "I won't be long."

She spent the morning trudging through the snow, looking for spots the storm had been unable to reach, and placed a few snare traps, hoping some unsuspecting creature would brave the cold looking for food. It seemed unlikely, but it was worth trying. She could do with something hot.

The enforced stop was frustrating. Yrsa's plan had been stalled after a few days, but if she couldn't move, nor could anyone else. Nobody would be coming to look for her in this weather. She'd made sure she'd gone on a few longer hunting trips recently. Two, three, four days. Her father didn't like it, but he mumbled and said no more. This would seem no different, and he knew she'd find shelter from the storm. It would be a while before he worked out she wasn't coming home this time.

The snow hadn't thawed much by the next morning. The sharp edges of some of the drifts had softened, but it was still a long way from passable. Yrsa set out to check her traps. Nothing in the first, but a rabbit in the second, dead and frozen stiff. The pot would soften it up.

The little hollow where she'd left the last snare was covered in a few inches of snow, with the trap to one side where the edge of some bushes was still exposed. The trap was sprung, with a leg in it. Just a leg. The leg of a small wild pig. But Yrsa wasn't looking at that. It was the prints in the snow around the trap which sent a chill through her. Her eyes widened and she cautiously looked around, scanning the trees, before bending to take a closer look.

She'd seen similar prints before. Many people in the Valleys had a dog or two. But no dog had paws that large. Even allowing for thawing around the edges, these prints were huge. She shivered and looked around again, half-expecting some hunger-crazed monster to be bearing down on her.

"Fool," she muttered to herself and turned back to the prints. They came into the hollow from the other end of the clearing, beyond the cabin, and were all mixed up around the trap. Then, whatever had stolen her dinner had set off towards the cabin again. Removing the leg from the trap, she reset it and cautiously followed the tracks.

She wished she'd brought her bow from the cabin, but hadn't dreamt of anything moving in this weather. Anyway, judging by the size of the prints, she wasn't sure her compact bow would have been much help. One of her arrows would have been unlikely to bring down an animal of this size, except at very close range. And she didn't fancy getting that close. The tracks led past the cabin, disappearing into the forest. Yrsa didn't follow them.

As she pulled apart the roasted rabbit hours later, enjoying its warmth and rich taste, she pondered the tracks. They were certainly dog-like, but far too big for any domestic animal. The pig must have been alive when it was taken, as there had been a lot of blood on the frozen ground. Whatever it was had the strength to kill the pig and sever its leg to free its prize.

She wondered about wolves. She'd never seen one as they'd been wiped out in this area long ago, and common opinion was they only survived far to the east and north. Even her father had never seen one. And this seemed to be a lone animal; wolves hunted in packs, as far as she knew. She had no answer to the riddle.

* * *

The snow hung around for several days. Yrsa was comfortable in the cabin and determined not to move until she could be sure the way forward was passable. Her traps supplied more game as the forest dwellers were forced out to look for food, and she ate well. Even Brimble was persuaded to leave her pen, though Yrsa could only clear a small area of rough grass for her.

As the light grew dim one afternoon and the cold began to bite again, Brimble took herself indoors, and Yrsa prepared to shut the world out for another night. As she did so, she heard a gentle whinny. So did Brimble, who gave a little snort in reply. Yrsa stepped outside the door and turned the corner to find a visitor.

"Room for another traveller, girl," he said. It was a statement rather than a question. "At least I won't have to start the fire from scratch."

The visitor slid gracefully from the largest horse Yrsa had ever seen. A huge black animal which was watching her closely, its head tilted slightly to one side. The man stretched carefully, loosening his arms and shoulders before curling and uncurling his fingers.

He tenderly stroked the horse's neck, whispering something which Yrsa couldn't hear, before leading it towards the stable door. As they disappeared inside, she heard a brief greeting between the horses.

"Any chance of more water, girl?" the man called out. Yrsa bristled at the word but decided to let it pass for the moment, and filled a pot with snow before putting it by the fire. As it melted, she watched the man put his saddlebag on the floor before removing a small crossbow and sheathed sword from his horse's caparison and placing them carefully on top. The caparison itself came off and was folded neatly to one side, with the saddle balanced on it.

He turned to Yrsa with a querying look, and she checked the water had melted before carrying it to the trough and pouring it in. The huge horse drank it almost before she'd emptied the pot, making her frown, but the animal raised its head and nuzzled her, its lips still wet.

"That will do for now," the man said as she wiped her face. "I'll get her more in a while."

The horse was watching her again, and Yrsa returned its gaze. The darkness was beginning to take hold, and she couldn't see the animal very well, but his words had surprised her. Given its size, she'd assumed it would be a stallion, but it was a mare. And it was still watching her.

Yrsa had never been unnerved by a horse before, but something made her give this one a brief stroke and move away to the other end of the cabin. She sat on the bench and watched the visitor groom his mount, muttering to her occasionally, though again, Yrsa was unable to hear what he was saying. At one point, Yrsa laughed when Brimble appeared almost underneath her new stablemate, so different were they in size.

"There, girl," the man finally said quietly. "That will do for tonight." He put his brush carefully in his saddlebag before slinging it over his shoulder. "Is there any chance of something hot?" he asked as he approached the fire. "Do not be afraid to say no."

"There is enough," Yrsa replied. "Help yourself."

He picked up a bowl, ladled some of the stew out, and sat on the opposite bench, bringing a metal spoon from his bag, and tasting it.

"That is welcome," he said.

As he ate, Yrsa studied him. A man of around fifty years, tall and broad-shouldered, though thin. His hair was greying and cut short, his clothes had once been rich and elegant, though now they were worn and even a little threadbare in places. The only weapons he wore were two curved daggers on a belt at his waist. Their intricate scabbards seemed out of place against the rest of his rather drab appearance. He knew she was watching him, but said nothing.

"There is plenty," she said as he finished and put the bowl down.

"That is enough for now," he replied. "The more one eats, the slower one gets."

"I'm Yrsa."

"Amluss."

It was clear he was not here for conversation, so she didn't push it and went to groom Brimble.

"Your horse is magnificent," she said as she squeezed past it to get to her pony. "What's she called?"

"Tennell."

"Where's she from? I've never seen her like."

"A long way from here."

Once more, Yrsa gave up trying to make conversation. As she brushed Brimble, she looked carefully at Tennell. Even in the dull light, she could see the animal had the sleek lines of fine breeding but was thin and tired. She recognised a weary horse when she saw one.

As they sat either side of the fire later in the evening, the man's eyes closed, and Yrsa wondered if he was asleep. He certainly wasn't talkative.

"Where did you come from today?" she asked quietly. "Is the track passable?"

"We left Yunkur two days ago," he replied without opening his eyes. "Tennell can pass with care, but you couldn't on foot. Nor could your pony. Still too deep for either of you. Perhaps the day after tomorrow."

"Where did you stay last night?"

"Under a tree."

"It must have been bitterly cold," Yrsa said, surprised.

"You get used to it, at least for a night or two."

She had a sudden thought.

"Did you know this cabin was here?" she asked.

"Yes."

"You stayed in it on your way to Yunkur?"

"Clever girl."

Yrsa bit her tongue. Something about this man told her not to pick a fight.

"What were you doing in Yunkur?" she asked as casually as she could.

"Asking questions," he replied, finally looking at her. "Which is a trait we seem to share."

"Just curious."

"I'll take up your offer of some more stew," he said and filled his bowl. "You trapped the meat?"

"Yes, though I'm not the only hunter in these woods."

"What makes you say that?" He stopped eating and studied her as she spoke.

"One day, there was just a leg left in the trap."

"What happened to the rest?"

"Something had stolen it."

He slowly put the bowl and spoon down.

"Tell me what happened."

Amluss made her tell him the whole story, and went over it a couple of times, checking and double-checking everything she could remember.

"Why are you interested?" she asked.

"Tomorrow, you can show me the trap," he replied, ignoring her question.

"There will be nothing there."

"I still want to see it."

The next morning, Yrsa showed Amluss the small clearing where the trap was. The snow had melted and there were no paw prints left, but he made her show him what they were like, and how large they were. He seemed fascinated by her story.

"Was it a wolf?" she asked.

"No," he replied slowly, looking around the forest. "There have been no wolves here for generations."

"Then what was it?"

"I can't say, but I have my suspicions."

"You're being very secretive."

"I have learned to keep my intentions to myself," Amluss replied. "My life would have been different if I had learnt that lesson a little earlier."

He turned and strode towards the cabin, Yrsa struggling to keep up.

"Sounds like quite a story," she said.

"But not a story for you, or for today. I must go."

He prepared Tennell and led her out of the stable.

"Where are you headed?" Yrsa asked.

"Somewhere where they ask fewer questions," he replied.

"Just curious," Yrsa said, giving Tennell's head a stroke as Amluss mounted. The mare turned and confidently picked her way through the snow to the track, and headed south.

Chapter 3

Yrsa knew Amluss was right. She'd have to wait at least another day before trying to force her way through the snow. So she uncovered some more grass for Brimble to graze and leaned against the cabin, watching her and smoking her pipe.

She didn't have the advantage of a horse like Tennell. But she gave a silent prayer for bringing Brimble. She could have brought Gusta. He was stronger than Brimble, younger, much faster and she could have ridden him. But he was also fidgety, cranky, a fussy eater and didn't like carrying baggage. She shook her head, imagining him being trapped in the cabin for five or six days. It would have driven him mad, and her with him.

No, Brimble had been the right choice. She hated being ridden, always had, tended to stubbornness, and had just one speed. But she could walk at that speed all day, with a heavy load strapped to her back, never complaining. She was the perfect companion for this journey. Besides, she had been Yrsa's first horse, and they had a special bond.

An unexpected sound made Brimble look up; Yrsa heard it, too. An image of some growling monster with huge claws flashed through her mind. But they were human sounds, the noise of someone trudging through snow and muttering to themselves, and they were getting closer. Another visitor to this isolated cabin in the forest.

Yrsa checked the knife on her belt as Brimble gave a little shimmy and whinnied, obviously able to see the visitor, but Yrsa was still hidden from view.

"Well, by all the Gods," a man's voice said, echoing off the snow in the clearing. "Where on earth did you spring from?"

The sound of feet on snow resumed, and moments later a man appeared heading for Brimble. He was dressed well for the weather, invisible in furs, a heavy hood covering his head, and a staff in his hand.

Brimble was always friendly, and as he reached her, she sniffed the hand exposed as he took a glove off, before letting him pet her neck.

"Who do you belong to, I wonder?" he said.

"She's mine," Yrsa replied.

The man spun around, and the dark hood looked at her for a few moments before being pulled back to expose its occupant. A handsome man, a little over thirty years, with a blond ponytail and beard.

"And who might you be?" he asked.

"Yrsa, and that's Brimble."

"Brimble. It suits her."

"We think so."

The man studied Yrsa as he stroked Brimble's neck.

"Who are you?" Yrsa asked when it was clear the man wasn't volunteering his name.

"Tosteg," he replied. "But everyone calls me Steg."

"Have you travelled far through this?"

"From Yunkur."

"Tough going?"

"Yes, but the snow's clearing."

"Where are you going?"
"You ask a lot of questions."
"I like to know who I'm dealing with," Yrsa said. "One visitor left this morning and now another turns up out of nowhere."
"Man on a black horse? He passed me yesterday. But I hardly came out of nowhere. I use this track often."
"Why?"
"To get to the market in Yunkur."
"From where?"
"I've answered enough of your questions for the moment. Now I have one." He looked up at the smoke coming from the chimney. "May I warm up by your fire?"
"It's not my cabin, anyone can use it."
Steg walked over, noting the knife at Yrsa's waist as she stood.
"I know," he replied, "but I thought it best to ask."

Yrsa let him go in and followed moments later. He'd removed his outer layers and was standing in front of the fire, rubbing his hands.
"Something smells good," he said.
"Help yourself," she replied, pointing to the pot warming on the edge of the fire. He found a bowl and ladled some of the contents into it. Taking a wooden spoon from the small bag he carried, he took a mouthful.
"This is good. You carried the meat with you?"
"We're in a forest," she replied, dismissively.
"You caught it?"
"Of course."
He fell silent as he ate the stew, clearly hungry. Yrsa had settled herself on one of the benches against the wall, and they studied each other as he filled his belly. Yrsa nodded when he gestured for more.
"Where are you from?" she asked.
"I have a farm near Malcot. Know it?"

"No," she replied. "Heard of it, though."

"And you, Yrsa. Where are you from? What brought you here?"

"I'm travelling. Found myself here when the storm set in."

"You've been here for a while, then?"

"Six days now."

"Well, you've made it cosy. I've passed this cabin many times but never set foot inside. I don't think I can remember ever seeing anyone here, and now I find you and hear of another visitor as well. Who was he, by the way?"

"Gave me his name and not much else. Why were you in Yunkur?"

"I wanted a few yearling pigs to fatten."

"Obviously didn't find any."

"That's where you're wrong. I bought six, but the snow's too deep to take them home, so they're keeping them for me. I'll go back when the track is clearer."

"Why not stay in Yunkur?"

"Need to get home to my family, it'll be hard for them without me in this weather. I've been away seven days as it is, and I should have been back in three."

"Will you reach home tonight?"

"It doesn't look like it now."

"There's plenty of room here if you don't mind sharing it with me and Brimble."

"Not sure I want to share Brimble's bed," he replied, with a cheeky grin.

"I'm going to check my traps before it gets dark," Yrsa said. "Brimble will keep you company."

"I'll come with you," Steg replied.

"There's no need."

"I'm interested, that's all. I'm no hunter."

She threw her cloak over her shoulders and waited for him to cover up again before they headed for the first of the traps. After the mysterious paw prints, she'd moved them closer to the cabin, but there had been no sign of the visitor returning.

"Who taught you to hunt?" Steg asked.

"My father."

"I didn't know Valley people hunted."

"What makes you think I'm from the Valleys?"

"A wild guess," he replied. "Seems I was right."

Yrsa was frustrated her identity was so obvious, but not surprised. She was still too near home.

The first two traps were empty, but the third yielded a nice coney. It was still alive, and she snapped its neck to end its misery. As they approached the last, the prize announced itself. They heard a pathetic squealing and found a young wild pig, its leg held tight.

It was bleeding and exhausted from its frantic efforts to escape. Steg watched in amusement as Yrsa took her knife, straddled the animal, pressing it to the ground and slit its throat. She held it until the gush of blood died down, then freed it from the wire.

"You've done that before," Steg said.

"A few times," she replied. "Are you going to be helpful and carry it?"

"If I get some roast pork in return."

When they got back to the cabin, Steg dropped the pig to the ground.

"I'll butcher it for you," he said. "That's one thing I can do. But I'll need to borrow a knife."

Yrsa hesitated. This man claimed to be a farmer, but was he? If she gave him her knife, she was giving him a weapon. He saw her doubt.

"I can think of several things I'd like to do to you, girl," he said. "But slaying or robbing you aren't among them."

She took the knife from its sheath and handed him the hilt. He took it and examined it closely.

"I've never seen anything like this," he said. "It's more like a smallsword, but it's not from the Valleys ... or anywhere around here."

"It still cuts," she replied.

He shrugged at the evasive response, squatted by the pig, and began his work. It was quickly in pieces.

"That's some blade," he said, passing it back to her after cleaning it in the snow. "Whoever made it knew what they were doing."

Yrsa said nothing but drew out a small cloth, carefully finished cleaning it and replaced it in the sheath.

"Are we cooking it all?" Steg asked.

"No," she replied. "I need to move on, and in this weather, it's better to carry it raw than cooked. I'm keeping the coney as well."

They chose a hind leg with plenty of rump attached, and stuck it on a spit over the fire, along with some belly for cold, putting the rest in a pile of clean snow near the door. The light was fading fast. Brimble had already taken herself into the pen, and Yrsa and Steg went inside and barred both doors.

She made a couple of beakers of the herb infusion and offered him one. He smelled it suspiciously.

"I can think of one or two things I'd like to do to you," she said. "But poisoning you isn't one of them."

He laughed; a deep, relaxed laugh, bringing a smile to her face. He raised the beaker in her direction and took a sip. Then another.

"This is good," he said. "What is it?"

"Herbs and dried fruit."

"It certainly warms you."

They settled on benches around the walls, facing the fire, the roasting pork already filling the room with its enticing aroma. Yrsa took a small whetstone from her bag and carefully ran her knife's edges over it. Then she took a few drops of oil from a flask, rubbing them onto the steel, before holding it in the fire briefly, causing it to fizz and burn off. After polishing it with a cloth, she put it back in the sheath.

"How often do you do that?" Steg asked.

"Whenever it's been used by an unfamiliar hand," Yrsa replied.

"Want to tell me where you're going?"

"Not really."

"Come on, girl. I'm not a threat. Perhaps I should be afraid of you."

"You should if you carry on calling me girl."

"I'm sorry," he said, raising his hands, "wrong word. Woman? Hunter? Warrior?"

"Yrsa will do," she replied.

"Yrsa, then," he said. "Where are you going from here?"

"Why do you want to know?"

"Why don't you want to tell me?"

"Because I'm not sure, to tell the truth."

"Running away?"

"Seeking something."

"What?"

"I'll know when I find it."

The pork was good. Yrsa's remaining bread was hard and dry, but the pork fat softened it, and their conversation lulled as they ate. There was little left but bones when they sat back, full and satisfied. Yrsa took out her pipe, filled it with leaf and lit it.

"Do all Valley women smoke?" Steg asked.

"I picked it up from my stepmother."

"I haven't smoked in years; good leaf is expensive."

"Want some?" she asked. "I have a spare pipe or two."

She retrieved one from her baggage, filled it and handed it to Steg, who lit it from a taper by the fire. At the first draw, he coughed a couple of times, bringing a laugh from Yrsa.

"Men!" she said.

The aroma of leaf filled the cabin as they enjoyed its taste.

"Is your farm large?" Yrsa asked.

"We've done well the last few years," he replied. "I've taken on more land, and there's always work to do."

"Big family, too?"

"I've ten children," he replied, and she noticed that cheeky grin on his face.

"Gods, I feel sorry for your wife."

"You're assuming she's mother to all of them."

It was Yrsa's turn to choke on her pipe, as she burst into a fit of coughing and laughing.

"I see," she finally replied. "Free with your seed, are you?"

"I've been happy to give it to anyone who wants it."

"I'm sure you have."

She tapped her pipe out on the fireplace, refilled it, and added a little powder.

"What's that?" Steg asked.

"Temkin," she replied. "It's a mushroom. You can eat it when it's fresh, but if you dry and powder it, it's rather good."

"What does it do?"

"Makes you feel relaxed. Want some?" He eyed her suspiciously again. "Come on, surely the local stallion isn't scared of a girl?"

He nodded gently, and she took his pipe, refreshing the leaf, and adding a small sprinkle of temkin.

"I've only added a little," she said. "The first draw might make you dizzy, but it only lasts a few breaths, then you'll feel mellow."

She returned the pipe, and he cautiously drew on it. A few moments later, he let out a strange grunt, his eyes widened, and he took a few deep breaths.

"I see what you mean," he croaked.

"Just relax."

Silence fell again as they concentrated on the task. Time passed as they puffed on their pipes, Steg refilling his, and adding a little more temkin. Yrsa watched in amusement. If you weren't used to it, the results could be interesting.

She felt more positive than at any time since arriving at the cabin. The snow was thawing fast, and she hoped to move on the next day. She had meat to take with her, the cabin was warm and cosy, and Steg had turned up to give her some much-needed company and conversation. Amluss had been company, but hardly talkative.

"Does your wife know about all your children?" she asked.

"Most of them. There are a couple whose mothers wouldn't want their husbands to know they aren't the father."

"I see."

"They're from before we were married."

"So, you don't stray from home anymore."

"I didn't say that."

"In Yunkur, perhaps?"

"Possibly."

Yrsa briefly considered finding out just how easily Steg would stray but decided against it. Tomorrow she'd be moving on and would need her strength and wits. So they spent the evening companionably by the fire until the dark and the temkin lulled them to sleep.

Chapter 4

Brimble stood patiently while Yrsa loaded her with the panniers, the remaining oats, and the meat recovered from the snow. Yrsa had accepted Steg's invitation to walk with him towards his home, though she warned him Brimble set her own pace and wouldn't be hurried.

"You could go to Yunkur," he'd suggested. "You'll be able to replenish your supplies easily there."

But it was one of the few inland towns regularly visited by Valley people, and she risked being seen. So, after they latched the cabin door, they headed south. The snow still lay around in drifts, but the path had largely cleared, and the walking was easy.

"How did you know I was from the Valleys?" Yrsa asked.

"Your clothes," Steg replied. "The cloak could be from almost anywhere, but the colours of your tunic and trousers I've seen in Yunkur on Valley people. They're not dyes common inland. If you want to blend in, you need to get some new clothes. And you and Brimble are too clean. You haven't been travelling for weeks on end."

Yrsa pondered his observations as they walked. She'd been to sea many times with her father and visited many trading ports. The variety of cultures they attracted had been obvious there. It was what had excited and enthralled her. But she hadn't thought how even small, local differences were noticeable, particularly to those who had never left their home village.

They stopped at midday and ate some of the belly pork.

"Tell me about Malcot," Yrsa said.

"It's fair enough," Steg replied. "Though it can be rough. It's on the Norsouth road, so caters to people passing through."

"How far is it?"

"It's a good day's walk from the farm."

"Why do you go to Yunkur and not Malcot?"

"There isn't a market in Malcot. I go in a few times a year, but Yunkur is altogether calmer."

"Trying to put me off?"

"No. But if you go to Malcot, go in, get what you need and head out as soon as you can. A single girl – sorry, woman – in Malcot may attract the wrong sort of attention."

"I can look after myself."

Steg turned to her.

"Yrsa, I believe you believe that, and you're no fool. But people die in Malcot, a throat slit here, a knife in the back there. And not just Malcot. When you travel, you put yourself at risk, and a lone woman more so. I don't know where you're going or why, but think carefully at every move. You'll come across people far less friendly than me."

They moved on, Yrsa deep in thought. He was right, she wasn't a fool, and had learnt to deal with the lads she grew up around. She could equal some of them in strength, many of them in agility, and almost all of them in brains. But ultimately, the Valleys were safe places. She couldn't remember the last time anyone had been murdered, though one or two died in drunken brawls.

The weather was clear and bright, though cold, and they walked at Brimble's pace. The snow hardly hindered them, but in a couple of places, they had to clear a way through. Yrsa was grateful for Steg's presence as his strength speeded their efforts. After forcing a particularly deep drift, they sat and rested on the other side.

"You need a staff," Steg said.

"I've never needed one before."

"They're a versatile tool," he replied. "You can rest on them, poke things with them and they're a useful weapon." He held his own up. "This can give someone a nasty pain in the balls." She frowned. "Yrsa, if someone attacks you, don't think of playing fair. Most men, even the big ones, will go down if you ram this between their legs. Here, give me your knife."

She hesitated for a moment, before handing it over, and Steg disappeared into the trees. It was some time before he returned with two branches.

"Stand up."

He held the branches by her and placed her hand on each in turn. Throwing one into the forest, he took the other and smoothed the sides. By the time he finished, it looked like a staff, with a thicker gnarl at the top.

"There you go," he said, handing it to her. "A good prodding point at the bottom, a fine cosh at the top." While he cleaned her knife, she took the staff and weighed it in her hand. "It'll feel heavy and awkward at first. The weight will drop as the wood dries out. You'll soon get used to it. Time to move on."

The path was still narrow, and they had to walk in single file. Yrsa wondered when she should say farewell to Steg and look for somewhere to spend the night. She wouldn't make Malcot today, so needed to find shelter.

"Are there any hunter's cabins around here?" she asked.

"You won't find any more. Few hunt here now, and only close to home."

"Is there a clear road to Malcot?"

"There's a well-worn track about half a league from the farm. You can set out in the morning."

"I need somewhere to shelter."

"You can stay with us; my wife won't mind. Tove welcomes everyone."

The settlement, when it appeared, wasn't vastly different from those in the Valleys. A few homes with stone foundations, wooden walls and thatched roofs dotted around, simple wooden fences marking out the separate steadings. They walked past the first homes, finally turning towards the last one. Yrsa realised Steg hadn't been lying. Beside the house was a second building, almost as large and not very old. He had been doing well.

Two children, a boy and a girl around seven or eight, came running from the door of this second building, heading for Steg. He scooped them up in his arms and headed for the house.

"Ulf!" he called out, and moments later, a lad of perhaps twelve or thirteen came from the barn. "Ulf, take this horse and make her comfortable in the barn. Her name's Brimble."

"Yes, Father," the boy replied, and as he took the reins from Yrsa, she went to unload her mare.

"Leave it," Steg said. "Ulf will unpack her."

Yrsa followed Steg towards the house. A figure appeared at the doorway, and she got a shock. She wasn't sure what she expected Steg's wife to look like, but the woman in front of her was one of the most beautiful she'd ever seen. Tall, with long blond hair framing a perfect face, and a figure that belied however many of Steg's children she'd actually given birth to.

She came forward and greeted her husband warmly, before casting her gaze on Yrsa.

"And who is this?" she asked.

"Tove, this is Yrsa," he replied, "and she provided me with shelter and food last night."

"Then we will do the same. Welcome, Yrsa. Come in from the cold."

Tove filled beakers of ale and Steg told her about Yunkur, the pigs and the cabin. A variety of children came and went. Six, as far as Yrsa could tell, but only the younger two showed any interest in their visitor. Ulf brought her baggage into the house and went off with his father to check the farm before the light faded.

Yrsa was left alone with Tove, who was preparing a meal.

"If you slept with my husband," Tove suddenly said, "don't feel embarrassed. I know his appetites more than anyone."

"I ... no ... we didn't," Yrsa stammered, surprised by her host's words. "You ... wouldn't mind?"

"He's a man, isn't he?" she replied with a wry shrug. "They can't help themselves. As long as he keeps me happy, he can stray once in a while. Did he tell you about his other children?"

"He did mention them, yes."

"So, you see, he's an honest man. He tells me everything, so I'd have heard all about it."

Yrsa wasn't sure she liked that idea but saw Tove's point. It was a pragmatic view.

"Where are you headed?" Tove asked.

"Malcot from here, I think."

Yrsa knew her journey would prompt questions. A man travelling alone would sometimes be challenged by suspicious locals. A woman doing the same would provoke even more curiosity. She'd have to prepare some believable answers to such questions. Thankfully, Tove didn't pursue the matter, and when Steg returned, the family assembled for their meal.

Afterwards, the children settled around their father who told them a story. It was one Yrsa hadn't heard before, but they'd probably heard it many times. Even so, they listened in rapt silence. It reminded her of her childhood, listening to the tales told by her father and grandfather.

They were what first opened her eyes to the world beyond her village and filled her with a desire to see the places and people who populated them. Her father's uncle in particular had endless stories to tell.

He'd left the Valleys as a young man, deserting his family. When he returned almost thirty years later, few believed the tales he told of his adventures, but Yrsa listened and took it all in, wishing she could follow in his footsteps.

The children gradually took themselves to one end of the house, where a raised platform covered in furs served as their communal sleeping place. Ulf wished them goodnight and went out through the door.

"He's nearly a man," Steg said, "or thinks he is. He's taken to sleeping in the barn."

This brought a chuckle from Tove.

"He's frozen out there," she said. "But too proud to come back in."

The three adults settled themselves by the fire still blazing and dancing in the hearth.

"Please smoke if you want to," Steg said to Yrsa. She went over to her baggage and retrieved her pipe and leaf. Tove watched as she filled the small bowl and lit it.

"I've never met a woman who smoked," she said.

"I picked it up from my stepmother. Want to try?"

She looked at her husband.

"I admit, wife," he replied, "I smoked a pipe or two last night, thanks to Yrsa. I cannot deny you the same."

Yrsa found two more pipes, handing them to Steg who filled them with leaf, and gave one to Tove. Two or three explosive coughs followed before she found the right depth of draw.

"Do we have any spare cloth?" he asked.

"Cloth?" Tove replied.

"I guessed Yrsa was from the Valleys from the colour of her clothes. I am wondering if we can do anything to help her be less conspicuous."

"Why, I have plenty. Most of it's plain, but you're welcome to whatever you need."

"Thank you," Yrsa replied, "but I'm not sure I'll be able to make clothes while I'm travelling."

"Why not stay with us tomorrow? We can make some trousers and tunics. I assume that's what you prefer to travel in?"

Yrsa wasn't sure she wanted to delay her journey, but it made sense, and after a few moments' thought, she accepted the offer, on condition they took fair payment for the cloth.

A little later, Tove went outside to relieve herself. Steg refilled her pipe, then took the temkin Yrsa had given him and sprinkled a little on top. She'd told him of its possible effects and shook her head as he winked at her. On Tove's return, he lit hers, and she took a draw.

"Ooh," she said, wide-eyed. "That made me dizzy."

"That's strange," he replied flatly.

Yrsa had been given a place by the fire to sleep and Steg laid some blankets on the ground. He and Tove slept on a small loft built around the chimney above the fireplace, screened off by more furs. It wasn't long before Yrsa began to regret introducing Steg to temkin. She spent a long time listening to the coupling above her. Again and again, Tove reached her peak.

Yrsa heard the occasional giggle from the children at the other end of the space, reminding her of hearing her own parents in the night. Finally, Steg reached his end, his cries echoing around the room, bringing more whispering and giggles from the far end. Then peace and sleep.

* * *

Steg and Ulf went off to work on the farm at dawn, the other children all had their jobs to do, and Tove and Yrsa set about making some clothes.

"I'll get my needles," Yrsa said.

"I've plenty," Tove replied, handing her one.

"Is this steel? I've never seen one before. We use bone."

"I do as well, but these are finer and sharper. Try it."

Tove was right, the steel needle was far better; it pierced the cloth more easily and left smaller holes.

"Take a couple with you," Tove said.

"Oh, I couldn't. You've already been more than generous."

"Consider it payment, then," Tove replied with a smile.

"Payment?"

"For introducing us to temkin. I hope we didn't keep you awake for too long."

"Didn't hear a thing."

They returned to their sewing, both smiling broadly.

The next morning, as Yrsa prepared to leave, she went to the purse hidden in her baggage to get silver to pay for the cloth. When she opened it, she frowned in surprise. It contained more than she expected, and the real shock was a small ingot of gold. Where had that come from?

Now wasn't the time to answer the question, so she took four solens and offered them to Tove as Steg loaded the panniers onto Brimble's back.

"No, Yrsa," Tove said. "We're comfortable here. You'll need them more than we will."

She gave Yrsa a hug, and Steg did the same, giving her a sly wink.

"Remember," he said. "Hit them with the staff, then ask questions. Not the other way around."

The children all said their farewells before running off to their errands or play, and Yrsa led her mare to the road. A last wave and she headed away from the steading.

Chapter 5

As soon as she was out of sight of the farm, Yrsa pulled up and rummaged in her baggage. Taking out the purse, she opened it again. She hadn't been dreaming. A small gold ingot, and more pieces of silver than she'd ever managed to save. She could think of no explanation as she put the purse away.

As Steg had said, she came to a broader track running east-west and turned towards Malcot. The sky was clear, the sun shining, and although it was cold, it was perfect walking weather. Yrsa was still getting used to walking with the staff, but it gradually became more natural, and she soon found herself doing it subconsciously, without having to think about each swing.

Her mind kept coming back to the coin. She'd told nobody about her stash of silver, nobody knew she was leaving. It couldn't be her father and certainly wasn't her brothers. The only other person in the house was … Hilda. Could it be?

Her stepmother was a perceptive woman who she'd got on with from the beginning. The same could not be said for her brothers. When their father remarried, they'd been unhappy, even though it was the usual practice after a man was widowed, and their father had left it five years.

Yrsa knew why. Hilda wasn't some old maid, desperate for a roof over her head. She was a young widow, with some land of her own, whose husband had been lost when his ship foundered on a trading voyage. Considerably younger than her new husband, she was only ten years older than his eldest son. Yrsa suspected both Erik and Leif were worried their father would start a new family. It hadn't happened, but they'd never warmed to Hilda.

Yrsa had learnt a lot from her stepmother besides the pleasures of smoking and temkin. They'd spent many hours talking about life, particularly about men. As Yrsa discovered her lust for life, Hilda had supported her, often placating her unhappy father. Hilda was the only person who might have the means to be so generous. But how did she know?

The path was firm, and the woodland on either side cut back, giving a clear view in both directions. They began to pass other people. A farmer with three cows, a richly clothed man on a fine horse, a couple of women gossiping as they walked. All acknowledged her briefly with a nod of the head or a 'good day'.

At midday, she stopped in a small clearing to one side of the track, and freed Brimble of her load, allowing her to wander off and graze. She took out some cold pork and broke off a piece of the bread Tove had given her.

Resuming their walk, the track dropped into a shallow depression where it was forced to narrow. Yrsa heard undergrowth being broken as something forced its way through. Turning, she saw a deer spring out of the trees some distance away. It stopped momentarily and looked at her, before running headlong into the forest on the other side of the path.

"Something's frightened her," Yrsa muttered to herself.

As she did so, another noise caused her to look around again. This time something crossed the track so quickly she didn't have time to focus clearly before it disappeared. But it was as large as the deer, pale grey and had needed no more than two or three strides to cross the track. The paw prints at the cabin flashed through her mind. She needed to get to Malcot before sunset.

The woodland slowly died out, replaced by open land, dotted with houses. Yrsa hesitated to call them farms, they were mostly small and rundown. She assumed their occupants struggled to get by on the small plots of land they sat on.

She could see the town in the distance. It would be dark soon after her arrival, so it was unlikely she could find what she needed today. And if she passed through, there would be nowhere to spend the night except the side of the track, and so close to the town, that wasn't an appealing prospect. Particularly if Steg's warning about the transient nature of Malcot's population was right.

She would have to find somewhere in the town to stay and remembered Steg's words.

"Look for the Dragon or the Castle," he'd said. "They're the best you'll find, though the Dragon is run by one, and the Castle doesn't live up to its name."

She picked up the smell of the town, slowly overpowering the fresh scent of the fields. It was mainly rotting garbage and effluent, and it got stronger the nearer she walked. The buildings grew closer together, the larger houses rubbing gables with the shacks. People milled here and there, some quiet and determined, others ambling along, exchanging shouts and greetings.

She was surprised there were no walls or gates, and before she knew it, they were well into the town, buildings crowding onto the street. Buildings unlike those she had left behind. Two, even three storeys high, rising precariously into the air.

The hustle and bustle overwhelmed her, and it took repeated oaths from a cart driver stuck behind her to get her moving again. Brimble, as usual, took it all in her stride, seemingly unconcerned by the crowds and the noise. A scruffy young lad no more than eight popped up in front of her.

"Looking for somewhere to rest your horse?" he asked.

"I'm looking for either the Dragon or Castle," Yrsa replied.

"Shitholes, both of them," the lad replied. "I know the best place in town."

"I'll bet you do, but I'll give you a copper kel if you take me to the Dragon or Castle, whichever is nearest."

She could see the boy was torn. Either his family owned another inn, or he was paid to lead customers to one, but she was sure he didn't get a kel for each one he conned. He thought for a moment or two, eyeing her shrewdly.

"Two kels," he finally said. "And I'll lead you to the best of the two."

"How far is it?"

"Three or four streets."

"And you'll charge me two kels for that?"

He had a cheeky grin, knowing she knew his game.

"It's worth it," he said. "There are some terrible places in this town."

"All right, but as we walk, you can tell me where I can buy food for both my horse and me tomorrow."

By the time they reached the Castle, the lad had told her so much there was no hope of remembering it all, but she did fix two or three streets in her head which would provide what they needed. Outside the yard, she took two kels from the purse on her belt and gave them to the boy. He grinned, did an awkward bow, and ran off.

Leading Brimble under the arch, she entered a square space behind the inn, with a wooden building beyond it, presumably the stable. Hitching the mare to a post, she wondered if it was safe to leave all her baggage, but people were coming and going, and she could see other animals laden with their packs, their owners nowhere to be seen. She'd take the risk.

The rear door to the inn was open and pulling her cloak around her, she ducked under the lintel, to be hit by the smell. Like the meeting house in the village, but ten times stronger. A heady mix of cheap ale, stale food, several varieties of leaf, and the sweat and grime of the customers.

She headed for the serving table and stood behind an old man in some sort of argument with the landlord. It allowed her to look around. Bare tables and benches, a few chairs, and a meagre fire in the hearth. The customers were mostly men, but she spotted a few women among them. That made her feel better, though she wondered if they were there for business or leisure.

The old man finally tottered off, and the landlord looked her up and down quickly, before putting on a false smile.

"Yes, young lady," he said.

"I need a room for the night," Yrsa replied, "and stabling for my horse."

His hearty laugh roused the interest of a few people nearby.

"Oh, indeed. With a feather mattress and your own fire, I suppose?"

"No," she replied, aware of the unwanted attention. "Just a room."

"Well, we don't have separate rooms, not much call for such luxury in Malcot. We do have one big room, with lots of beds for hire. Don't usually have girls using them, though. Least, not unless they're being paid by the hirer." He was enjoying teasing her, as were those listening. "You can always sleep in my bed," he continued. "I'm sure we can come to some arrangement."

More ribald laughter.

"Can I sleep in the stable with my horse?"

He rubbed his chin, looked her up and down again, then shrugged.

"Don't see why not," he said, his hand shooting out. "A silver solen. Includes water and fodder for the horse."

She handed it over, both of them knowing she'd been robbed, but she needed somewhere to bed down. He handed her a wooden tally.

"Give this to Gaut in the stable, he'll take care of you."

She stepped outside and took a deep breath. The air in the town might be foul, but it felt sweeter than in the inn. She unhitched Brimble and led her over to the stable, where a lad of about eighteen was sitting idly on a barrel.

"Are you Gaut?" she asked.

"I am," he replied cheerily and jumped down to meet her. She handed him the tally which he threw in a wooden pail. "This way," he said and disappeared through the large doors.

The stable was cleaner than the inn. It was a large building with open-fronted stalls along the back wall, and large windows in the front, letting light in. It appeared the horses were better served than their owners. Gaut led her to the end stall. It was large enough for two horses and filled with clean straw. A long water trough ran the length of the wall.

"I'm sleeping here as well," Yrsa said.

"Fair enough," he replied, looking around furtively before lowering his voice. "I keep it clean."

"I can see that."

"Cleaner than inside."

His face was full of pride, and he stood beaming at her. She unloaded Brimble and put the panniers on the floor at the back of the stall. There was a risk they'd get soiled but leaving them anywhere else risked them disappearing altogether.

Gaut was still watching her; she recognised him as a child of the Gods. A child in a man's body, uncorrupted by adulthood. She'd met a couple in the Valleys. Whatever else they lacked, they were without guile, she could trust him.

After tending to Brimble, she needed to eat. She had some meat from the forest left, and bread Tove had given her, but the warmth of the fire in the inn and some hot food was too tempting. As she walked past the stalls to the door, she looked at the horses occupying them. A mix of solid working animals, many like Brimble, and a couple of mules in a small stall at one end.

Coming out of the stable doors, she came across Gaut on his barrel.

"There'll be a few kels if you keep an eye on my baggage," she said.

"I'll watch it," he replied. "Nobody goes in there without me knowing."

She crossed the yard and dipped under the beam into the inn. At the table, the landlord was talking to the same men who'd been there earlier.

"Well," he said, still grinning, "have you settled into the stable?"

A few laughs, but they seemed friendly enough.

"I have. Gaut keeps them clean."

His face broke for a moment, uncertain if she was goading him.

"He's a good lad," he finally replied.

"I'd like ale and something to eat."

"Ale, I can do, and I can offer some roast pork and bread. Take it or leave it."

"I'll take it."

Yrsa picked up the tankard the landlord slammed on the counter and looked for somewhere to sit. She wanted to avoid unnecessary conversation and spotted a small empty table and two stools squashed into a corner. Taking the weight off her feet, she could feel her body slowly warming. A girl looking remarkably like the landlord brought a wooden board with the food and slammed it on the table. It was clearly a family skill.

Both the pork and the bread were tough, but the meat was hot and the bread filling. As she lit her pipe, she sat back and surveyed the room. If Steg felt this was one of the better inns in Malcot, she wondered what the others were like. There didn't seem anything threatening about the atmosphere, but she suspected that might change by the end of the night. By which time, she would make sure she was safely in the stable.

Yrsa noticed a man enter the room. His clothes were muddy and wet, his hair straggly and lank. He peered around, looking for someone, and headed to the high-backed bench on her left. As he passed, he spotted her and leered. She couldn't see who he'd joined, nor make sense of their muted conversation.

When she went to refill her tankard, she could see them both clearly: the bedraggled newcomer, with his partner. Amluss. It was Amluss. They were talking quietly, their heads close together. Had he seen her? Did he know she was here? She looked around quickly to find someplace to hide from his sight, then relaxed, frowning.

Why did she need to hide? What was it about this Amluss that made her feel uncomfortable? She didn't know, but determined not to give in to it. Picking up her ale, she returned to her table on the other side of their enclosed bench.

The two men were joined later by another, who looked out of place in the inn. Clearly a countryman, he was poorly dressed and nervous. The sidekick went to get more ale while Amluss tried to make conversation.

Yrsa couldn't hear everything being said. The high back made it difficult, so she gave up trying until she heard the word 'beast'. The disputes and laughter around the room often drowned out the quiet conversation, but she picked up bits. Tales of a huge beast roaming the district, killing livestock.

Such tales often grew from the slimmest evidence, and the two men tried to get their visitor to give them details. He lived near Clister, one of his cows had been attacked, and one of his neighbour's. They'd been torn apart. Nothing left but skin and bones. The usual wild exaggerations, but the man believed his own story and was frightened.

Soon after, she heard the sound of coin on the table, and the countryman left the inn. The two men dropped their voices and

Yrsa could follow no longer. There wasn't much to go on, just wild country rumours. She didn't even know where Clister was. But the two men were interested in the man's information; interested enough to pay him for it. She wondered why.

Chapter 6

The warmth and ale had led Yrsa to let her guard down, and Amluss's companion suddenly appeared at her table, his hair still unkempt, his hands filthy. He dropped himself onto the other stool and leaned forward.

"How much, girl?"

His voice was no more than a hoarse whisper, though it dripped contempt. Her initial surprise was replaced by a wary amusement.

"What?"

"How much?"

"For what?"

"Don't play games, girl."

"I'm not for sale."

His chuckle made her shiver.

"You're all for sale if the price is right. If I like you, my master might want you too. Double the coin."

"Go and piss in the fire."

"I like the fiery ones."

"I reckon you like the cheap ones."

He raised his arm to strike her, but a hand gripped it from over the back of the bench. His face fell as Amluss pulled the arm away.

"Forgive my companion," he said. "He forgets himself at times. Hagrat, come and sit down."

"Yes, Amluss."

Hagrat gave her a dark look as he returned to his seat, and Amluss gave Yrsa no more than the slightest nod of recognition before dropping out of sight again.

This Hagrat had called Amluss master. Who called another man that? An apprentice might, but Hagrat was far too old to be an apprentice. A slave? Yes, but slavery was illegal almost everywhere now. In the trading ports she'd visited with her father they'd met people who'd been born slaves, but they'd been freed long ago. Why else would a man call another master?

When Yrsa returned to the stables, Gaut was still on his barrel.

"Do you sleep up there, as well?" she asked.

"No, in the stable." He jumped down, led her inside and pointed to a small loft above the entrance. "Up there, so I can look after the horses."

As she headed towards her stall, she found Tennell in another with a smaller gelding, presumably Hagrat's mount. The mare spotted her and came to the bar, where Yrsa stroked her head and met her eyes again, sensing a keen intelligence behind them.

She checked on Brimble who was dozing, pulled an armful of straw to the entrance of the stall and spread it out. Pulling her two cloaks from her baggage, she sat on the ground, thinking about what she'd heard. If there was a beast about, she'd been lucky to avoid it and wanted it to stay that way. Had she not seen the prints, she'd have laughed at the idea.

Stretching out on the floor, she covered herself with the cloaks and fell asleep.

* * *

Brimble woke her. A little whinny Yrsa knew well, a warning sign. She lay still and opened her eyes to get them accustomed to the dark. She listened; lots of breathing horses, little movements as they swayed in their sleep. A few stalls away, one was having a long piss. All natural sounds. Then she picked up something else. A soft crunching, the sound of a foot on straw. Someone cautiously moving around, getting closer.

It couldn't be Gaut. He wouldn't be moving about so slowly. She tried to work out the direction of the sound, but the horses' activities made that difficult. Gently checking the knife in her belt and the staff she'd laid beside her, she tried to breathe normally and watched Brimble, visible in the moonlight coming through the windows.

A shadow passed over the mare's back, and moments later a foot appeared in her view, standing level with her waist. Someone was standing astride her prone body. She remembered Steg's advice; hit first, question later. But when to hit?

The question was forgotten as a rough hand smothered her mouth, and another rolled her onto her back. She looked up to see Hagrat, a triumphant leer on his face, bring a knifepoint close to her throat.

"Now, girl," he whispered. "Last chance to agree a price."

A thousand thoughts went through Yrsa's head, but only one mattered. He wasn't getting anything from her. She gave a nod, which prompted a grunt from her assailant.

"Good girl."

Unwrapping the cloak as he watched her every move, she undid her belt and laid it to one side, before pulling up her tunic. His focus turning to her bare skin was all she needed. Rolling enough to free the staff, she brought it up between his legs with all her might.

A scream filled the stable, waking the horses, who shifted about, unsettled. Hagrat collapsed to his knees, hands over his groin, wailing. Yrsa hurriedly got to her feet, staff still in hand and she brought its heavy top down on the back of his head. He rolled forward, stunned.

She heard a noise behind her and turned ready to fight, but it was only Gaut, staring at the figure on the ground.

"I'll get uncle," he said, before rushing off.

Yrsa closed her eyes and took a few deep breaths to steady her nerves. Going towards Hagrat, she remembered another of Steg's uses for the staff and poked him hard. A few moans came from the body; at least he wasn't dead. She rolled him over with her foot, picked up a bucket, filled it from the trough and threw it over him.

He spluttered, opened his eyes, rolled into a ball, and began howling again, his hands going back to his groin. He slowly focussed on her and tried to move away, but she knelt by his head and put her knife across his throat.

"By the Gods," the landlord cried, running into the stable. "What's going on here?"

"I'm just deciding if this bastard lives or not," Yrsa replied, as calmly as she could.

"Are you now?" The landlord walked over and looked at the man who was still rocking in agony. "He's one of them in the top room. Gaut, go get the other. You can let him go, girl."

"No thanks, I like him right here."

"Fair enough."

When Amluss appeared, he looked at Hagrat, then at Yrsa holding the knife to his neck.

"What's going on?" he asked.

"Your friend wouldn't take no for an answer," she replied.

"I'm sure it was a misunderstanding."

"Would it be misunderstood if I cut out his balls?"

"All right," the landlord said. "That's enough. Let him go, girl, and you," he turned to Amluss, "get your friend to your room, and the pair of you will move on in the morning."

Amluss shrugged as Yrsa let Hagrat go. He didn't move.

"Gaut," the landlord said. "Give him a hand."

Between them, they lifted Hagrat to his feet, though that brought more screams. Yrsa saw with a shock his trousers were soaked in blood. They took his arms over their shoulders and dragged him forward. As they passed her, Amluss paused and looked at her knife.

"Be careful girl," he said calmly. "Hagrat's a fool and I apologise for his actions as he seems unable to at the moment. But you may not be so lucky next time."

When they were all gone, Yrsa flopped to the floor, exhausted and shaking. She'd discouraged many lads in her life with a slap or a kick. But she'd never used her full strength to injure someone, never had to fight for her life. There was a rush about it, something that made her feel good, and that puzzled her. She slid the knife into its sheath and checked on Brimble, who was already asleep again. It was time to get away from Malcot.

Yrsa didn't try to sleep. It was nearly light, and as soon as the merchants were open, she wanted to leave. She thought about what had happened. Hagrat had wanted her, but what if his intention had been robbery? Her purse was a tempting prize.

She split the contents between her panniers. If they were all stolen, the result would be the same, but if someone managed to search one or two, she'd at least keep something. Putting a few more silver solens and copper kels into the purse at her waist, she loaded her baggage onto Brimble.

Gaut appeared, climbing down the ladder from his loft. He didn't look at her and went to the other end of the stable to begin work.

"Good morning," she said.

"Morning," he replied, not stopping.

"Are you all right?"

Gaut paused and leaned on his rake. He was crying.

"What is it?" she asked.

"It's terrible," he replied. "What happened."

"Women are used to it." He looked at her, puzzled. "Men can be bastards."

"I'm not," he protested.

"I know, Gaut. In fact, you could be extremely helpful to me."

* * *

When she reached the Norsouth road, she saw people hadn't been exaggerating. It was a major thoroughfare. A wide central track, partly cobbled, with a grass verge on either side which was as wide again. Admittedly where she joined the track on the edge of Malcot, there wasn't much grass, but it was clear the road was regularly maintained.

Although it was early, there was a steady stream of people moving in both directions. She soon saw that carts used the central road, with everyone else going wherever they chose. She led Brimble to the grass verge and turned south, as she'd told Gaut she would.

The lad had indeed been helpful. He may have been unworldly in many ways, but he knew the area. He'd told her where the Norsouth road went and what was on the other side. He'd told her the traders who opened earliest, and she'd managed to pick up a sack of oats for Brimble, some bread, cheese and sausage and a large bag of acceptable leaf. It was all she needed.

She'd assured him what happened hadn't been his fault and he might have been hurt if he'd tried to stop the man. He brightened up at that, brightened up some more when she kissed him on the cheek and beamed when she gave him two silver solens.

"They're yours, Gaut," she'd said. "Don't tell your uncle."

"I won't, he'll have them otherwise."

Quite where he'd spend them without his uncle knowing, she wasn't sure, but she figured Gaut was smarter than people realised. He'd find a use for them. Having made peace with him, she didn't

Yrsa and the Zeffen Hunter

feel too bad lying about her plans. He was a nice lad, but a few coins would open his mouth. In that way, he was the same as everyone else.

So, she'd told him she was going south, all the way to the great river, but had no intention of doing so. She'd thought long and hard about her next destination, and was already in lands she knew little about. Valley people were seafarers, they rarely ventured far inland, except for a few eccentric souls like her uncle. The river called to her, and she'd feel at home on a boat, but she decided to continue east, away from the water and away from her home.

She'd travelled a wandering path and was probably only thirty leagues from the Valleys as the birds flew. She wanted to extend that distance. Gaut had mentioned a track branching off to the east a league or so from Malcot. That was her destination this morning.

There was no trace of snow here, but the nights were still cold, and the grass crunched where it had not already been trodden. Yrsa ambled along at Brimble's pace. It could seem frustratingly slow at times, but it gave her time to look around and take in the country. She'd just begun to look out for the eastern track when she sensed someone approaching.

"Well, well," a deep male voice said. "It seems our paths must cross once more."

She spun around and saw the horse first. Tennell, with the packhorse tied on behind. Amluss slid from the mare's saddle, and she let her hand fall to the hilt of her knife.

"Don't worry, girl," he said. "I'm not here to avenge Hagrat."

"Is he dead?" she asked, letting her hand drop.

"He was alive when I left him, though his balls were swollen like a sheep's bladder with blood everywhere."

"And you just left him?"

Amluss was level with her on Brimble's other flank, leading his horses and keeping pace.

"Why not? He always was a fool," he said. "A useful fool, but a fool nonetheless."

"Do you normally leave your friends behind?"

"He wasn't a friend. He was my bondsman." That explained a few things. "I spared his life, and he gave me two years' service."

"Which, I suppose, were nearly up."

He looked at her and nodded.

"You're a smart girl. Yes, a moon or so to go. I'll have to do without him."

"You don't care what happens to him?"

"No. Should I?"

"Your conscience is your own."

He studied her as they walked.

"Where are you going?" he asked finally.

"South."

"So the stable lad told me." She smiled inwardly. "Anywhere in particular?"

"No."

"All right, girl, keep your secrets."

Yrsa was riled by him always calling her girl, but something about him made her let it pass. Again, silence fell, and Yrsa wondered why he had stopped to talk.

"Show me your knife," he demanded suddenly. She hesitated. "I'm not going to repeat Hagrat's mistake, if that's what you're worried about."

"You might steal it."

He stopped and pulled his riding cloak open. Today he wore not only the two daggers but an impressive sword as well.

"Expecting trouble?" Yrsa asked.

"Travelling can be dangerous," he replied, with a cool smile. "You never know who you might come across in a stable."

He held out his hand, and she passed him her knife which he examined closely, turning it in his hand, before removing his glove and checking the point and the edges.

"Do you know what this is?" he asked.

"A knife," she replied glibly, but the way he stared at her made her feel small.

"You don't know, do you?"

"So, what is it?"

"This is a Flengaran szanka. I haven't seen one in years. How does a mere girl come by such a weapon?"

"Perhaps I've been there."

"Ha!" He gave her a contemptuous look as he returned the szanka. "I'll wager you've never been anywhere near Flengara. Nor done anything to warrant wearing such a symbol of honour."

"Where are you going?" Yrsa asked, hoping to change the subject.

"Something is killing farmer's cattle, as you no doubt overheard. I'm going to help rid them of it."

"Farmer's rumours," she scoffed. "They see wolves in every shadow."

"Maybe, but I've nothing better to do."

"No home, no family?"

He tightened briefly before shaking his head.

"You ask too many questions, girl. Time I went about my business."

"Chasing shadows?"

"Perhaps. We'll see." He strode back and mounted his horse. "Take care, girl. Not every danger in this world is as easy to overcome as Hagrat."

He nudged Tennell on and trotted away. As they passed her, Yrsa took a good look at the horses. Amluss's saddle was past its best but had once been impressive. The caparison now had two small crossbows and another sword hanging from it. The trailing horse was loaded with baggage, a couple of hunting spears strapped to the side. If he was hunting a beast, he was well-equipped.

Chapter 7

The conversation with Amluss had taken Yrsa past the eastern track, but she hadn't wanted to give away her intentions. The main road in front of her was straight at this point, and it would be a while before he was out of sight. So, she led Brimble off to the side and stopped for a break. There was no water nearby for the mare, but she let her graze some sweet grass.

Amluss had said he was after the beast, but she didn't believe he was some selfless hunter, riding to the aid of a few farmers. What did he know that others didn't? Perhaps he was simply seeking another trophy; the rich had time for such things. Finally, she shook her head. It didn't matter, all she needed to do was stay away from whatever it was.

When Amluss was no longer in sight, she turned back towards the track. It was a rougher path, with the forest much closer, but regularly used, and the going was easy. It made a change from the open farmland.

Gaut had said the track led to a succession of settlements, and she passed the first in mid-afternoon. A few houses clustered along a stream; the forest felled to make room for some rough fields.

One or two people turned to stare as she walked through, wary of an unknown face.

An hour before dusk, she led Brimble off the path and a little way into the forest. Gathering a few fallen branches, she built a shelter against a tree. It seemed safe enough to build a fire, and she roasted the last of the pork. It was a bit high, but edible. As the fire slowly died, she wrapped her cloaks around her and fell asleep.

* * *

They travelled for three days and found sheltered places to camp each night. Spring was visible in the forest, with touches of light green where the trees and undergrowth were beginning to sprout. The nights were still cool, but during the day, the steady walking and strengthening sunshine made Yrsa happier.

Her mood was changing, and she was beginning to feel more positive about her journey. Thinking about where she was going, and what she wanted to do, rather than where she'd come from. The planning of the previous year was slipping away, replaced by the dreams of distant lands from her younger years.

The following morning was misty, and as they rejoined the track, Yrsa could only see a few steps in front of her. This slowed their pace, as she had to concentrate on the path. At around midday, still surrounded by fog, she heard a horse repeatedly shrieking in the distance, and stopped and peered into the mist, calming a restless Brimble.

After the sounds faded, deadened by the moisture in the air, she cautiously moved on. Then another shriek rose, still far off, but this time, it sent a shiver up her back, and thoughts of the beast floated through her head.

"Well," she said, calming Brimble again, "if it's over there, it's not going to pounce on us here."

As the fog lifted, the path widened, allowing Yrsa to guide Brimble off the muddy centre to the firmer grass. Coming across a stream, they stopped for a break, and she let the mare wander to drink and graze. Yrsa leaned against a tree and filled her pipe. They were in no hurry; she'd take her time. As she was getting comfortable, Brimble whinnied, and her ears rose. Yrsa heard something moving in the forest.

She untied her bow, loosely notched an arrow and waited, crouched between the sound and Brimble. Something heavy was crashing through the undergrowth, breaking branches and bushes, and it was getting nearer. It wasn't coming directly towards her, and she tried to pinpoint the sound.

Just as she did, a horse crashed out of the forest fifty paces ahead and thundered away along the track. Amluss's horse. As it disappeared, she strained to hear anything else. But as the sound of the horse's hooves diminished, there was only silence. Nothing was chasing it.

She cautiously led Brimble to the point the horse had appeared where there was a discernible line of broken undergrowth between the trees. Yrsa considered her next move. Clearly, something untoward had happened, as Amluss's horse wasn't going to gallop off without him for no reason.

"Well, old girl," she said to Brimble. "I'll probably regret this …"

She led her pony into the forest, following the snapped branches. It was quite a trail of destruction, and she wondered if the black horse was injured. It led her deep into the forest, and as the undergrowth thinned out, it became harder to follow.

She was about to give up when she spotted another horse standing in a small clearing, apparently frozen, and not moving a muscle. It was the horse Amluss had been using for his baggage, most of which was spread over the forest floor. She headed for it, and it still didn't move. When she got within a few paces, she saw why. It had a huge, bloody wound from its hip to its hock.

She hitched Brimble to a branch, circled the horse so it could see her, and slowly walked towards it. Nothing. The animal didn't move. It wasn't even looking at her. She approached carefully, holding her hand out. When she reached it, it allowed her to stroke its neck and she moved around to its rump.

Something had cut the flesh in a single line for an arm's length and two knuckles deep. She wondered what to do. Such wounds could be sewn together, and it was straight and clean enough to try. But she'd never done it, and although she had needles, she had no gut to sew with. Perhaps she should have walked on, after all.

"It's in shock, girl."

The rasped words made her spin around, angry she'd let her guard down again. Propped against a rock was Amluss, and he was in a far worse state than the horse. His left arm was hanging limply from his shoulder, the whole joint exposed. The cloth on his right leg was torn to shreds, exposing a large open wound on his thigh. Again, she could see bone.

"What happened?" she asked.

"I tracked it." His speech was halting, his breathing shallow. The shoulder wasn't bleeding much, but the thigh wound was. "After three years, I found one. Followed it here. But I thought it would run." He coughed, a weak smile crossing his face. "I got that wrong. It decided to fight."

"It? What?"

"A zeffen."

Zeffen. The stuff of nightmares. A creature of legend used by parents to scare their naughty children. A creature of myth. Now apparently real.

"Is it still here?" she whispered, backing towards the rock, and anxiously looking around.

"It hauled itself away, wounded. I got at least one bolt into it."

"What can I do?"

"Nothing, girl. Leave me to die."

"You won't get rid of me that easily."

Yrsa went to fetch Brimble and took out one of her tunics. As she tore it into strips, she looked around at every sound, fearing a monster flying towards her. To Amluss's annoyance, she tried to bind his thigh.

"You won't stop it," he grumbled.

"We'll see."

She wasn't sure what to do about the shoulder. It wasn't bleeding heavily but the arm was useless and would have to come off. That was something she'd never witnessed and had no stomach for, let alone the skill. He smiled at her quandary.

"Forget it, girl, I'm finished. Just go."

"I'll not leave anyone like this."

She took out her spare cloak and bundled it up, putting it between his head and the rock.

"Got anything to drink?" he asked.

"Only water."

"That won't help."

"I do have something which might."

She found her pipe, filled it with leaf, and then sprinkled a generous amount of temkin on top. Placing it in his mouth, he managed to hold it with his right hand. She lit it, and he breathed in as deeply as he could, the subsequent cough wracking him with pain.

"What is it?" he asked.

"It's temkin. In small amounts it relaxes you. I've given you quite a lot."

He gave a dry chuckle.

"I hope you've got more."

She did, but not a huge amount; it would have to do. She took a water skin and went to hold it to his mouth, but he handed her the pipe and took the skin, drinking from it, before taking the pipe back.

"I'm not dead yet," he said.

"Do you want to eat?"

"Not worth it, girl. I'll be dead by morning."

She said nothing, knowing he was right. There was nothing she could do to prevent it. But she'd stay, so she might as well make the best of it. Gathering some wood, she built a fire close to Amluss, more to keep her courage up than keep them warm.

She flinched at every sound and hoped Amluss had been right when he said the zeffen had hauled itself away to recover. If he hadn't been able to defend himself against it, she stood no chance. She unloaded Brimble, and Amluss watched her with amusement.

"You'd better use that szanka of yours to put that wounded horse out of its misery," he said.

"That animal will live. Got any catgut?"

"I haven't, but that was Hagrat's horse. Only the Gods know what the wretch had with him."

She went through the baggage on the forest floor, but there was little of value. Then she found a leather roll and breathed a prayer. A couple of large bone needles and a roll of corded gut. Not enough to sew the wound neatly, but she should be able to pull it together well enough until she could find help.

She brought Brimble closer so the packhorse could see her, and cut lengths of gut, threading the first. Offering another prayer to the Gods, she flushed the top of the wound, grabbed the skin with her fingers and plunged the needle through it.

Any normal horse would have kicked her twenty paces, but this one merely twitched. She brought the needle back through the other side of the wound, crossed the ends and pulled the gut tight before tying a knot. She put several stitches along the wound, and when she'd finished, it looked better. Still a mess, but it was mostly closed.

"Waste of time," Amluss muttered. "Any more of this stuff?"

She refilled the pipe. The temkin was having an effect, but she didn't want to knock him out, merely dull his pain, so put less in this time.

"I could try and get you to help," she suggested.

He looked at her with a weary smile.

"The journey would kill me quicker. And where in this backward country would we find anyone to put me back together?"

Amluss closed his eyes and Yrsa thought for a moment he had passed. But he was still breathing. Whether he was unconscious or the effects of the temkin had sent him to sleep she didn't know, but there didn't seem much point trying to wake him. She rubbed Brimble down, leaving her in view of Hagrat's horse, in case it was any comfort to the animal. There was no water here, but Brimble would cope until the morning.

Squatting by the fire, she forced herself to eat. Hunger had left her when she saw the horse's wounds, and then Amluss's. But it was something to do. The day hadn't turned out as planned. She found herself sitting by a fire with a man who would surely die, and a horse which seemed destined to do the same. All she could do was wait.

She'd seen people die often enough. Sat with them, held their hands as they passed from this world to the next. Her people feared dying alone, and it was considered a privilege to witness their final breaths. She would now do it for this man she hardly knew.

She wondered where he came from, why he was here, why he was hunting the zeffen. Gods, she'd almost forgotten about the zeffen, and the memory made her jump and look around. It was dark, but the moon was bright, and even with the tree canopy, enough light filtered through to see some distance. Nothing stirred, and she hoped it stayed that way.

She vividly remembered the stories of the zeffen from childhood. A mythical beast from the north, twice as big as a man. It was said they made wolves flee in terror. But even in their wildest drunken boasts, she never heard any man claim to have seen one. Many a child had gone to bed terrified of being taken in the night by this fearsome creature.

Yet this man believed there was one close by. That it had torn his arm off, ripped his leg open and sliced through a horse's rump like a knife. Who was she to doubt him? She couldn't think of any other creature capable of inflicting those wounds, and hoped he'd been right when he said it had a crossbow bolt lodged in its body. It would be licking its wounds somewhere.

She took out her pipe, filled it with leaf, and took a deep draw. She wouldn't use temkin tonight. There wasn't much left, Amluss might need more, and she feared she might need her wits about her.

Amluss stirred, pain evident in his groan. He opened his eyes, looked about him, and frowned at her.

"Still here?" he asked.

"Until you need me no longer."

He narrowed his eyes, looking intently at her.

"Thank you," he finally said softly, with surprising emotion. "Is there any more of that … what did you call it?"

"Temkin, yes."

She refilled his pipe and handed it to him, holding a twig from the fire so he could light it. He took three deep draws on the pipe.

"Pain bad?" Yrsa asked.

"Not so bad now," he replied. "They say the pain lessens as you near death."

She said nothing. She'd heard the same.

"Will the zeffen return?" she asked.

"I doubt it. It'll be hiding somewhere in the same state as me. Though without a companion."

"Why were you hunting it?"

"Why not?"

"That's no answer."

"It may be the truth."

"You're just a simple hunter, then?"

"Why do you doubt it?"

"Your clothes, your horse, your weapons. They're not those of a common hunter."

"Where do you come from?" he asked.

"The Valleys, to the west." She saw no harm in being honest with a dying man.

"Are all the girls there as smart as you?"

"I like to think not."

His laugh made him wince in pain.

"Why is a Valleys girl travelling so far from home?"

"I want to see more of the world. I'm curious."

"I see." He took a few more puffs on his pipe. "Does a curious girl want to hear a curious tale?"

Yrsa listened as Amluss told her his story. As he did so, she wavered between fascination and disbelief. Was he still in his right mind, or had his wounds shattered his wits? A tale of princes, a sorcerer, and a cursed king. And a three-year quest for zeffen blood.

Chapter 8

Yrsa woke as the first rays of the sun found their way through the forest canopy. She stretched, rolled over to look at Amluss, and knew instantly he was dead, his body slumped sideways, his head hanging on his chest. She cursed herself for falling asleep and letting him pass away without company. They'd both known he wouldn't last the night, but to see him now was a reminder of the fragility of life.

She sat up and looked around. Brimble was standing where she'd been the previous evening, apparently asleep. Hagrat's horse was also unmoved, although seemed to be awake. She stood and pulled her cloak around her; it was a chilly morning.

Brimble woke as she approached and shook her head in greeting, her fringe waving over her eyes as it always did. Yrsa hugged her neck, needing some comfort on this melancholy morning. Now, she had to decide what to do.

Amluss had been clear. Take what he'd gifted to her, anything else she wanted, and leave. She wanted to do something with his body and had asked two or three times what his death rituals were, but he refused to tell her. The ground was too solid to bury him with the small shovel she had, and it would take a long time to gather enough wood for a pyre. And a pyre's smoke would be visible for leagues.

No, she had to leave him. She gathered her own things together first, loading the panniers, and fastening them on Brimble's back. Then she went over to Amluss. He hadn't given her any details of the battle with the zeffen, but it must have taken him by surprise, because his daggers were still in his belt and his sword lay by him, unmarked by blood.

When he'd finished his tale, he'd told her to take those weapons when he died. After a moment's hesitation, she shifted his body away from the rock and laid it on the ground. Unbuckling the belt, she rolled him over until it came free, laying it to one side, and quickly searched his body. She eased out the leather cord around his neck, freeing the crystal phial he had shown her the night before. If he was right, it possessed power, but it lay inert in her hand, and she put the cord around her own neck, pushing the phial beneath her tunic.

There was nothing in the other baggage worth taking, but she did find Amluss's riding cloak. It was made from a heavy, finely woven material, far better than hers. But she knew what purpose it should serve.

Laying Amluss at the base of the rock, with his good arm over his chest, she laid the cloak over him. She doubted they prayed to the same Gods, but quietly sang the death rhymes anyway. It couldn't do any harm.

She thought about strapping Amluss's belt and weapons around her waist but smiled at her presumption. The belt would be far too big, and she didn't have the skill to use a sword. She'd look ridiculous, like a child playing with its father's tools. Instead, she rolled the belt and weapons in one of her cloaks and strapped it to her panniers.

Yrsa and the Zeffen Hunter

The only thing delaying her now was Hagrat's horse. She went to it, trying to work out how to bring it out of its stupor.

"This is your one chance, old lad," she muttered. "If you won't move, I'm leaving you."

She laid her hand on its neck, and it trembled slightly. She cursed herself for not asking Amluss its name. He'd talked briefly of Tennell, even asking her to look out for the mare when she moved on. But Hagrat's gelding had not been important to him. She made her way along the animal's flank and inspected the wound. It had stopped bleeding, at least her sewing had achieved that. Her hand slid along its flank and went towards the top of the wound.

At which point, the horse came to life. It shrieked and its injured leg kicked out, the hoof catching Yrsa's left hand on the way up. It tried to rear, squealed as its wounded leg gave way, and landed in a scrabbling heap on the ground. Yrsa managed to grab the rein with her good hand, realising in the process the other was numb and useless, and hurt like nothing she'd ever felt.

She had to get the horse back on its feet, otherwise, it was doomed. She pulled on the reins, talking to it all the time. Eventually, the horse righted itself and frantically looked around, trying to find an escape. She continued talking calmly to it, stepping a little closer until she could pass the rein to her damaged hand, trying to stroke it with the other.

To her surprise, Brimble came over and nudged the horse. Instantly calmer, it nuzzled Brimble, and Yrsa backed slowly away.

"I'll leave them to it," she muttered, as her hand reminded her of the kick. There was a gash across the wrist which was bleeding a little, but much worse was the shape of the two middle fingers. They were clearly broken. She cursed the horse, cursed Hagrat, cursed the forest.

She needed to find someone to put them straight, she couldn't do it herself. Looking for something to bind them, she found some old rags and wrapped them around her hand as tightly as she could.

It would be virtually useless for some time. Another round of curses.

She had a final look around to see if she'd missed anything useful. She was disappointed she hadn't found a crossbow. She had no experience with them, her people preferring the longbow, but they were a useful weapon and easily concealed.

When she returned to the horses, the injured gelding was calm, standing close to Brimble. It appeared they'd become friends which would make life easier. Yrsa picked up the horse's reins and gently led him on, knowing Brimble would follow on her own.

They made their way back to the track, where she swapped the horses around. She wouldn't abandon the packhorse, but Brimble was her priority. She lengthened his rein and tucked a loose end into a pannier strap. It wasn't secure; if he wanted to run off, he could. If he wanted to follow, so be it.

"Right, girl," she said, ruffling Brimble's mane, "let's go."

They hadn't gone a hundred paces when she stopped, and Brimble let out a little snort of impatience. Yrsa could see a trail of blood, dark and thick, on the ground. She followed it to the right of the track, then to the left. She couldn't be certain which direction the bleeding creature had been going, but she had a good idea.

Curiosity piqued, she hitched the two horses to branches and entered the forest on the opposite side of the track to where she'd left Amluss. This animal had been bleeding heavily, and the trail was easy to follow for someone used to hunting.

She walked slowly, looking around and stopping frequently to listen. Nothing but the sounds of the forest; no alarms from animals or birds. The trail disappeared at one point, but a few moments of circling found it again.

An injured animal moving in such a straight line had a destination. It wasn't wandering around looking for somewhere to hide. It had a lair, and eventually, she found it. The trail suddenly ended on the edge of a sheer drop, about the height of a man. It was a small, rocky depression twenty paces across.

Yrsa made her way around the edge and found the ground levelled out at the bottom. The hole was densely covered in shrubs and undergrowth, but there were signs of something coming and going. She hesitated, knowing the danger she was putting herself in, but realised she felt no fear, just curiosity driving her on. Pushing between the bushes, she made her way forward until she came to an open space backed by a hollow in the rock.

There she stopped, frozen by the scene before her. Lying on the ground was the creature she knew she'd find. A zeffen, looking straight at her with brilliant green eyes. It was like nothing she'd ever seen. And it was dying. A crossbow bolt was stuck in its leg, and this wound had produced the trail of blood, it was bleeding still. But it was the bolt embedded deep in its chest which was killing it.

It didn't move as she crawled forward, sure now this animal could do her little harm. But it watched, and the creature's stare made her feel small. It was panting, each breath catching long before its giant lungs were full. It wasn't afraid of her, merely tolerating her presence, knowing it had no choice. They stared at each other for what seemed like an eternity before Yrsa had to look away.

She studied the zeffen. It was huge, at least twice the size of even the largest hunting dog. As big as a pony, but leaner. Powerfully built, with muscles visible even through a rough coat of mixed greys. She was fascinated by its head, broad and long, with large erect ears, its snout ending in a black nose. Its mouth was open, tongue hanging out, revealing teeth that could have ripped any animal apart.

It occasionally scraped weakly at the ground as pain rippled through its body, and Yrsa looked at the massive paws which had left the prints she'd seen near the cabin. But here she could see its claws, each bigger than a man's finger. They were fearsome to look at. She didn't doubt the power which had taken Amluss's arm off with one swipe. Now, that power was waning.

As she noticed the zeffen was female, its teats swollen enough to appear through the fur on its belly, she heard rustling. Turning, she saw the undergrowth move, and her heart flew into her throat before she saw a pair of eyes, followed by another.

The dying zeffen made her jump when it gave a surprisingly tender call, and two small cubs hesitantly crawled out from the bushes. They were torn between going to their mother and fear of the intruder. Yrsa reached out, and the cubs allowed her to pick them up and place them by their mother, where they started suckling.

Yrsa felt tears running down her face. This magnificent creature was indeed the stuff of nightmares and seeing it made her understand why. But it was also beautiful, almost beyond imagining. And she was witnessing its death, and the death of its cubs, for they were too young to survive without their mother.

She looked into the zeffen's eyes again, their green depths drawing her in as they gradually lost their light. Then something extraordinary happened. An understanding, a promise, a bond. She felt this creature's soul touch her own, before leaving its body, which relaxed as one long, last exhalation signalled its death.

Yrsa reached out and stroked the creature's shoulder. The coat was surprisingly soft and warm. The cubs were still feeding, oblivious to their mother's death. She gently lifted them and placed them by her head, her eyes lifeless and still. Even at their age, they finally understood, licking her face, letting out little mews, trying to bring her back to life.

Yrsa waited, letting them have their moment, then calmly picked them up and left the hollow.

* * *

Yrsa and the Zeffen Hunter

The wounded horse was where she'd left him, and Brimble was quietly grazing. That was a good sign. They looked up as she approached and became curious when they saw the cubs. She had to find some way to keep them safe as they walked. Deciding a pannier would have to do, she emptied one and gently placed the cubs in their temporary home. Whether they stayed there remained to be seen.

As they walked on, her fingers throbbed more and more. She thought about smoking some temkin but had little left and preferred to save it. As they turned a corner, a farm appeared, and she saw a couple of cows. She didn't know if the cubs would take their milk, but she had to try.

A woman at the farm warily sold Yrsa half a waterskin of milk, and as the sun began to set, she knew she wouldn't find any help that day. So she walked until they came across a small stream, turned into the forest, and found a suitable place to spend the night. After she'd led the horses to the stream to drink, she cut a few branches for a shelter and built a fire.

Now to deal with the cubs. They'd filled the base of the pannier with their waste, so she lifted them out, put them on her lap and did her best to clean them up. As she wiped their paws, she was surprised to find their little claws were fully retractable, sheathed within their toes. They were already sharp, and she pondered their eventual size. If she could keep them alive.

So far, they hadn't been any trouble, but when they got hungry, they'd be a handful. She tried putting some milk in her palm to see if they would lap it. No, they wouldn't. She tried holding the skin up and letting the milk run down her finger, but this simply led to little teeth marks in her skin.

She had an idea. Taking Hagrat's leather roll, she cut a square, pierced a small hole in the middle and wrapped it around the top of the skin. Holding it upside down, the milk dripped out, and she tried putting one of the cubs to it. After some hesitation, it began to suck at it. Success. The other followed, and she let them drink about half the milk. It wouldn't last long.

She put them on the forest floor, where they wandered around, showing great interest in the fire. She had no idea how old they were. Not new-born, certainly. They were steady on their feet and already the size of a cat, each with a mouth full of tiny, sharp teeth. But she had to assume they were still dependent on milk. That was going to be difficult.

She didn't understand what had passed between her and their mother, but something told her she didn't need to tie them up or confine them. They wouldn't run away.

Her hand was almost numb, still throbbing and sore, and she could only move the thumb. A few more soft curses filled the air as she struggled first to eat, then to fill her pipe. Why couldn't it have been her right hand? The cubs were already curled together between her and the fire. She checked the horses. Brimble had moved to stand by Hagrat's horse who seemed calmer and happier, though Yrsa noted he often lifted his leg jerkily. The animal was still in pain.

Returning to the fire, the cubs were awake again and playing. They shrank away a little as she passed, waiting until she sat, then resuming their play. They seemed remarkably unworried by their precarious position. Yrsa spent most of a sleepless night worrying for all of them.

By first light, her fingers were swelling. If she didn't get them straightened and bound that day, it would be too late. The night had produced mixed blessings. As the fire died, the cubs started shivering. Three times, she tried placing them on her lap, but three times they crept off and lay a step or two away, eyeing her warily.

Eventually, she rolled her cloak into a cushion by her side and laid them on it. After a lot of scuffing and pulling at the material which made her wince, they settled, curled around each other, and slept. But several times in the night, they stepped off the material, going a little way to defecate. What came out was almost raw milk; it was going straight through them.

After she loaded Brimble, she put the cubs in the pannier and led the horses back onto the track. She had to find a settlement of some kind.

Around mid-morning, she stopped to let everyone rest. Lifting the cubs out, she put them on the ground and let them loose, every action forcing her to use her right hand as the left reminded her of its injury. They hesitantly padded about, sniffing everything, including the horses. Yrsa realised they'd spent their brief lives hidden in the hollow, and everything was new to them. Brimble didn't mind them, but the injured packhorse did and stamped his foot a few times, sending the cubs scuttling away.

She was still surprised how readily they let her pick them up and put them in the pannier before they moved on. She ate some sausage as they walked, not wanting to stop again. By mid-afternoon, she was giving up hope. They'd walked all day and seen nobody, nor any sign of life. The packhorse was slowing and limping more, the cubs were hungry if their occasional mewing was anything to go by, and her fingers were in danger of being bent forever.

As all these things went through her mind, she saw smoke rising above the trees. It appeared to be to the left of the track in front of them, so she spurred Brimble on, keeping a careful eye on the smoke.

They found a well-used path leading off the track, as clear and trodden as the one she was on. She followed it until the forest suddenly opened to reveal a large clearing, with a substantial thatched house, surrounded by greenery, a few fat fowl pecking around. A green field held a pony, a cow, and a few goats. She was astonished when she saw Amluss's horse was with them, calmly grazing.

Her eye was drawn to a large area fenced in by some sort of reeds, which was home to a wide variety of plants. There were drooping, ragged stems from last season, but plenty of new green shoots poking through the soil. Whoever lived here put a lot of effort into tending them.

She led her horses towards the cottage and looked for the industrious owner. No sign, so she called out a greeting. Then repeated it, louder. Her shoulders were dropping in disappointment when the door swung open, and a woman stepped into the light.

"Good day, my dear," she said. "I wondered when you'd get here."

Chapter 9

"You ... you were expecting me?" Yrsa said.

"I didn't know who would come, but I knew someone would. It's not every day I come across a horse as fine as that wandering in the forest. 'Well, Luna,' I said to myself, 'we'll have visitors before the day's over'. And here you are."

"It's not my horse," Yrsa replied. The woman stared at her until she wilted. "But I do know whose horse it is ... was."

"It sounds an interesting tale. Why not stop and tell me?"

"I don't have time. Is there a healer anywhere nearby? I need one urgently."

"That would be me, dear. Lunata's my name, but everyone calls me Luna. What is your need?"

Yrsa breathed a sigh of relief, hardly believing her luck.

"I have a broken finger or two, the gelding has a bad wound, and ..." She lifted the cubs out of the panniers, one under each arm, and turned back to Luna. "I need to find a way of keeping these two alive."

Luna's eyes widened, and her mouth dropped open.

"By the spirits," she said. "Are they what I think they are? Are they zeffen?"

Yrsa nodded, and half-expected Luna to send her on her way. She'd feared this reaction. But instead, the healer broke into an excited laugh, chuckling and clapping her hands.

"Well, you have brought a gift indeed, dear," she said. "I've always wanted to see one, and you appear with not one, but two."

She stared at the cubs, clearly entranced by them. The silence was broken by a whinny, and they looked over to the field, where Amluss's mare was trotting to the fence. The wounded gelding turned and shook his head, before limping over to greet his friend.

Luna remembered Yrsa's needs.

"Right, my dear. Put them down and let me see your hand."

As the cubs hesitantly explored their new world, Luna undid Yrsa's temporary binding. Yrsa cursed the world, cursed the Gods, and cursed the damn packhorse as the healer pulled and prodded.

"How did you do this?" Luna asked.

"That beast kicked me," Yrsa replied, pointing to the offender.

"Frisky, is he?"

"I was inspecting his wound and he took exception."

"At least it's your left hand."

"That's the one I use most."

Luna let go of Yrsa's fingers and went over to inspect the horse. She whispered close to his head, words Yrsa couldn't hear, and made her way to the wound. The horse twitched and snorted but let her gently stretch and prod it.

"What did this?" Luna asked.

"Their mother," Yrsa replied, leaning her head towards the cubs.

"Dead?"

"Yes."

"You put these stitches in?" she asked.

"I'm afraid so."

Yrsa and the Zeffen Hunter

"Nonsense, dear. You probably saved its life. We'll need to tidy them up, though." She came back to Yrsa. "And what's the problem with these two?"

"I don't know what to feed them. I tried cow's milk, but it passed straight through."

"Oh, that's easy," Luna replied without elaborating. "I think your hand comes first. The others can wait."

Luna helped Yrsa remove the baggage from Brimble and put it by the door.

"Put this one – Brimble, did you say? - into the field with the others."

"And the injured one?"

"Better keep him separate for now. The goats can be a bit rough, though they don't mean it."

Yrsa gave Brimble's neck a hug as she left her to make friends with the little flock. On her way back to the house, she scooped up the cubs.

"What shall I do with these two?"

"Bring them inside dear, the poor things."

Yrsa followed Luna into the house and the smell hit her. Not foul, but sweet and fragrant. The scent of the forest and the meadow, ten times over. It was overwhelming at first. She looked around, not knowing where to begin. Baskets in rows, sacks lined up against the wall, all sorts of objects hanging from the beams and nails on the wall.

"Come, dear. Let's sort your hand out."

Yrsa put the cubs on the floor and walked over to Luna, who was standing by a table.

"Sit. Drink this," Luna said, handing her a beaker. She looked at it suspiciously. "Drink it, this will hurt."

Yrsa shrugged and swallowed the contents in one go, immediately feeling a little dizzy, and cried out as Luna yanked a finger. The next moments were the worst Yrsa could remember. Without pausing, Luna worked quickly, pulling, stretching, and rearranging the broken fingers. The sound of bone scraping bone was almost as bad as the pain. She wrapped each one tightly in linen, before placing pieces of animal bone between them and wrapping them tightly together.

"There," Luna said. "All done."

"Thank you," Yrsa muttered, not sure she was grateful at all.

"I'm afraid the pain will get worse before it gets better, but I can give you something if it gets too bad."

"What's next?"

"The gelding will be fine until tomorrow. We need to think about these two." The cubs were lying on the floor a few steps away, watching. "They're already fond of you."

"They are?"

"They were hissing when I was mending your fingers. They thought I was hurting you."

"You were."

"Sometimes pain is good," she replied. "I see they have teeth."

"Yes, I tried running milk down my finger, but all I got were scratches."

"I think we can try some meat."

Luna scuttled over to a large, raised hearth in the end wall, grabbed a bowl and ladled something from a large pot, before returning to the table. It was some kind of stew, and she'd picked out a few lumps of meat. She went to pick one of the cubs up, but it hissed at her and backed away.

"You try, my dear. They're not sure of me yet."

With her good hand, Yrsa picked one up and put it on her lap. Luna took some meat and broke it into tiny pieces, passing a few over. Yrsa offered it to the cub in her hand. It sniffed it, licked it, but didn't take it.

"Put it in your mouth," Luna said. Yrsa placed the meat between her lips and bent towards the cub. It scrunched its nose, sniffed, and took the meat. After trying this a few times with success, Yrsa felt a wave of relief. She swapped the cubs over, and the other was as keen as the first.

"They probably still need some milk as well," Luna said. "But with their mother dead, they'll have to grow up fast. We could try some goat's milk. I've raised fox cubs on it."

Yrsa fed the cubs until their interest waned, while Luna went to milk one of the goats and offered it to the cubs in a bowl. They sniffed it and made pathetic attempts to suck it. Yrsa tried the water skin trick again, and they took it.

"All we can do now is wait and see," Luna said.

It was beginning to get dark, and Yrsa went out to the horses. The injured gelding was still standing outside the fence, with Tennell on the other side. Brimble was ignoring them both, grazing happily with the goats and Luna's pony.

When she went back into the house, Luna was watching the cubs who were fast asleep after their meal, clearly fascinated by them.

"As everyone else has eaten," she said, "It's time for us to do the same."

She ladled out two bowls of stew, and set them on the table, along with some chunks of bread. Yrsa realised she was starving, and sat down, accepting the offered spoon. The stew was delicious, the bread heavy and filling.

"Now, dear," Luna said. "What might your name be?"

Yrsa could have kicked herself.

"I'm so sorry," she replied. "I'm Yrsa."

"Yrsa, a good name. And don't worry, when people come to me, they're often too desperate to remember their manners." She saw Luna was teasing her. "Where are you from, Yrsa?"

"The Valleys."

"And where are you going?"

"I'm not sure," Yrsa replied, looking over at the sleeping cubs. "At least, not as sure as I was yesterday."

***

Yrsa woke refreshed in the morning. Her hand hurt, but Luna had given her something to dull the pain when she needed it. She didn't ask what it was. She'd fed the cubs again before they went to bed and judging by the solid deposits she saw on the floor of the house, they'd liked it better than the cow's milk.

"I'm sorry," she mumbled, as she cleared it up.

When she went out to the horses, Brimble was still apart from the other two, though whether she was keeping her distance, or they were snubbing her, she couldn't tell.

She wondered what to do with Amluss's horses. The injured gelding needed rest, and time to heal. His black mare needed rest, too. She'd been a magnificent animal once, but Yrsa guessed years on the road had worn her down. Ribs too visible, she needed good grazing and oats. Coat a little thin in places, particularly where the saddle and caparison had rubbed day after day.

But she found one area where Amluss had not neglected her. The animal allowed her to lift a leg, and Yrsa found a foot in good condition, carefully clipped. Iron shoes as well, which looked fairly new. Most people still bought brads and hammered them in themselves. They were good enough for working horses. Shoes were the preserve of the wealthy or those who rode long distances.

Luna came out of the house, and seeing Yrsa, walked over, stroking the injured gelding when she arrived.

"What might his name be?" she asked, examining the wound.

"I don't know," Yrsa replied.

"You should give him one."

"Why me? I'm not even sure who owns him now."

"He's been through a lot; he needs some love."

"But I can't take either of them with me. This one's injured, and that one needs a long rest."

Luna looked at Amluss's horse.

"That one has no name, either?"

"She does, she's called Tennell."

"Well, they can both recover while you stay with me."

"Oh, thank you, but I need to move on."

Luna looked at Yrsa with mild pity.

"My dear," she said. "You cannot go anywhere with your hand in that state. One wrong move and it will all slip out of place again. And it is your strong hand, too. Who will reset it? You need to stay here for at least a moon, probably two."

That hit Yrsa hard.

"Two moons? I don't want … I can't … impose myself on you."

"Nonsense, dear. Besides, those little terrors need some stability, too, until they can walk alongside you. They won't fit in your baggage forever."

Yrsa hung her head, knowing Luna was right. Whatever she'd planned, wherever she was going, it would have to wait.

Chapter 10

Yrsa had to make the best of her enforced stay. She needed her hand to heal, it was useless as it was. She had to use her right hand to brush the horses, feed the cubs, and eat. It made her laugh and cry in equal measure to begin with, but she was surprised how quickly she adapted, automatically using her right without thinking.

When Luna treated the injured horse's wound, Yrsa watched in disbelief as the healer persuaded him to lie on his side, while she washed the wound with a concoction she'd made, and carefully stitched the areas which were still open. She had to re-open it in a few places, but the animal merely twitched, without further complaint.

"Well, dear," she said, getting the horse to its feet, "that should do. We need to hobble him, though. If he runs around, it'll open up."

When they put him in the field with the others, Tennell greeted him like a long-lost friend, and even Brimble did a little jig.

"Have you thought of a name for him yet?" Luna asked.

"I can't keep him, so I'm not sure I need to name him."

"What about Lucky?"

"If you like."

"Well, he has been. Surviving the attack and finding his way to you."

"You can have him."

"I've got Apple, dear. She's all I need. But I'd love to hear how you came by them."

Yrsa saw no reason to keep the story from her host and gave an account of her journey so far. The only thing she omitted was the tale Amluss told her on his last night on earth. She was still considering what to do about that.

"You've packed a lot into a brief time," Luna said when she finished. "Quite a start to your journey."

"More than I planned."

"Life is like that. I find it's best if I don't plan at all."

"But you plan your steading here. You have all you need."

"I do, but beyond that, I never know what each dawn will bring."

Yrsa saw how true that was over the coming days. Local people came seeking Luna's advice, and a remedy for their ills, real or imagined. Animals were brought to receive her attention as well. She treated everyone the same, talking to them, reassuring them, and doing what she could. They mainly paid in kind: a few eggs, some cheese, a scrawny hen.

Most paid Yrsa little attention, and although she tried to keep the cubs out of sight when visitors appeared, those who saw them saw nothing unusual in a couple of young dogs. Young dogs who were learning fast.

After taking food from her lips the first few days, they were soon happily taking it from her hand. She had to reprimand them a few times for being a little too snappy, but they learned quickly and could be remarkably gentle. It had taken even less time to train them not to soil the house, and they took to using a patch of rough ground at the edge of the forest.

Their confidence grew, and they started to explore the steading, going a little further on their own each time. One day, Yrsa almost cried when for the first time, they went with her as she tended the horses. Staying a few steps behind, they followed her to the field, laid a few paces away as she brushed each horse, then moved with her to the next.

Lucky was still nervous of them, which Yrsa understood, but Tennell treated them with disdain. Yrsa wondered if that would diminish when the cubs were fully grown. And they were growing, it was visible almost every day. They were eating well, and she began to think about providing meat for them.

Luna had refused any offer of payment, but with herself, three horses and the two cubs, Yrsa was an expensive guest. There was no way she could use her bow yet, but she went into the forest and set some traps. At least she could provide some game for the pot.

There was something about Luna that fascinated Yrsa. It was her way with everyone and everything she encountered. People seemed relieved to see her, to have her pay them attention. Even she knew some of the things they came to the healer with were incurable, yet they went away happy.

But her way with animals was what intrigued Yrsa. She spoke to them, but never loud enough for others to hear.

"What do you say to them?" she asked one day.

"I tell them of my day, ask them how they are."

"Do they respond?"

"In their way. They seem to find it soothing."

They did. The incident with Lucky was repeated several times with other animals which came and went, and the cubs had quickly gotten over any shyness of her.

"I sometimes wish I could talk to animals," Yrsa said one evening, sitting on the floor near the fire. A cub lay on either side, their heads on her lap. "It would make looking after these two easier."

"There are some who can," Luna replied.

"Oh, I've heard such tales, too."

"I've seen it. I've met two people who could communicate with animals."

"Who?" Yrsa was interested now.

"One is distant kin of mine. Something of an outcast, now calls himself a seer."

"Is he not?"

"Oh, he sees things," Luna replied, laughing. "Mostly the bottom of a tankard, or the hand of a girl before it hits his face refusing an invitation to his bed."

"But he can talk to animals?"

"Not all, but yes, I believe he can communicate with them."

"And the other?"

"The other I will not name. A woman of tremendous skill and guile, but a heart of pure malice. I beg the spirits daily I never come across her again."

Yrsa wanted to ask why but resisted.

"Do they just talk to them? Can they hear the animal speak?"

"My kinsman wouldn't discuss it. But my guess is it's some form of vaying."

"Vaying?"

"It's said there were those long ago who could read minds, even put ideas into people's heads. I think these people can do it with animals."

"I can't believe that."

"Don't you communicate with Brimble? Talk to her?"

"But that's different. She doesn't understand or reply."

"Are you sure? Doesn't she hear your commands and carry them out? Doesn't she look at you sometimes and you know what she's thinking?"

"Brimble does make her opinion very clear at times. But it's not talking."

"There are other forms of communication than talking."

They fell silent, Yrsa thinking about what Luna had said. Luna watching her. Yrsa shifted position and the cubs voiced their displeasure.

"Do you have any temkin?" Yrsa asked.

"I don't think I know it," Luna replied.

"It's a mushroom. Quite small, almost black with white spots. Usually grows around dead oaks."

"I think I know the one you mean. What do you use it for?"

"Dried and powdered it's good to smoke. It's calming."

"Sleepy top, I'll bet that's it. That's what we call it, anyway. I've got some somewhere, it was in the draught I gave you when I set your hand. I didn't know about smoking it. I'll find it tomorrow, though it won't be powdered."

"I'll prepare some if I can borrow a mortar."

"Of course, if you will help me."

"With what?"

"I think it's time you learnt some of my skills."

So, the next day, Yrsa worked with Luna. She joined her when people came to seek her help, listened to the advice she gave, and helped her prepare a myriad of ointments and potions to relieve their ills. Every few days, Luna ambled off with her pony, Apple, and visited the nearest villages. She went off with bundles of aid for some regular patients and came back laden with supplies, both those received in payment and those she'd bought.

"I wonder if the cubs would be all right on their own for a day?" Yrsa asked when Luna returned from one of her trips.

"Why, dear?"

"I'd like to come with you next time."

"Let's find out."

The next day, after they'd eaten and played outside, Yrsa shut the cubs in one of Luna's storerooms while the two women got on with their work. There was a little whining at first, but then they went quiet. At lunchtime, Yrsa let them out, nearly falling over under the weight of the cubs launching themselves at her in greeting.

A couple of days later, she shut them in for longer, and again, they seemed fine when she let them out, though she was now prepared for their vigorous welcome.

The following week, the two women set off together, with Apple and Brimble. The first village was half a league away. A prosperous place, with lots of small plots around a couple of communal buildings, and larger fields further out. Luna visited three houses, dispensing calming advice and some medicine, and checked a goat which another villager brought to her.

"You seem to be popular," Yrsa said, teasingly, as they walked on to the next village.

"Sometimes," Luna replied. "But it's always the same with my kind. They love me when they need me but think I'm up to no good when something bad happens."

The next village was much larger. Luna visited several farms, and Yrsa had the opportunity to buy two sacks of oats. The centre had a communal hall, a small inn, and a smithy. Luna stopped at the latter, waiting for the smith to pause in his work.

"Good day, Grenk," she called over the noise of the forge. The man looked up, saw her, and came out of his shop.

"Good day, Luna," he replied. "How is your world?"

"Well, thank the spirits."

Yrsa couldn't help admiring the man. Stripped to his trousers to cope with the heat in his shop, his body was glistening with sweat. He looked different to the other locals. His skin was darker, and he wore his long reddish hair loose with no beard. He was tall and immensely strong, his body built by the arduous work of his trade.

"Grenk, this is Yrsa. She's helping me for a while."

"Greetings, Yrsa," he said, giving a slight bow.

"Good day, Grenk," she replied. "I may need your services shortly."

"For yourself, or a horse?" he asked with a twinkle.

"Watch him," Luna said, laughing.

"A horse," Yrsa replied, "or three. I'll need their hooves checked and possibly one or two shod."

"Three horses? Needing shoes? Luna, is your guest a noblewoman?"

"If she is, you'd do well to be polite, lest she finds another smith."

As the women moved on, he returned to his work.

"He's young to be the village smith," Yrsa said.

"He was an apprentice to his father, but the old man was killed by a kick from a horse. I couldn't save him. Grenk was skilled enough to take over and the people like him."

"I can see why," Yrsa replied, making Luna chuckle.

By the time they got home, their horses were loaded with supplies which they put by the door. Yrsa heard scratching from the storeroom.

"Go on," Luna said. "I'll take the horses."

When Yrsa opened the door, the cubs rushed out, heading for their patch of ground. Looking inside the store, she found they hadn't soiled it in the long hours she and Luna had been away. The cubs rushed back, jumping, running around her, giving lots of little yaps. She sat on the ground and made a fuss of them.

* * *

"You're definitely their mother now," Luna said that evening.

Yrsa was in her usual position, sitting on the floor with the cubs on either side of her.

"It seems so," she replied, "though it worries me."

"Why, dear?"

"What's going to happen to them? Wherever I go, they'll be in danger."

"Most people won't have a clue what they are. Tell them they're hunting dogs, and they'll believe you."

"But you recognised them."

"A wild guess, and a lot of luck," Luna replied, dismissively. "They're finding their voices, as well."

"I know, they're very vocal. I'm trying to work them out."

"And what have you discovered?"

"Well, there's a whimper." Yrsa tried to imitate the sound, and the cubs immediately responded, raising their heads, and looking at her. She stroked them and they relaxed. "That's when they're uncertain. There's a hiss when they feel threatened, a yap when they're excited, and a purr when they're content that's almost like a cat."

"You see, you do understand them."

"But I've not heard anything like a bark or a howl. They're not much like any dog I've ever known."

"If the old stories are true, they're solitary creatures. Most dogs are pack animals and need to hear each other over long distances. These don't."

"I wonder what their mother was doing here?"

"I don't know, I've never heard of any sightings in my lifetime. But I guess she gave birth to these two earlier than expected and couldn't go back north."

Yrsa recalled the scene in the hollow when she first found the cubs. It brought a tear to her eye thinking about it, but also something else. A determination to fulfil her promise to their mother. These cubs would only leave her if they wanted to.

"They're with you now," Luna said. "You made a pact with their mother, and it's going to change your life, and theirs."

"But how?"

"You need to discover that yourself, my dear."

Chapter 11

Yrsa checked her traps every morning, and they yielded plenty of meat, mostly coney with the odd wild pig. The cubs accompanied her, frolicking in the forest, relishing every new experience. They were always interested in the contents of the traps. The first time they went with her, she had to stop them from eating the coney she released. But they were keen for her praise and didn't try it again.

One day, she tried giving them each a coney to carry back and they trotted along, gently holding them in their mouths. When they reached the house, they went inside and dropped them in front of Luna, before sitting expectantly. Luna thanked them and gave them each a piece of meat from the pot. It became a regular ritual.

The horses flourished in their new environment. Brimble was Brimble: the same level mood, the same air of contented resignation. Lucky's wound was healing, and although he would always carry an ugly scar, he seemed to have gotten over the terror of its infliction.

But the biggest change was in Tennell. She looked a different horse. She was filling out, her muscles regaining their strength and definition. Her coat was recovering, and a good daily grooming had begun to make it shine. She was proving very trusting, and Yrsa was itching to try riding her.

She'd been delighted when Luna had shown her Amluss's saddle and caparison which she'd removed when she brought the horse home. There were leather stirrups, as well. Yrsa had never used them, making do with a couple of looped ropes.

She spent hours working on the saddle, using some ill-smelling lotion Luna gave her. But it worked, and although you could see it was old, the leather now had a glossy sheen.

The caparison was an unusual design Yrsa hadn't seen before. It covered most of the horse's back but only came partway down its flank. There were loops to hold things, and she remembered seeing the small crossbows and a sword hanging from it when she'd met him on the Norsouth road.

Where those weapons were, she didn't know, but she spent time cleaning and polishing those he had bequeathed her. She marvelled at the obvious skill needed to make both the blades and the scabbards. The sword blade had an odd profile, with patterns etched into it, but she couldn't tell if they were some kind of script or merely decorative.

All the blades were incredibly sharp, like her own szanka, which wasn't surprising now she knew they may all have come from the same place. When she finished, she found the courage to add one of the curved daggers to her belt.

Her fingers were healing. The pain had almost gone unless she tried to do something stupid. So, one day, she took the saddle, caparison and bridle out to the field. Tennell calmly allowed her to set it all up, and Yrsa gently mounted the mare, who fidgeted a little under the unfamiliar rider.

Calmly talking to her and stroking her neck, Yrsa steadied her and walked her around the field. After that first time, she rode her every day, horse and rider getting to know each other until she felt confident enough to take her along the forest path.

Subsequent forays introduced the trot and even the canter on a couple of days. Yrsa loved it; Tennell was a powerful, agile animal, a joy to ride. It reminded her of Gusta, the stallion she'd left behind, though without his often frustrating temperament.

"I think I'll take the horses to the village tomorrow," Yrsa said to Luna. "Lucky needs attention, and I'll get Grenk to tidy the others."

"Very well, dear. Will you be staying the night?"

"No, why?" she replied. The smile on the healer's face gave her the answer.

"Luna!"

After they'd eaten, they settled for the evening.

"Yrsa, my dear," Luna said after a lengthy period of contented silence. "How is it you didn't find some sturdy young man like Grenk to settle with and raise children?"

Yrsa didn't reply for some time, thinking about the question and whether she wanted to answer it.

"My father had selected a man for me to marry," she finally said. "I didn't like him."

"Is that the custom in your land?"

"It is for women in my state."

"What state is that, dear?"

"My blessing never came."

"Blessing?" Luna asked, puzzled.

"I don't bleed. I never have."

Luna gave her a strange look briefly, then chuckled, but it was a warm sound.

"Blessing!" she said. "By the spirits. Around here, it's often called the curse. Most women would feel blessed if they didn't bleed. Besides, women who cannot bear children have other gifts. But surely it doesn't mean you cannot marry?"

"No man wants a woman who cannot bear him children, but all men desire such a woman as a lover."

"Ah, I understand."

"I've never been shy with men. My state allowed me to be. I've taken it when I wanted it and used it to my advantage. But no young man was going to want me as his wife."

"Where does your father come into this?"

"Our tradition is for women who don't find a husband from the unmarried men to become replacement wives, marrying those who have lost the mothers of their children. It means you often marry an older man, and many are happy with the arrangement."

"But you weren't?"

"The latest man my father had in mind was more than twice my age and a drunken dolt. I want more from life than that."

"What do you want, dear?"

Yrsa thought for a moment.

"To see the world. I know it sounds childish, but after my mother died, Father took me with him on his voyages, along with my brothers. I loved travelling to all the places he visited to trade, meeting different people. I would have been happy doing it forever. But it all stopped when he remarried five years later. My brothers were useful in his work by then, but I had to stay at home with my stepmother."

"You'd lost your freedom."

"And when it was certain I couldn't have children, he blamed himself."

"Why is that?"

"He thought it was because he'd brought me up too much like a boy."

"Men can be stupid, dear."

"He decided it was his duty to find me a husband. I couldn't change his mind, neither could my stepmother. He's suggested one after another, each worse than the last."

"So, you escaped. I think you made the right decision."

"I hope so, I can't go back."

"That is your pride talking."

"No, Luna. I've sworn to the Gods I will never go back. I've left that life behind."

* * *

As she rode Tennell along the path to the village, Yrsa remembered Luna's words. Other gifts. What did she mean? She hadn't picked it up at the time, but as she lay waiting for sleep, it had come into her mind. She'd long accepted the traditional role of her sex – as wife and mother - was not to be a part of her life, but still wasn't sure what her role was.

Lucky and Brimble were loosely tethered behind her, and they were walking at the pace of the slowest. Brimble, of course. Yrsa didn't want to draw attention to herself in the village, and Tennell had the saddle, with some sacking under it. Amluss's caparison was rather showy for a trip to the smith.

As she reached the edge of the village, she dismounted and led the chain of horses to the centre, where she found only disappointment. The smithy was closed, with no sign of smoke from the forge. Knocking on the door brought no answer, and she was wondering what to do when a man passed by.

"If you're looking for the smith," he said, "you'll find him around the back."

She walked around the side and found a smaller building standing ten paces or so from the back of the forge. It looked new, the thatch still showing signs of its natural colour.

"Hello?" she called, knocking on the door. "Grenk? Are you here?"

She heard whispering, and stood back a few paces, not wanting to intrude. A few moments later, the door opened and Grenk appeared, tying his trousers, his tunic over his shoulder.

"Yrsa," he said. "Good day."

"Good day, Grenk. I'm sorry to disturb you."

"It's nothing. Time I did some work. What can I do for you?"

"I was hoping you could look at my horses, but I see you're not fired today."

"There's not enough work to light it every day but let me see what you need."

They walked around to the front of the smithy, where the horses stood patiently, tied to the rail.

"Well," Grenk said, laughing. "There's a mixed crew."

Yrsa let him examine them. There was little smiths didn't know about horses, and she didn't need to explain their needs.

"So," he said, after a quick evaluation. "Introduce me, this little lady first."

"That's Brimble, we've grown up together. Hates being ridden, a bit stubborn, one pace, but can walk all day."

"And this one?"

"That's Lucky. A recent … rescue. I know nothing about him."

"And this beauty?" He stood by the big black mare, gently stroking her neck, and nuzzling her nose.

"Tennell, another new find."

"She's a magnificent animal. I've only seen her like once before, several years ago now, when some soldiers from the east passed through. She's a bit special."

"Sometimes she lets you know it."

"The best always do."

He looked up and over Yrsa's shoulder, and she turned to follow his gaze. A woman of perhaps thirty years had appeared from the side of the forge carrying a small basket. She was smiling at Grenk, saw Yrsa watching her, and blushed.

"I'll be going," she said. "You have work to do."

"Fair enough," he replied. "Bodira, this is Yrsa."

"Good day," Bodira said.

"Good day, Bodira," Yrsa replied. "I'm sorry for disturbing you."

"Oh," the woman replied, blushing deeper, "we weren't busy."

Grenk chuckled, earning a scolding look from his lover before she turned and walked away. When Yrsa turned back, he had a broad smile on his face.

"Your wife?" she asked.

"No," he replied, shaking his head. "I'm not married. Bodira's a widow, and she and I enjoy each other's company."

Grenk opened the smithy, put an apron on, and began his assessment, starting with Brimble.

"She needs a little clipping, and these studs need replacing. Or I could shoe her?"

"Studs will do, she's never been shod."

Lucky was next.

"He needs some work. Clipping, cleaning out, and a bit of shaving. He's missing most of his studs."

Tennell came last.

"These are good shoes, but they're too small. Looks like someone's fitted a set they had lying idle. They're not fully supporting her hooves."

"Do what you think is best."

"I can do everything but the shoes now if you're happy to wait."

As Grenk set to work, Yrsa sat on the boards at the front of the forge, quite happy to watch him. He'd been working with horses from the cradle, and even Brimble calmly let him lift each leg, trim her hooves, and hammer in new studs. Lucky proved more reluctant, but he was used to flighty horses.

"Do you work here alone?" Yrsa asked.

"Yes, since my father died."

"Luna told me, I'm sorry."

"He taught me everything he knew. He was a good smith."

"It must have been hard."

"He was also a drunkard and a chaser of women."

"Ah. Have you followed in his footsteps?"

He looked back at her, with Lucky's leg still between his thighs. Yrsa was hit by his dazzling grin.

"No," he replied, "I hardly drink at all."
She couldn't help laughing. She was growing to like Grenk.

* * *

On her way back to the village the next day, the clouds looked heavy and grim. Light rain was being blown around by an increasingly gusty wind. Arriving at the smithy, she found Grenk hard at work, stripped to the waist, his forge glowing. He was hammering an iron flange, a carter waiting outside, his cart propped up while the wheel sat in a frame awaiting its outer rim.

He spotted her, waved, and continued his hammering. Yrsa stood and watched, enjoying the way his muscles moved and flexed as he brought the hammer down on the thin metal. The man was beautiful, and she imagined his body sliding over her own.

"Tha's a fine 'orse."

The voice brought her back from her daydream. The carter was standing next to her, looking at Tennell.

"Thank you. Yes, she is."

"Where's 'er from? Sh'aint from round 'ere."

"I'm not sure, to be honest. Her last owner was from the east."

"Bet 'er could pull a load."

"I'm not sure she'd take well to pulling a cart."

"Nowt wrong wi' pulling a cart, girl."

"No, no, I didn't mean that. I'm sorry. She wouldn't be used to it. That's a fine horse you have there."

"Tis too. Bred it m'self. I've another like her at 'ome."

"A fine animal."

It was. A true workhorse, big, heavy, and stupid, if the carthorses she'd known were anything to go by. Grenk came out with the glowing band and worked quickly to force it over the wooden rim. Checking it was exactly where he wanted it, he lifted the wheel, his shoulders and arms tensing nicely under the weight, and dropped it into the large trough at the side of the forge.

The iron hissed as it shrank onto the wood, sending clouds of steam into the air, the wood creaking as it was constricted by the iron. He rolled the wheel over to the cart, pushed it onto the axle and knocked the pins in.

"There you are, Bo," he said. "Good as new."

"Better be," the carter replied, handing Grenk a small basket. "I'll be wanting tha' basket back, mind," he said before leading his horse and cart away.

"Good day, Yrsa," Grenk said, coming over and stroking Tennell's neck.

"Good day, Grenk. What's in the basket?"

He lifted the lid; three chickens, looking very unhappy in their confined home.

"I'll put them round the back."

When he returned, he set to work on Tennell. The weather was worsening, the rain coming down heavily, and they moved into the forge, the mare standing in the stall at one end. He removed her old shoes and trimmed and shaved her hooves, before starting some new ones. By that time, Yrsa was sure he was strutting a little more than necessary for her benefit, but she didn't mind.

Now she was in the forge, it wasn't only Grenk who was sweating. The fire was glowing red, filling the space with its heat, sucking in all the air. Yrsa's clothes stuck to her skin and Grenk's trousers were clinging to him, his buttocks visibly flexing as he beat the iron. He noticed her gaze, and she saw that dazzling grin again.

"Get on with your work," she mouthed over the noise of the forge.

"Yes, lady," he replied with a mock bow.

Chapter 12

By the time Tennell's shoes were finished, the rain was audible over the sound of the fire. Even though only the middle of the afternoon, it was dark and heavy.

"Nobody will be out in this," Grenk said. "I'll have no more work today."

He spread the fire, closed the vents, and brought down the shutters along the front of the smithy. They'd been letting some of the heat out, and with them closed, the temperature rose dramatically.

"I don't know how you work in here," Yrsa said. "It's so hot."

"That's why I take my tunic off," he said.

Yrsa hesitated for a moment, before pulling hers over her head. Grenk watched her, his arms folded, admiring the female form fully revealed to him as she let her trousers drop to the floor. She wanted him, and his interest was visible under his soaking trousers, which quickly followed hers.

As their bodies came together, he lifted her off the ground and dropped her onto his worktable, sending tools flying everywhere. It wasn't an ideal platform for their lust. Neither was the anvil, after he turned her around and bent her over it, but they didn't care. They ignored the sound of the rain beating on the roof as they satisfied each other, almost reaching their peak together.

As she recovered, Yrsa could feel the cold from the anvil under her tummy. Grenk lifted her from it and gently stood her up, a satisfied smile on his face. Now the frantic activity had ended, they could hear the rain outside. The noise was overwhelming, as it beat down on the ground, the wooden shutters, and the roof.

Yrsa was covered in the debris from the table and the anvil, stuck to her body by the sweat.

"Look," she said, "I'm filthy."

Before she could react, Grenk picked up a bucket of water and threw it over her. She wiped her eyes, blew water out of her nose, and saw him standing in front of her, laughing. So she pushed him backwards into the trough.

Dripping wet, Grenk opened the little door at the back of the smithy, and they looked out. The rain was still coming down in torrents. So heavy, they could hardly make out his home a mere ten paces away.

"You can't travel in this," he said.

The journey was a little less than a league, but most of it was on grass or muddy paths. They'd be treacherous in this weather, and she hadn't seen Tennell in heavy rain. Most horses didn't like it.

"You can stay with me," he said with a grin.

Yrsa checked Tennell had food and water; she'd be fine in the smithy for the night. They didn't even dress to cross the yard between the buildings. Grenk made a dash for it, but Yrsa stopped halfway, looking up to the heavens, stretching her arms and feeling the weight of the rain on her naked body. It felt good, natural, sensual even.

When she moved again, she saw him standing undercover in his doorway, watching her. The sight of his naked body thrilled her all over again, making her think about what was to come.

Yrsa and the Zeffen Hunter

Grenk built a fire, and they dried off as it grew. His home was thatched, unlike the forge, and it deadened the sound of the rain.

"I'm no cook," he said. "But I've got some bread and meat. People often pay me in food, and Bodira sometimes brings me a meal."

They ate what he had; it was fine enough. After eating, they rested, and little was said. Without discussing it, they were soon cuddled up and beginning to explore each other's bodies. Grenk proved to be a keen and experienced lover, slowly bringing her joy again.

She settled herself to exploring and teasing him when the noise of the wind burst in, and Bodira appeared in the doorway, still carrying her basket. Yrsa jumped up and tried to cover herself, but Bodira seemed unconcerned.

"Good day, Yrsa," she said. "It appears I've disturbed you, this time."

Grenk laughed and walked over to Bodira naked, giving her a hug and a kiss.

"Has the rain stopped?" he asked. "You're not wet."

"It has, but it'll be back. I've brought something to eat while I have the chance."

"Why don't you share it with us?"

Bodira blushed but didn't refuse.

"I could," she said. "There's enough for three."

She shut the door and headed towards the fire, where she dropped the basket.

"Besides," she said, surprising Yrsa by pulling her dress over her head. "He has enough for both of us."

* * *

Yrsa was still smiling as she headed home in the morning. The storm had cleared the air, and it was a bright day. The tracks were sticky and muddy, but Tennell was a sure-footed animal, and they made good progress. It gave Yrsa time to reflect on the night.

Bodira had been right, Grenk could cope with them both. She'd often seen people having sex. Communal living halls meant little privacy, and her people weren't shy about it. But she'd not been in that situation before, being watched by and watching another woman with a shared lover.

Bodira had proved enthusiastic and vocal with Grenk. She was shorter and plumper than Yrsa and watching her breasts bouncing around as she rode him had been an interesting experience. That and the thunder crashing around the house had made it all seem a little unreal.

By the time she reached Luna's, it was mid-morning. The cubs spotted her and bounded out to greet her, getting a few indignant snorts from Tennell as they raced around her legs. When Yrsa dismounted, she dropped to greet them and was soon knocked to the ground by their exuberance. Tennell took herself off to the field, greeting her friends, and Yrsa had to go over and retrieve the saddle.

"There you are, my dear," Luna said. "Did you get everything you wanted?"

"Yes, thank you," she replied. They both grinned but said no more.

"I'm glad you're back," Luna continued. "I'll be away tonight."

"Anything I can help you with?"

"No, thank you, dear."

Before dark, Luna wrapped herself in a heavy cloak and picked up a stout stick.

"I'll be off," she said. "Will you be all right?"

"Of course. Are you taking Apple?"

"No, not tonight. I'll be home in the morning."

After she left, Yrsa wondered where the healer was going. It was nearly dark, and she'd taken little with her, so she couldn't be visiting patients. Luna hadn't mentioned any friends, and the nearest home was a good walk on foot, particularly with the ground sodden from the storm.

When she returned the next morning, Luna appeared especially cheerful. As they worked, Yrsa studied her. She looked younger, brighter, her movements quicker and lighter. Luna wasn't old, but Yrsa couldn't work out her age. On their first meeting, Yrsa had guessed the healer was approaching fifty years. This morning, she looked younger.

"How long have you lived here?" Yrsa asked casually. Luna wasn't fooled.

"Longer than you've been on this earth," she replied.

"Were you born here?"

"No. I came into this world a long way from here."

"And long ago, I suppose."

"Long enough."

"How long?"

Luna stopped her pounding on the pestle and looked at Yrsa.

"How long do you think?"

Yrsa studied her for a moment. She still couldn't decide. There was a calming air about Luna, an air usually acquired with time and experience.

"I guess somewhere between forty and fifty years," she replied, hoping she wasn't insulting her host.

"Well, I must be doing something right, my dear," Luna replied, resuming her pounding.

"You can't leave it like that."

"I don't tell people my age. It leads to too many questions."

Yrsa had abandoned her work, too intrigued by the healer's words.

"Come on, Luna. You took me in, along with my horses and two little terrors. You healed me – and them – without question and without payment. And now you're teaching me some of your secrets. Why keep this to yourself?"

"I'm not telling you everything."

"I couldn't take it all in, anyway. I'm not sure I'm destined to be a healer."

Luna stopped again, looking closely at Yrsa.

"No, dear. I don't think that's your destiny, either."

"Then why teach me?"

"Because it kept you busy, because otherwise you'd have rushed off before you and your animals were healthy enough for your next journey, and got yourself in trouble again."

"So, it's all been pointless?"

"No, Yrsa, dear," Luna replied, placing her hand on her helper's arm. "Everything I've taught you will prove useful. You'll know how to deal with your own illnesses and injuries, and your animal's. No knowledge is pointless."

She released Yrsa and went back to her work.

"Did you have a good night?" Yrsa asked.

"Yes, thank you," Luna replied, a smile on her face.

"Is he nice?"

"I wasn't meeting any man. I gave up on them long ago."

"You seem refreshed this morning."

"Thank you, dear."

* * *

Yrsa's hand was almost fully healed. She hadn't regained all the strength in her fingers yet, but she was exercising them all the time, even testing her bow, pulling it a little further each day. She'd been surprised how easily she'd managed with her right hand, and found herself able to use either for most things.

She knew it was time to think about leaving this place, but she was torn. Luna had welcomed her and offered her a sanctuary. Part of her could imagine staying, becoming the healer's assistant. But their discussion had confirmed her suspicion it wasn't what the Gods had in store for her.

Besides, she'd set out to see more of the world. The horses were fully refreshed, and Tennell and Lucky had put on weight and muscle. Even Brimble had found a sense of fun from somewhere.

And the cubs … well, she wondered how much longer she could call them cubs. They were bigger and stronger than most dogs. Still nowhere near the size of their mother, and being boys, she guessed they might outgrow her. But they were a handful, and she had to watch out for their surprise pounces. They were always in fun, but they didn't realise their own strength.

"You haven't named them, dear," Luna said to her one day for the umpteenth time.

"I know. I didn't want to at first in case anything happened. Now, I'm not sure it's right."

"Don't your people name their dogs?"

"Yes."

"So," Luna said, watching Yrsa closely, "what's different about these two?"

"I think they have names. I just wish I knew what they were."

* * *

Summer brought longer days, and she spent some of them exploring the forest with the cubs, where they followed any tracks they came across instinctively.

"Do you think they know how to hunt?" she'd asked Luna. "Or do they need to learn?"

"I suspect it's a bit of both, dear."

"Gods, how am I going to train them? I can't even keep up with them."

She'd tried hiding dead game and leading them close to it. They invariably found it but didn't know what to do with it once they had, usually carrying it back to Luna. How could she teach them to stalk? To pounce? To kill? Even Luna hadn't been able to come up with a solution.

Grenk was also a satisfying diversion. They met at least every few days, and those encounters were invariably filled with laughter and passion. She'd rarely come across a man who could thrill her as much as he did, and his open manner was refreshing. She shared him with Bidora, who was happy with the arrangement, and indeed seemed to relish those occasions when the three of them were together.

Those nights were something of a revelation for Yrsa. Watching Bidora and Grenk aroused her, as did Bidora's open and casual approach to her own nakedness and sexuality. And she was aroused when Bidora watched her with Grenk, the plump widow even running her hand over Yrsa's nakedness. That reaction had surprised her, and Bidora had appeared in one or two dreams.

Chapter 13

"I need to move on soon," Yrsa told Luna one evening.
"Are you sure, dear?" Luna replied.
"I love it here, but it's time."
"Grenk cannot persuade you to stay?"
"He has Bidora."
"She won't marry him."
"Possibly not, but they're happy as they are."
After a few moments silence, Luna turned to face her guest.
"There's something I need to talk to you about, Yrsa," she said. "Something I've thought long and hard about since you arrived. You asked me a question a while ago, a question I avoided."
Yrsa had to think before recalling it.
"Your age?" she said.
"It's not something I talk about, and I don't think there is anyone left who knows. But I've been in this world one hundred and nineteen years, and I hope to remain here for many more yet."
Yrsa laughed, but something told her Luna wasn't joking, and she looked at the healer in awe.
"How is that possible?" she asked.

"I am blessed with long life."

"So are my family, but I don't recall any of them living much beyond eighty years. One or two passed their ninetieth, I believe."

"When I say blessed, I don't use the word lightly, dear."

"What do you mean?"

Luna sighed, shifted in her chair, and made herself comfortable.

"I was born in the southern lands. My parents were nothing special, just a poor couple scraping a living on a patch of scrubland. My father would take his goats up into the hills in spring and bring them down again in autumn. The plains were too dry to feed them in summer. When I was about eight, he took me with him when he went to bring them down, a task which took many days.

"One evening, something scared the goats and they dispersed, and he spent the night rounding them all up. I wandered off. I found a cave. Children are never frightened by such things, and I went in. It was deep and long, and something drew me on.

"In the darkness, I saw a dim light and followed it. Eventually, it opened onto a green space. It felt like a dream, like something I'd imagined. I was in an oasis, with a stream, verdant trees and bushes. I was spellbound, and danced around, laughing.

"Eventually, I tired and lay on the ground. I have no idea how long I was asleep, but I will never forget the dreams. Dreams so intense they hurt; so intense, they changed my life."

Yrsa went to ask a question, but Luna quieted her with a wave of her hand.

"When I emerged from the cave, my father scolded me for running off. I tried to tell him of the oasis, the greenery, but he dismissed it as the imagination of a child. And when I began to see and hear things he couldn't, he scolded me further. He didn't understand. But my perception of the world had changed. I heard the birds and animals more clearly; I felt plants and trees growing and spreading.

"My parents thought I was possessed, and in a way, I suppose I was. They tried to talk me out of it, my father tried to beat it out of me. They failed. I won't tell you the whole tale, but it took me many years to discover what happened, to discover who I was. When I was old enough, I left my land and travelled, looking for answers, as you are. I eventually found them here in the northern lands, though far to the east. I am a spirit melder."

"What's that?"

"It's hard to explain, but the spirits give me access to parts of their world. I feel the life around me; I use it in my work. I honour the spirits, and they protect me."

"They give you long life?"

"That seems to be true for some, but there are no two spirit melders the same. I have come across quite a few in my life, and we are all different. Some are herbalists, making potions to save a life. Or take it. Others are thinkers, devoting their lives to philosophical matters.

"Some seem able to conjure the spirits to perform acts which common folk will call magic. But most of us simply have skills that exceed those around us. Mine is healing, and it's been my purpose for nearly one hundred years."

Yrsa had so many questions but didn't know where to begin. So, she started with the first which popped into her head.

"Do you live forever?"

"No," Luna replied. "And not all melders have extended lives. But for some of us, the spirits are gracious enough to prolong our time here."

"You speak as if you live apart ... as if you inhabit another place. Oh, I don't know what I mean."

"Do any of us understand the world around us? We accept what we can explain, and leave everything else to what? Gods ... spirits ... magic. It's easier that way. I've had more time than most to think about it, and I have no answer, but I believe I may find out one day when my time here is at an end."

"What has all this to do with me?" Yrsa asked.

"I believe you may be a spirit melder, too."

Yrsa began to laugh but saw Luna was deadly serious.

"Me? I'm a girl from the Valleys who wants more from life than a drunken old letch for a husband."

"I've watched you, my dear. You're an instinctive learner, you know things almost before I tell you. You perceive things others don't. And you use your left hand."

"Does that matter?"

"Not all those who use the wrong hand are melders, but most melders I've met have their strength in their left side. I do myself. But it's the animals who tell me I'm right. They are drawn to you, they trust you. I don't believe the mother of these two would have given them to you if she didn't know."

"She didn't give them to me. She died, and I rescued them."

"Do you really believe that? Do you think they would have been so easy to rear if their mother hadn't given you her blessing? She told them to go with you. She told them to trust you. She told them you were their mother now."

Yrsa was stunned, and her breath caught when she turned to the cubs. They were lying on the floor, side by side, and looking straight at her as if listening and understanding what Luna was saying. She dismissed the notion, but the memory of what happened between her and their mother replayed clearly in her mind.

Luna sat back in her chair, allowing Yrsa to think. To take in everything she'd heard.

"But there's nothing like this in my family," Yrsa said.

"It doesn't run in the blood, dear. My kinsman – the one who can vay – is a very distant cousin. No, something arises within us, and the spirits see it."

"What are these spirits? People talk about spirits all the time, but I don't think they're what you mean."

"I cannot give you an easy answer, for I don't know. Perhaps they are what you would call Gods. Perhaps they are something different. But I do know they care for me."

"They are good?"

"They make no judgements. They see something in you and help you to release it. What you do with it is up to you. Some melders care less for their fellow men than their own advantage."

"The other vayer you have met, for example?"

"Perhaps," she replied with a shiver. "I beg the spirits you never encounter that woman. There is more to her than mere melder."

"I still don't understand how this affects me. How will I know?"

"You remember the oasis? Where I saw my destiny? There is a similar place near here."

"You were there the other night," Yrsa said, as realisation dawned.

"Yes," Luna replied. "I go sometimes to clear my mind, clear my worries, and consult the spirits."

"Do they speak to you?"

"They take no form. As I sleep, they enter my mind and cleanse it, renew it. But it is a mixed blessing."

"How so?"

"You know what people are like. I've lived here for over thirty years, and the gossip will soon start. 'That Luna,' they'll say, 'she never seems to get any older. Something odd about her.' I have to move on every so often, and it won't be long before I have to leave this place."

"But they love you."

"They need me, I ease their lives. But old superstitions are powerful things. I've been accused of magic practices more than once."

"You could come with me."

"You don't know where you're going."

They lapsed into silence as Luna left Yrsa with her thoughts.

"Do I need to visit this place?" she eventually asked.

"That, my dear, is up to you."

"That's not very helpful."

"It is your choice because there are grave risks. You must open your mind to the spirits, and let them in. For some, it is too much, and they return without their wits."

* * *

Yrsa spent the following days thinking about what Luna had told her. She'd never thought deeply about her beliefs, about the other world. The Gods of her people were a part of their everyday lives. They asked for good fortune, for protection. They cursed their enemies in their Gods' names. But they didn't think deeply about them, about what they were. They didn't believe they could connect with them in the way Luna had talked about the spirits.

Yrsa had always felt close to the forest and its inhabitants. Most of her people were focused on the sea at their doorstep. Since they'd turned from foreign raids to trade, and peace had reigned, some had turned towards the land, but they never ventured far into the forest, still wary of its reputation.

Yrsa had always felt at home there, more even than her father, who had been among the first to appreciate its potential. From the day he first took her hunting in the forest above their home, she fell in love with it, felt an affinity with its strength and age. Where others found it a tiring, forbidding place, she drew strength and energy from it.

She quickly understood the connections between the plants and animals, that their lives depended on each other. Her brothers were sometimes baffled by the ease with which she found her way around, by her skill at predicting where they would find prey.

She'd never believed this was anything other than watching and listening, but perhaps it was. As she worked with Luna, the idea of being tested by the spirits became more and more appealing. She didn't discount the risk, but she'd left home to experience life, to challenge herself. How could she refuse the first challenge laid before her?

"What do I have to do?" Yrsa asked Luna one evening.
"You go to the glade, and whatever happens, happens."
"Where is it?"
"I will tell you when it's time."
"When will that be?"
"The next full moon."
Luna hadn't told her that part. It meant another three weeks of waiting.

* * *

"Are there any open spaces in the forest?" Yrsa asked one day.
"What for, dear?"
"I want to train the cubs to run alongside the horses." She was healed, the horses were all in prime condition, and the zeffen were easily capable of keeping up. They could probably run as fast as Tennell.
"You could use the tracks to the villages."
"They're a bit too visible."
Luna thought for a moment.
"Do you remember a dead tree in the middle of the track you arrived on?" she said. "Where the path has to split around it."
"Yes, I wondered why no one had removed it."
"There's an old path going down the hill nearby. It leads to some water meadows. Providing we haven't had too much rain, that might be suitable."

Yrsa found the tree easily enough but had to search for the path. Eventually finding it, Tennell pushed her way through, seemingly unworried by the overgrown branches. The trees suddenly ended, and in front of her was a grassy clearing, surrounded by the forest, with a small stream running through the middle.

The ground wasn't quite hard, and she had to be careful, but Tennell was a smart horse. They were soon speeding around the clearing, and to her delight, the cubs naturally followed her, keeping and matching her pace.

While she waited for the full moon, she visited the clearing each afternoon, taking Lucky and Brimble as well. Lucky would sometimes have a canter, snorting and frolicking, while Brimble happily stood by, watching all the activity, and grazing. All three loved rolling in the long grass.

But the real joy was riding Tennell at almost full pace. She was a powerful beast and had been well-trained by someone. Whether it was Amluss, Yrsa didn't know, but she only needed the smallest nudge to understand what was required of her. She was so easy to ride. At the end of their third trip to the clearing, Yrsa dismounted to give the cubs some praise.

As she turned her back, Tennell nudged her shoulder, which she'd never done before, and pulled lightly on the reins in Yrsa's hands. A moment's puzzlement, then understanding.

She slipped the bridle from Tennell's head and watched in amusement as she trotted away, then in amazement as the mare gathered speed and proceeded to tear around the large clearing, stopping occasionally to prance and stamp the ground. When she'd finished, she returned and calmly accepted the bridle again. It became a daily ritual.

* * *

With a week until the full moon, Yrsa was busy preparing for her departure. She intended to leave after her visit to the glade, whatever happened, though Luna warned her it might not work like that. She carefully cleaned and repaired her equipment, washed her clothes, and made a few more. She wished she had more panniers, but there was nowhere nearby to buy any.

Yrsa and the Zeffen Hunter

She'd thought long and hard about the horses. There was no question about Brimble. She was a part of Yrsa's life, and they would never be parted. Tennell was every rider's dream; a smart, sure-footed animal with incredible strength. It was Lucky she was unsure about.

The packhorse had fully recovered from his ordeal and was very compliant, but Yrsa didn't need him. Tennell could carry her and her immediate needs, and Brimble would happily handle the rest. And three horses needed a lot of feed.

"You should take him, dear," Luna said when Yrsa again offered to leave him. "You never know when that horse might surprise you. You saved him, and he loves you."

"But three horses are harder to manage, Luna."

"They're all used to travelling, they'll give you no trouble."

Yrsa had no choice. Luna didn't want Lucky. She thought about offering him for sale in the villages, but something stopped her. She took them all to Grenk again for a final check, though they only needed two studs hammered home between them.

She didn't return home that night. Grenk was as keen as she was, and their meetings were as frequent and satisfying as they had been at the beginning. Bidora was nearly always there as well; she seemed to spend most nights with him.

But the two women were never jealous of each other and had taken the opportunity to explore each other's bodies, though something unsaid had always stopped them from fully indulging their curiosity.

Three days before the full moon, Luna left one morning to help a farmer with a cow that was having a difficult birth. Yrsa had gained enough experience to deal with any simple cases which turned up. She spent the morning crushing and mixing some herbs and played with the cubs over lunch.

As she continued her work in the afternoon, she heard an unfamiliar whinny, followed by her own horses' replies. Time to see a patient. She walked to the door, looked out and froze. It was a few moments before she could collect herself and move forward.

"Leif …"

"Greetings, sister."

Chapter 14

They stood looking at each other, unsure of their next move until finally, Yrsa relented and went to her brother, embracing him. She greeted Fallon, Leif's horse, who seemed pleased to see her.

"You were not easy to find," he said, looking around the steading, taking in the house and the fields. "This is your home now?"

"It has been for a while, but it's time I moved on."

"Because I have found you?"

"No," she replied. "Let's introduce Fallon to some new field mates, and you can come inside and warm up."

She led Leif to the field, where he removed the baggage from his horse. Brimble got excited when she saw Fallon, and they greeted each other.

"Gods," Leif said, looking at Tennell. "That's a magnificent animal. Your host must be a rich man."

"My host is not a rich woman," she said. He acknowledged the rebuke. "That horse is called Tennell ... and she's mine."

"But how-"

"All in good time, brother."

They headed for the house, Leif carrying his packs over his shoulder. As they strode along, Yrsa remembered the long walks they'd shared growing up. She'd always been closer to Leif than Erik.

The cubs came trotting from the forest, spotted Yrsa and her visitor and bounded towards them. Leif dropped his baggage and rested his hand on his sword. She had to stifle a laugh as she gently took it from the pommel. The cubs greeted her but were more interested in her companion, who was standing stock still, not sure what to make of the large dogs nosing him.

"Sister?" he said quietly, a tremor in his voice.

"Don't mind them," she replied. "They're only young."

"Gods, protect us."

"Come on, boys," she said, and the cubs followed her towards the house, leaving Leif to slowly pick up his baggage and shadow them.

"How long have you been on the road?" Yrsa asked as she made a warming herbal brew.

"Nearly two moons," Leif replied. "I was close to giving up. I've spent the last few weeks travelling to every town and village I could find east of the Norsouth road. Then this morning, I came upon a couple hurrying into the village with a pony. I described you and asked if they'd seen you. The man was keen to move on, but the woman studied me and when I told her I was your brother, she directed me here."

"That," Yrsa replied, a little bitterly, "would be Luna, my host." Why had the healer done it? Why hadn't she kept quiet?

"With her husband?"

"No, Luna's a healer. She was going to help a farmer with a cow birth."

"I have told you my tale, perhaps you will tell me yours."

Yrsa considered what to tell him. Perhaps omit Hagrat's true intentions … and best to mention Amluss only in passing … and to gloss over her encounter with the cub's mother. It didn't leave a lot, but she told him as much as she wanted him to hear.

"But how did this Amluss die?" he asked.

"A hunting accident."

"And he gave you his horses and dogs?"

"His horses seem to have come to me, yes. But these weren't his dogs."

"Where did they come from, then?" he asked, looking over to the cubs, who were lying quietly in front of the fire, awake and alert. She thought carefully before replying.

"Their mother was Amluss's quarry. It was she who inflicted his injuries."

"And these cubs were with her?"

"I found them a little way away."

"I've never seen dogs like them. If they fled their owner, he'll come looking for them."

"Nobody will be looking for them. They come from far to the north. They're zeffen."

Leif turned his gaze from the cubs to Yrsa, his face frozen in horrified amazement.

"Zeffen?" he finally managed in a strangled voice, visibly trying to pull away from the animals through the back of his chair. "Zeffen? They're monsters ... they're killers ... they're-"

"Loveable scamps," Luna interjected, coming through the door.

He stood, trying to be polite, but his attempt to face Luna without turning his back on the cubs made Yrsa laugh out loud.

"Oh, brother," she said. "Sit down. They won't hurt you. A beaker of warmth, Luna?"

"Oh, yes please, dear."

Luna removed her cloak and sat by the table, clutching the beaker.

"I believe you two have already met," Yrsa said.

"Yes, dear, we have, but not properly."

Yrsa took the hint.

"Luna, this is my brother, Leif. Brother, this is Luna, my host … and friend."

After Luna told them how she'd got on with the cow – both mother and calf would live – Leif excused himself.

"My boys have frightened you that much?" Yrsa called after him before turning to Luna.

"Why did you tell him I was here?" she asked.

"I thought you'd like to see your brother."

"But I chose to leave my family behind."

"Yes, dear. But I think you need to see him."

"Why?"

"To make peace. So you can spend the rest of your life looking forward, with their blessing, rather than constantly looking over your shoulder."

The healer was right, as always. But why was Leif here?

"At first," he told them later that evening, "we assumed you'd gone hunting and got snowed in. But after the snow cleared, our father started to worry. Then he found you'd taken everything you owned and began to fume. 'She's run away,' he kept on saying. 'Why? Why?' Well, Hilda had a thing or two to say about that. She told him why."

"How did he take it?" Yrsa asked.

"He couldn't understand. He still thinks Ando is a good match."

"Ando?" Luna said.

"The drunken dolt I told you about," Yrsa replied.

"Oh, yes. I remember. Sorry, Leif, do go on."

"He found one of the watch lads who admitted to letting you out. That confirmed it, and Father was all set to come and find you himself."

"Why didn't he?"

"We had more snow, which delayed his departure, and Hilda worked on him. Tell me, sister, did she know you were going?"

"I didn't tell her," she replied. "But I think she knew."

"I thought as much. Anyway, she calmed him down, we got together, and I volunteered to try and find you."

"What for?"

"So I can tell our confused father you are safe and know what you're doing."

"He wants you to bring me back."

"He does, but he's the only one who thinks that's going to happen, isn't he?"

"Yes, Leif, he is."

"At least I can report to our father I found you. And tell him you've gelded a man, acquired a horse the like of which he's never seen, and adopted two zeffen. I'm sure that will make him feel a lot better."

Luna cackled.

"What you tell him is up to you, brother," Yrsa replied, but couldn't hide her smile.

"I think by the time I return, Hilda will have made him face reality."

"She's a good woman."

"She is, I've come to see that. She sends you a message, by the way. Her blessing and the hope her gift will help you find your destiny, if that makes any sense."

"It does."

"Going to tell me?"

"Better you don't know, but thank her for me."

By the end of the evening, Leif had relaxed around the cubs, and when one of them walked over and stared at him, he hesitantly stroked its head. To his consternation, it promptly flopped down by his side and laid its head on his lap. His face was an amusing mix of delight and unease.

* * *

Yrsa persuaded Leif to stay a few days before returning home. He and Fallon needed a rest, but she was also aware this was the last time she was ever likely to see any of her family.

They went to the meadow, with all their horses. Fallon was a stallion, and by the measure of Valley people, an impressive one. But Tennell stood head and shoulders above him, something Fallon was unhappy about. Once or twice, he tried to assert himself, but Tennell put him in his place. He didn't try again.

At the meadow, they raced their horses, Yrsa having to hold her mare back so much she switched to Lucky. But the old packhorse, though enjoying the challenge, wasn't ever going to be a winner. As they rested, watching the horses roaming the grass, Tennell decided to show off, thundering around the clearing.

"Where is she from, I wonder?" Leif asked.

"Amluss was from a land way to the east, so I can only assume she comes from there too."

"She's like a force of nature. I don't know how you control her."

"She's a joy. Want to try?"

He looked at her, uncertain. He rode to get from place to place and had never thought of it as an end in itself. But Yrsa called Tennell, who came trotting over.

"Now, girl," she said softly. "My brother's going to ride you. Be good."

The mare stood still as Leif slowly mounted her and Yrsa gave him the reins.

"Be gentle," she said. "You only need to guide her."

He carefully turned her and walked off, once or twice pulling the reins too hard and Tennell turned sharply. But eventually, he succeeded in maintaining a straight line.

"Tap her flank," Yrsa called.

Tennell's instant response was to move to a trot.

Yrsa and the Zeffen Hunter

"Again," Yrsa shouted.

The mare moved to a canter.

"Again."

This time, Tennell shot forward, galloping on, with Leif desperately hanging on. He'd lost control, and the mare was enjoying herself.

"Tennell!" Yrsa shouted, and the horse slowed to a trot, Leif composing himself. But her brother had courage. Once he'd caught his breath, he tried again, slowly increasing the animal's speed and guiding her around the clearing, but at no more than a gentle canter. By the time he returned, he was grinning.

"Sister, she's a mount worthy of the Gods."

They gathered the horses and led their mounts up the overgrown path, the others following on. The cubs were off exploring the forest. When they reached the main track, they turned for home and approached the dead tree stranded in their path.

A sound made Yrsa drop instinctively, and something whistled past her. A moment later, she heard a thud as something hit a tree. The horses sensed danger and huddled closer, Tennell stamping her foot hard on the ground two or three times. Yrsa looked around hurriedly, and Leif was doing the same. Nothing. But when they looked in front of them again, a figure stepped out from behind the dead tree.

"Found you, girl."

Chapter 15

Yrsa couldn't believe what she was seeing. Hagrat, as large as life, standing in her path with a loaded crossbow. Another bear of a man appeared beside him, carrying a heavy stave.

"I've been looking for you, girl," Hagrat said. "And your brother there, well, he's been extremely helpful. So helpful, I might let him live." She looked at Leif, whose expression told her he didn't know what Hagrat was talking about. "Oh, he hasn't been telling tales. But he's been asking about you everywhere, and I couldn't help myself. I had to follow his trail. And he's led me right to you."

"What do you want?" Leif asked.

"Keep quiet, lad. My business is with this bitch, not you."

"If you-"

"Leif," Yrsa said quietly, stopping her brother. "What do you want, Hagrat?"

"If I can't have you, I'm going to enjoy watching Rolf here have his fun with you."

"You must be mad." She tried to sound confident but was stalling for time, trying to work out what to do. A crossbow bolt would be fatal at this range. Rolf was a huge man but had only his staff, and his permanent grin indicated he was probably slow in both body and wits. Hagrat was the main threat.

"Am I?" he replied. "Maybe. I don't care anymore. But you're going to pay with your life for what you did to me. After Rolf's finished with you, that is."

The path was fairly wide, but she and Leif had four horses and two of those were loose. There was no chance of mounting and riding away.

"You can tell me one thing, girl," Hagrat said. "Where's Amluss?"

"What do you care?"

"I don't. The bastard left me for dead. But you've got his horse …" He looked behind her. "And mine too."

"He gave them to me."

"He never gave anyone anything in his life."

"Perhaps he only gave to those he trusted."

"Why would he trust you? Give yourself to him, did you?"

"No, but at least he would have been a whole man."

Hagrat's expression changed, furious at the insult.

"I was a whole man," he said, his voice rising. She could see the crossbow trembling slightly in his hand. "If you hadn't fought back, you'd have found that out, bitch."

"I choose who I fuck and when, Hagrat," she replied, causing Leif to splutter. "And I wasn't fucking you, and I'm not fucking your patsy here."

Stepping to one side, she slapped Tennell's flank three times. To Hagrat's astonishment, the mare shot forward, heading straight for him and Rolf. He raised the crossbow, but before he could aim it properly, the mare took out his companion, knocking him to the ground.

As this was happening, Leif jumped on his horse and headed for Hagrat who finally managed to fire the crossbow. The bolt caught Leif on the shoulder, but it didn't stop him from launching himself into the air and landing on Hagrat. They fell to the ground, both temporarily winded. Leif recovered first, in time to land a blow on Hagrat, stunning him.

Yrsa went over to Rolf. He was dead, killed by Tennell's weight and speed. She turned to Hagrat, being held on the floor by Leif's boot. He looked at her with such hatred she turned away.

"Get him up," she said, and Leif pulled him to his feet, holding his wrists behind his back, his arm around his neck. Hagrat may have been a cunning, malicious bastard, but her brother was far stronger. Yrsa took a few deep breaths. She was angrier than she could remember, but it was tempered by a deep sense of calm, a feeling of … what? Triumph? She stood in front of their attacker, still sneering at her.

"Amluss is dead," she said. "Want to know what killed him?"

She gave two short whistles, and a puzzled look crossed his face before she heard rustling. His face showed fear for the first time as the cubs came bounding out of the undergrowth, coming to a halt on either side of her.

"Their mother killed him. Not quickly mind. She took his arm off at the shoulder, ripped his thigh open, and left him to die."

Hagrat had lost his fight for the moment. He was looking at the zeffen with a mixture of fear and calculation. She knew what he was thinking. How valuable they were. How they could change his life.

"Amluss told me why he was hunting their mother," she said.

"Liar," he replied, spitting in her face. She wiped it away.

"He wanted her for her blood." His eyes told her he believed her now. "But she's dead, and you're never going to get these two."

"I never give up, girl. I'll get you next time."

She knew it was true. He'd pursue her and the cubs constantly. She stepped forward, her face close to his.

"First you tried to rape me," she said quietly. "Now you've tried to kill me. There won't be a next time."

Her hand swept up, pulling the curved dagger from her belt, and thrusting it into Hagrat's belly, his face twisting into agony as she forced it under his ribs with all her strength. A brief cry left his mouth, his body arching as the point searched for his heart.

Leif let out a gasp when he realised what was happening, and he stepped backwards horrified, allowing the mortally wounded man to drop to his knees. The movement wrenched Yrsa's hand from the hilt, and Hagrat feebly tried to pull it out. She pushed his shoulder with her boot, and he fell to the ground. Bending over him, she closed her hand around the hilt again and stared into his eyes.

"Don't ever call me girl," she spat, giving the dagger a final push. The cry which followed was short. His body twitched again before relaxing as its life flowed away. She had to put her boot on Hagrat's belly to withdraw the weapon, before lifting the corner of his cloak and calmly wiping the blade.

"What have you done, sister?" Leif whispered.

"It'll do for now. I can clean it better when I get home."

He looked confused for a moment.

"No, no," he said, gathering his wits. "Not the dagger. The man … the men."

"Killed them."

"Does that not bother you?"

"They attacked us. This one," she kicked Hagrat's body, "for the second time."

"What do we do now?"

"Bury them, I suppose."

The cubs came over, drawn by the smell of blood, and moved towards the bodies.

"No," Yrsa said firmly, and they retreated.

Leif was still in shock, and Yrsa went to pull the first corpse from the path.

"Well, help me then," she said.

Together they dragged both bodies into the undergrowth. She mounted Tennell and moved off. Leif caught up on Fallon, with Lucky and Brimble bringing up the rear. The cubs needed calling twice before they followed.

Nothing was said as they returned to the steading, but Yrsa couldn't clear her head of the look on Hagrat's face as she stabbed him. The shock in his eyes. She felt a certain elation at his demise, at what she'd done, and she wasn't sure that was right.

Luna was feeding her goats when they arrived and was about to offer a cheery greeting when she sensed the subdued mood.

"Is everything all right, dear?" she asked.

"We were attacked," Yrsa replied. "Leif's injured."

"Let me see," the healer said, coming over as Leif dismounted. "It's not serious," she said after looking at it. "Come inside and I'll wash and dress it."

"It'll have to wait," Yrsa replied. "We've got two bodies to bury."

* * *

Their meal was eaten in silence. Yrsa had given Luna a brief account of what happened, and the healer had treated Leif's shoulder.

"You're quiet, brother," Yrsa said gently.

"I still can't get it out of my mind," he replied.

"A good night's sleep and you'll feel better," Luna said.

"I doubt that. I still can't believe it."

"Believe what?" Yrsa asked.

"You. What you did."

"Was I to accept their plan? Were you to watch as they tortured and killed me in front of your eyes?"

"No, no. I don't mean that." Yrsa stayed quiet, unsure of her brother's meaning. He looked deep in thought. "It's just … it should have been … I shouldn't have …"

"Guilt, brother?"

"Yes," he replied sharply. She laid her hand on his arm. "Leif, it was me he wanted. He used you to find me. That wasn't your fault."

"I should have been more careful."

"How were you to know anyone was looking for me?"

"And I couldn't protect you."

"Brother, have I asked for your protection?"

"No, but …"

"But you're a man, and you should have protected your little sister."

"Something like that," he said sheepishly.

"It seems your sister isn't currently in need of protection," Luna said, which at least brought a weak smile to Leif's face.

"I don't think I could have done it," he said to Yrsa. "Killed a man like that. Erik would, without a thought."

"Perhaps," she replied. "But don't compare yourself to him. He got the muscles; we got the brains."

"There is truth in that," he said ruefully.

"Leif, I'm not looking for trouble, I never have. But I'll defend myself anyway I can."

"Including using your horse as a weapon?"

"She was rather good, wasn't she?"

"Like she'd done it before."

"I have a suspicion that animal has seen a fight or two."

"I don't know, dear," Luna said. "I think she understands you."

"What do you mean?" Leif asked.

"Your sister has a way with animals."

"Whatever it is," Yrsa put in, not wanting to pursue the subject, "she helped save us today."

"Did you know Rolf?" Leif asked.

"Never seen him before. Hagrat probably found him in an inn somewhere and offered him a few coins." And me, she thought.

"His clothes were falling apart, and he had nothing but his staff, a knife, and two copper kels."

"Which you took."

"He had no further use for them."

"And this Hagrat," Luna said, watching Yrsa carefully. "What was he carrying?"

"Oh, his bag. I almost forgot." She jumped up and went to the door where she'd dropped it when they'd come in. Clearing a space on the table, she emptied the contents. They were meagre. Two knives, a spoon, a couple of amulets and a purse with a few solens and kels.

But what drew their attention was lying in the centre of the table. Yrsa recognised it immediately. Leif picked it up.

"What is it?" he asked.

"A crystal phial," Luna replied. "And a fine one. May I?"

Leif passed her the object, and the healer took a long, assessing look. It was a finely carved piece of crystal the length of a man's middle finger, but twice as broad. Almost transparent, it was hollowed out and topped with a chased silver stopper, locked in place by a sprung clip.

"This is a rare find," Luna said quietly. "Few have the skill to make this."

"Did he steal it?" Leif asked.

"Who knows?" Yrsa replied as lightly as she could, seeing immediately Luna wasn't fooled, though she said nothing. "Anyway, I got the thing I wanted."

"Which was?"

"The crossbow. Amluss had two, but I couldn't find them where he died. It looks like he left one with Hagrat, and now it's mine."

"He might have an heir."

"Who's going to search for them?" she spat back. "Who's going to tell them the bastard's dead?" Leif leaned back slightly, surprised by the venom in his sister's words. "He's where he belongs and,

Gods willing, he'll never be found. Leave your sense of honour behind, brother. That's fine where people uphold it. Hagrat didn't, and I beat him by his own rules. That's the end of it."

Chapter 16

"It's the full moon tonight, dear," Luna said over their midday meal.

"Is that important?" Leif asked. The healer let Yrsa answer.

"It is for me, brother," she replied. "There is something I must do tonight."

"Can I help?"

"Not this time. I must do it alone."

Before the sun set, Yrsa prepared herself. Leif tactfully went to check on the animals, leaving her with Luna. She threw a cloak over her clothes and picked up her staff.

"This is it?" Yrsa asked. "I need nothing else?"

"It is you the spirits are concerned with, not any worldly belongings."

Yrsa went to put on her belt with one of Amluss's curved daggers and her szanka attached to it.

"You won't need that," Luna said. "It isn't polite to take weapons into the realm of the spirits."

Yrsa shrugged and laid the belt down.

"Shall I take something to eat?"

"You have everything you need. Now go."
"You still haven't told me where I'm going."

Yrsa walked along the path muttering to herself. Luna's directions had been far from inspiring. Simply follow the path to the stream, and follow the stream west.

"What then?" she'd asked.

"You'll know," Luna replied.

She'd know? How? She'd walked along that stream before and never found anything unusual. Why would tonight be any different?

She'd said goodbye to Leif, who was quiet and worried. The cubs briefly thought they were going hunting, but a soft word had disabused them. They'd given her a few licks, then laid down and calmly gone back to grooming themselves.

Striding along the path, her mood wasn't the best to commune with spirits. Her frustration was rising. What was she doing? It was madness. Perhaps Luna was just a mad old woman. The thought of Hagrat raised her ire further, and she found herself walking faster until she stumbled over a tree root and returned her attention to the task at hand.

The sky was clear, and the full moon flooded through the gaps in the canopy, illuminating the forest underneath in infinite shades of grey. She came to the stream and turned west. After a while, it became difficult to follow the water. The trees and undergrowth spilled over the banks. She'd have to walk in the stream, so sat and removed her boots, tying the straps and hanging them around her neck.

After a few steps, she realised her mistake. There were sharp stones in the bed of the stream, and the light wasn't good enough to see and avoid them. She'd have to get her boots wet.

Once she'd put them back on, it was easier, and she walked, still carefully, for some time. But the frustration rose again. What was she looking for? At one point she stopped, lifted her head to the sky and screamed. It seemed to help; she stayed still, trying to clear her emotions.

"Think, Yrsa, think."

She pushed everything from her mind and tried to listen to the forest. There was little sound at night. Most creatures were safely hidden. A few night operators were out and about but they were stealthy and silent. She closed her eyes and took slow deliberate breaths. She'd hunted at night often enough, knew how to find the few active animals, or those too big to hide. Use those skills, she told herself.

She moved on, trying to walk through the stream as quietly as possible, and began to hear tiny sounds around her. This was better. She had to duck to pass under several branches hanging low, and when they cleared, she was brought to a halt by the view in front of her.

A large pool of still water, the moonlight reflecting from it so brightly, she had to shield her eyes until they got used to it. The forest seemed to grow right to its edge, almost sliding under the surface. The only break in the trees was a small waterfall on the other side of the pool.

"Where now?" she asked herself, looking around. There didn't seem to be any paths leading from the pool, and taking a step forward and prodding with her staff, she found the floor was shelving away, the water deeper.

She closed her eyes again, trying to find inspiration somewhere. The only thing she could hear was the waterfall, eternally pouring water into the pool, and it was the sound that finally gave her the answer. She had to go to the waterfall.

It meant getting wet. As she walked carefully on, the water rose above her knees. It was icy cold, and as it flowed over her groin, she shivered at its touch. Then above her waist, slowly rising to her chest. Luna was a good deal shorter than her, and she wondered how the healer managed this depth.

But it didn't rise further, and she pushed through the water until she was standing a few paces in front of the waterfall. Could it be this simple? She stepped nearer and pushed the staff into the flowing water. It went straight through. No rock, nothing.

Taking a deep breath, she moved forward. The waterfall was more powerful than she expected, and the weight of the water drilled into her head and shoulders, making her speed up. When the weight disappeared, she opened her eyes to darkness.

Turning back, she could see light shining through the waterfall from the outside, and her eyes slowly adjusted. The water was still up to her chest, so feeling the bed with her staff, she walked slowly forward, emerging from this hidden pool.

Finding herself on a dry floor, she tried to see where she was. A small cave, the sound of the waterfall echoing around it. She reached for the wall and found it smooth and dry.

"What now?" she whispered, looking around for clues and finding none. "Well," she answered herself in a louder voice. "I came in that way, so I might as well try this way."

Half seeing, half following the wall, she moved away from the waterfall. The cave turned sharply, and the sound of tumbling water receded. She saw a glow of light and headed for it until she could see an opening.

This is what Luna had talked about, she wasn't a mad old woman after all. What would she find? What would happen? Her frustration had gone, replaced by anticipation. She wanted to do this, whatever it was.

The sight which greeted her at the cave entrance was unlike anything she'd ever seen. She shielded her eyes from the intense colours. Green. Green everywhere, but a myriad of other colours bombarded her eyes. As she became accustomed to it, she stepped out of the cave, hit by the contrast of the hard stone floor inside with the soft landing of her feet outside.

Outside. Was she outside? She looked up but couldn't make anything out. The bright colours seemed to go on forever, she couldn't see a night sky. Her feet seemed to sink into softness with every step, and looking down she saw long, lush grass. She removed her boots, letting her bare feet luxuriate in its soft touch.

She came to trees, instantly struck by their weirdness. Every tree was different: different leaves, different flowers, different fruits. But the strangest thing was they carried all seasons together. On each tree were buds, open flowers, and fruit, from young, to ripe, to rotting.

There was so much life here, but was this place real or conjured for her? Was this part of the test or merely the setting? Having allowed herself some moments of pure wonder, she tried to bring her senses back to the present. She was here for a reason. But what was it?

She walked around this delightful place, taking in the colours. And the scents; the trees and plants were fragrant. A variety of intoxicating aromas, mingling in her nostrils, filling her mind. There was sound too. Was it music? Something like it, but sweeter and more delicate than any she'd heard.

She picked a fruit, unable to identify it, but when she bit into it, its taste was unlike anything she'd ever eaten. She could have spent the rest of her life eating that one fruit.

She closed her eyes to take it all in. Her senses were struggling to deal with the onslaught. Images, smells, and sounds filled her head, each more vivid than the last. They were taking over, pushing everything else from her mind.

Her head swayed, she felt dizzy. Her body spinning, the glade spinning. A moment's panic before she gave in to it. Faster and faster, overwhelming sense after sense, until she passed into unconsciousness.

Stillness.

Silence.

Peace.

Yrsa slowly opened her eyes. She was still in the glade, lying on the grass. But the colours were muted, the music gone. She could smell nothing. She went to sit up and found she couldn't. She tried again. Nothing moved, her body not responding to her will. She could move her eyes, but nothing else.

A moment's panic. Was this the loss of her wits Luna had spoken of? No, she told herself. If I'd lost my wits, I wouldn't be asking the question.

A gentle breeze flowed over her body, and she realised she was naked. It was a wonderful feeling, her skin reacting to the invisible streams. She saw wisps forming in the air, the breeze sculpting them into tendrils of light or mist, weaving and soaring over her.

They were mesmerizing, and she tried to follow one, but it vanished, only for another to form in its place. They were rushing around her, caressing and stroking her skin. She could feel their pressure, their movements beginning to reach her muscles.

She felt them on her face, running over her cheeks, her forehead, racing through her hair. They were all around her, every part of her body feeling their touch. She felt her body rise from the ground. No fear, no panic. A few fingers' width at first, held aloft by the gentle streams of light.

Then a feeling of exhilaration as she soared upwards, rising higher and higher, finally bursting from the glade into the night sky. Travelling over the forest, passing tree after tree, clearing after clearing. Faster and faster, over villages and towns, their fields and buildings visible in the moonlight.

And all the time, the wisps of light were carrying her, caressing her … exploring her. Yes, they were exploring her: entering her mouth, her nose, her ears, and every other orifice. No pain, no discomfort. Just a warmth, an enveloping tenderness.

The land was moving under her so fast, she couldn't make out the details. Images formed in her head. Images of her past: family, friends, events from long ago, from her childhood. Images more recent, events of the present. Images she couldn't make out: joyous, sad, violent, disturbing. All flashing by, overwhelming her.

Physical effects too. She felt her heart beating; could picture it in her mind, watching it pulsate slowly, pumping blood through her body. Her lungs slowly filling and emptying in her chest. Other organs she didn't know quietly working to power her being.

Pleasant feelings too. The wisps between her legs stroking and caressing, so gently they were hardly there, yet so powerful she seemed to peak again and again, her mouth opening wide, but emitting no sound.

But gradually the pleasure turned to pain which began to flow through her body. It was all too much. Pain everywhere, agonising and real. Her skin burned; her head ached. Her chest tightened as her body tried to cope with the invasion. Her groin was swollen and too sensitive for even the lightest touch. She cried out, but still no sound came.

The world beneath her had gone, the sky was no longer there. She was wrapped in light and touch, and it was all she was aware of. Something told her this was it; this was the crucial moment. She somehow found a part of her mind still under her control and tried to use it. Forcing herself to fill it with her own thoughts, her own feelings, her own memories.

Slowly, awareness returned. The sky came first, the stars reappearing one by one. Then the land beneath her, hurtling by. The wisps left, driven out by the power of her thoughts reclaiming her mind and body. As they departed, each vanished in a puff of light, until none remained.

Falling.

Falling through the air.

Falling into unconsciousness once again.

* * *

Yrsa opened her eyes with a start and a sharp intake of breath. All she could see was grass, then some trees further off. A dream, she thought. But what a dream.

She tried to move. Nothing. She panicked and tried again. Relief as her legs slowly answered her. But they hurt, they felt heavy. She pushed at the ground, her arms complaining at the effort, and rolled herself onto her back.

Every part of her body was sore. Her muscles ached, her joints were stiff and painful, she had a blinding headache, and her ears hurt. With effort, she sat up. She was still naked, her clothes strewn around her. It hadn't been a dream. She knew it, accepted it. The question was what to do now.

Looking around, she was still in the glade, but now it was no different from any other part of the forest.

She slowly reached for her clothes, and under her tunic were three fruits she didn't know. Eyeing them suspiciously, she debated whether to try them, or whether they would repeat the whole experience. Deciding they were there for a reason, she bit into one. Nothing like the flavour of those from the previous evening, but good nonetheless, and she finished the first, before starting the second.

She stood and stretched, still having to force her muscles to answer her requests. She put a finger in a painful ear, only to find blood. As she moved to collect her clothes, she winced as her groin reminded her of the wisps' attentions. It felt like she'd been used by a God, possibly more than one.

Looking at her skin, she thought it was covered in sweat, but when she brushed it with her fingers, it floated away and disappeared. She spent several moments repeating the process, unable to explain it.

After dressing and finding her staff, she sat and finished the second fruit. Whether it was their effect, she didn't know, but she already felt stronger. It was time to leave. Reaching the cave entrance, she took one last look at the glade and went in. Finding her way through was easier this time, and she soon found herself behind the waterfall.

On an impulse, she stripped again, waded into the small pool, and stood under the gentlest part of the cascade. She washed herself, before closing her eyes and letting the sound and touch of the falling water shut everything else out.

How long she stood there, she didn't know, but as she rose from the other end of the pool, having walked through holding her dry clothes aloft, she felt refreshed. Dressing quickly, she set out for home. The sun was already high in the sky, and it would be afternoon before she reached the steading.

The renewed energy from the fruit and the waterfall didn't last long. As Yrsa walked along the stream, her legs began to stiffen. Her head was still aching, and every sound from the forest seemed to pierce her skull. Birds singing, trees rustling, even the sound of the water running in the stream. They were all painful.

She wanted to sleep and considered simply lying down and giving in to the need, but the thought of the steading, a warming fire and some food drove her on. Food. She remembered the third fruit and its energy flowed into her, making the final leg of the journey easier.

She hadn't realised how far she'd walked the night before, but eventually saw the smoke from Luna's house and pushed on. As she emerged from the forest into the open, she spotted the cubs as they spotted her. Their exuberant welcome was overpowering, but they always made her happy, and they seemed to sense her weariness, following her quietly to the door.

The look of relief on Leif's face was clear as he welcomed his sister, asking how she was, whether she needed anything. Even Luna's concern was obvious, and they sat quietly as she ate the bowl of stew the healer gave her and drank several beakers of ale before lying on a pile of blankets and furs and falling asleep.

Chapter 17

It was mid-morning before Yrsa stirred, gradually coming to, and tentatively stretching. Her body felt more like its usual self. A few aches and pains, some stiffness, but nothing like the day before. As she moved, she hit something: the cubs. One in front of her curled form, the other behind.

"How do you feel, dear?" Luna said quietly.

"Better than I did yesterday." She pushed the cubs gently. "Come on, boys, move over."

"They haven't left you."

"Really?"

"Only to go outside, they haven't even eaten."

"That's odd."

"They sense something different about you."

"Nonsense," Yrsa replied, yawning. "I'm no different."

"If you say so, dear."

Leif came through the door.

"Sister, you're awake. Are you hurt? Are you injured?"

"No, brother, I was simply tired."

"Tired? You have slept unmoving for nearly a full day."

"She was exhausted, Leif," Luna said. "Meeting the spirits is hard for those of us without their strength."

Yrsa was shocked. Had Luna told Leif of her purpose in the forest?

"All right, Luna," he said, laughing. "If you must persist with your ghost stories."

Yrsa sat up, and the cubs rolled over, resting by her side. They were looking at her expectantly, though she wasn't sure why.

"Want to go outside?" she asked. They didn't move. "Play?" Nothing. "What do they want, I wonder?"

"Ask them," Luna said softly.

"Well, boys," Yrsa said, ruffling the fur on their broad heads. "What do you want? I wish I knew. I don't even know your names."

'Bodro.'

'Pek.'

She froze as the words formed in her head. The world seemed to still around her, and she looked at the cubs. First one …

'Bodro.'

… then the other.

'Pek.'

It all suddenly made sense. She didn't know how, but it made sense, and she began laughing. Loud, uncontrolled laughter. Leif looked concerned, wondering if whatever had happened in the forest had turned her mad. But Luna was sitting quietly, a warm smile on her face.

"Well, dear?" she asked.

"This one is Bodro," Yrsa said, "and this one is Pek."

The cubs went mad, pushing her over onto the floor, frantically licking and nibbling her, rolling over her.

"Enough," she managed to say through her joyous laughter. "Enough."

The cubs stopped, laying by her as she hauled herself back to a sitting position.

"How do you know?" Leif asked, bewildered.
"They told me."

Yrsa wouldn't answer any of Leif's questions until she'd eaten, which involved a large bowl of Luna's stew, as well as two each for Bodro and Pek. She made him swear by the Gods he would never reveal anything to the rest of their family. He was an intelligent man, but his belief in the Gods was total, and he wouldn't break such a promise.

He listened as Luna explained the spirits to him. She kept it simple and brief, not going into detail, but it was difficult for him to comprehend, though he no longer dismissed it as a ghost story. As the healer was talking, he looked at Yrsa every so often, as if seeing her in a new light.

"You believe all this?" he asked her when Luna fell silent.

"I don't know, brother," she replied. "It's almost as strange to me as it is to you. But I can only tell you what happened. These two told me their names. You can see the truth of it."

"You can talk to animals?"

"I don't think it's as simple as that," she said, looking at Luna.

"It's not," the healer replied. "It may be these two are the only ones she can communicate with."

Yrsa was shocked by that, she hadn't had time to think about it. Was it only Bodro and Pek she would ever understand?

"Why?" Leif asked.

"There I cannot help you," Luna answered. "I don't possess the gift your sister has. Few do."

* * *

Leif's time with them was coming to an end. One afternoon, he was with Yrsa in the storeroom she'd used for her baggage. She picked up the szanka.

"Do you remember when Father gave me this?" she asked.

"Yes," he replied. "You'd been pestering him for your own sword."

"And he wouldn't give me one."

"You were only about ten."

"Eleven, I think."

"You could hardly lift a sword."

"He looked in the store and found this dirty old knife and sheath. Too short to be called a sword and covered in years of grime."

"I remember your face when he gave it to you," he said.

"I was so disappointed."

"I think I laughed."

"You did. I could have hit you."

"You did."

"Did I? Sorry." She shook her head gently and smiled. "But I was determined to make the best of it."

"You spent hours cleaning it."

"I didn't tell Father, he thought I'd put it away and given up the idea."

"Until you wore it one day."

"He stopped me in the yard. 'Where did you get that?' he bellowed."

"'You gave it to me' you said, so sweetly," Leif said, imitating his sister.

"He took it from me and examined it."

"He was angry, you know."

"With me?"

"No, with himself. He could see its value."

"Do you know how he got it?"

"It was probably in a basket of old metal. You know how he used to buy odds and ends when he was trading, in the hope of finding silver or gold."

"Well, he missed this one. Do you know where it comes from?"

"No idea."

"Amluss told me it comes from Flengara. It's called a szanka."

"Where's Flengara?"

"Far to the east. Hundreds of leagues, I think."

She took the curved dagger from her belt and handed it to him.

"This comes from Flengara, too." Unrolling one of her cloaks, she revealed Amluss's belt, the other dagger, and his sword. "As do these."

He was immediately drawn to the sword.

"May I?" he asked.

He picked up the scabbard and examined it. Yrsa had spent hours cleaning and polishing Amluss's weapons, bringing back much of their original lustre.

"This is skilled work, sister," he said, marvelling at the intricate metalwork.

"Isn't it beautiful?"

He slowly drew the sword from the scabbard, surprised by the ease with which it slid out. He looked at the blade, a wondrous example of the swordsmith's art with its unusual profile and strange symbols. Leif let out a long whistle.

"I've never seen it's like," he said. "What are you going to do with it?"

"I'm not giving it away, if that's what you're wondering," she replied, laughing. He looked suitably embarrassed. "No, I'm going to find someone who will teach me to use it."

He gently slid the sword into its scabbard and laid it down.

"Where are you going, sister?" he asked.

"I'm not certain," she replied. "And I'm not sure I'd tell you if I was."

"You don't trust me?" He looked hurt.

"It's not that, Leif. If you go back to our father, tell him you found me and I was safe, what happens if he asks you where I was going?"

"I wouldn't tell him."

"And you'd be lying. If you don't know, you have no need to lie." She took his hand. "Brother, this is the last time we will see each other. Your future is in the Valleys with our family. Better you have no need to hide things from them."

"What shall I tell them?"

"About what you have seen, tell them what you will. They may not believe it and think you as mad as they think me." He smiled. "But tell them I love them, that I will remember them in my heart, and I will ask the Gods and the spirits to keep you all safe."

Leif departed early one morning, his horse laden with enough supplies from Luna's stores to last him the journey if he was lucky with the weather. Bodro and Pek knew what was happening and insisted on one last romp with the man who was now their friend. He said farewell to Luna, and she left them to say their goodbyes, but they'd already said everything that needed to be said.

"Have a safe journey, brother."

"You too, sister, wherever your life leads you."

They embraced, and she watched him walk away along the path. As he approached the first bend, they waved one last time.

"Goodbye, brother," she whispered to herself, before turning and heading for the house. Luna left Yrsa to her thoughts for the rest of the day and held her in the evening as the emotion came out.

* * *

"Now you are leaving, too," Luna said the next morning.

"Yes, but I am in no hurry. I need to understand what has happened and make a decision. I need your help."

Yrsa told Luna the tale Amluss had told her, about his quest for zeffen blood and the reason for that quest.

"Did you believe him?" Luna asked when she finished.

"It sounded like a bard's tale, filled with distant lands and a whiff of magic. But as he told it, I saw in his eyes he believed it. But are such things real? Can they really happen?"

"I have seen things I cannot explain, things that seem impossible. Remember your night in the glade. Would you have believed that a few moons ago? He had a reason for hunting the zeffen. When I saw the phial, I thought it might be something touching the spirits."

"Amluss had one on a cord around his neck. He believed they had the power to keep the zeffen's blood fresh. I'm surprised he trusted Hagrat enough to give him one as well."

"In case he got there first, you mean?" Luna said.

"Yes."

"Hagrat was a coward. He would never have stood up to Amluss."

"He might have killed him in the night."

"I suspect Amluss had the measure of Hagrat. That man was only prepared to take on defenceless women." They both smiled at his error of judgement. "Having made his promise, Amluss made provision for it to be fulfilled, even if he were killed."

"Now, they're both dead and I feel I should take up his task."

"You owe Amluss nothing," Luna said.

"Perhaps not," Yrsa replied. "Though I now find myself heir to his animals and weapons, and something tells me they will come with a cost. But I owe it to their mother, as well." She stroked the cubs, lying either side of her, apparently asleep. "What will happen to them if I do nothing? Someone else may take Amluss's place and track them down, and I won't let that happen. If his story is true, there must be some other way to break the curse."

"Curses are beyond my knowledge. I have met a few of those who can cast them, and seen their results. If you decide to follow this path, you must realise the danger you're putting yourself in. Curses, and those who deal in them, are not to be meddled with lightly."

"I think I have little choice. If I want to protect these two, I must at least find out the truth of Amluss's story and what has happened since he left his land."

"You are already decided, I think," Luna said with a chuckle. "You do not need my advice."

"Talking it through clears the mind, but I still need your help with another problem."

"What is that, my dear?"

"The spirits' gift is weighing heavily on me."

Yrsa told Luna of her experience in the glade, recalling the wonder and the power of the spirits, and of her fight to control that power.

"It seems the spirits really tested you," the healer said. "I don't remember anything like that from my dream. I think they pushed you as far as anyone could go and safely return."

"My senses are overwhelming at times. Some of it's fine. I can see better; flavours and smells are more intense. But when I go into the forest, the noise is almost terrifying. I can't tell one sound from another.

"Then there's these two." She motioned to the cubs. "They told me their names, and I pick up a few things from them. I seem to know when they're hungry or want something. But I'm not sensing it as I did their names. All I get is a vague idea drifting into my mind."

"They seem to hear you," Luna replied, as Bodro and Pek both opened their eyes and looked at Yrsa.

"They do, that's for sure," she said, ruffling their heads. "They even obey me occasionally."

"I wonder how much they understand?"

"I wish I knew. You may have been right, perhaps I'll only feel this with them. I'm not getting anything from the horses, although I think Tennell looks at me in a different way."

"There is something special about that animal. But what you need is guidance."

"Can you help me?"

"No," Luna replied. "I can't. You need a vayer."

"But where do I find one?"

Luna took a deep breath and let it out as a long sigh.

"I only know one, apart from she who I won't name. That is my kinsman."

"You said he was a fraud."

"I said he isn't everything he claims to be. But he can vay and has had the skill for many years."

"Can I trust him?"

"No," Luna replied, laughing, "not for a moment. He'll trick the coin from your purse and the food from your bowl. Oh, and your body into bed, given half a chance. But he's neither malicious nor dangerous."

"He sounds dangerous to me," Yrsa said.

"You'll handle him easily enough."

"Where can I find him?"

"As to that, I cannot be certain, but last I heard of him, he was settled in Lonithrya."

Chapter 18

Yrsa had mixed feelings about being back on the road. There was excitement at the prospect of unfamiliar places and new people, and not a little trepidation about the task she'd set herself. But the last two weeks had been hard. After leaving the Valleys secretly, she hadn't expected to see any of her family again. Leif's time at Luna's had brought back so many memories, and their parting had been painful.

Then there was Grenk. When her brother had been there, Yrsa hadn't visited the smith at all, but after he left, she made up for it. They'd spent several nights, along with Bidora, making some happy memories. As she left his house for the last time, there was little emotion – their relationship had been friendly and physical – but she wondered when she might next find a man who excited her so much.

The final wrench had been saying goodbye to Luna. This woman had taken her in, healed her, healed her animals, and given her so much. She'd given her skills and knowledge which would stay with her, but the introduction to the spirits would change her life, she knew it. She still didn't know how, but as she rode away, she felt different.

The main difference currently was confusion. When she'd set out on her journey, Yrsa had no idea where her life would lead. But she knew it would be simple. Travelling where she wanted, finding work if she needed food or a few coins. Enough for herself and Brimble, that was all she sought.

How things had changed. Turning from the forest path onto a larger track that headed south, she was riding Tennell covered in her plush caparison and rejuvenated saddle. Trailing behind were Lucky the packhorse, and the faithful Brimble, loosely tethered in line. Both were carrying heavy loads, but her main concern was how to feed and water this walking collection of stomachs.

And somewhere in the forest to the side were two large, powerful animals lacking the skills their real mother would have taught them. Skills Yrsa had so far failed to impart. They'd got to the stage where they searched out potential prey, but as soon as they saw it, they got excited, giving the lucky victim more than enough time to escape.

She was becoming accustomed to her heightened senses. Her sight astonished her; she could see things clearly at a distance she thought impossible. Her other senses were also keener. Food tasted and smelled different, the individual ingredients coming through. And sex had been an interesting experience since her night in the glade, as well. Everything felt more intense, more powerful, and her pleasure had risen to new heights.

But her hearing still disturbed her. As she rode along, there was so much noise. The sounds of the forest assaulted her ears, leaving her barely able to distinguish between the gentle sound of the trees, the movement of birds and animals, or the danger of some unknown threat, should there be one.

Spotting a settlement ahead on the track, she gave two whistles, and moments later, Bodro and Pek appeared on the path in front of her. They were inexhaustible, seeming to have endless energy.

They slept long when there was nothing to interest them. At Luna's, they'd spent every evening lying by the fire. But take them to the forest, and they'd race around for hours.

She planned to pass them off as hunting dogs. To her own eyes, that was ridiculous, they were already too big. But Luna had been right. Nobody she was likely to meet had ever encountered a zeffen. If they knew of them at all, it would be as mythical creatures dreamt up to frighten children. They would never guess the cubs' identity.

On impulse, she'd sat down with the zeffen and talked through her plans. Whether they were hearing her, she didn't know. She still hadn't got anything clear from them since their names. She told them she needed to hide their real identity, that she'd tell people they were her dogs, and they needed to behave when others were around. She'd tested it out, by taking them into the village on one of her visits to Grenk.

Several people had greeted her as she was now a familiar face, and they'd shown only brief interest in Bodro and Pek, who had been on their best behaviour, trotting beautifully by her side. A few were wary of these huge animals, but nobody had run shrieking in fear.

"Gods," Grenk had said, seeing them for the first time, even though she'd asked if she could bring them. "What do they hunt? People?" She'd let it pass, and they took to the big smith, happily curling up by his fire while she, Bidora and Grenk spent an evening tiring each other out.

As they now walked through the settlement, the horses in single file, Bodro and Pek took up station on either side of Tennell and kept pace with her. A few people turned to look at the visitor, one or two offering a greeting. But they were more interested in who this lone woman was, with three horses and two dogs, than in identifying those dogs as terrors from the north.

Her first destination was the Great River. She needed to reach Lonithrya, and if she could find passage on a boat, the journey would be much easier than taking the winding land route.

Luna had suggested returning to the Norsouth Road, but Yrsa didn't want to go back. So she chose this track. Nothing like as solid as the main road, but easily passable now summer had arrived, and it took them five days to cover the distance.

She knew the Great River. Her people traded with several of the towns at its mouth. The river was immense; a slow-moving body of water, which opened into a huge delta as it reached the sea. It broke into several main channels and each of those had at least one busy port on it. She'd visited many of them with her father.

But she'd never travelled up the river, and when she finally saw it from the brow of a hill, she was impressed. At this point, it was still a broad waterway, the other side visible, but far in the distance. As she surveyed the land in front of her, she could see three settlements. Two smaller villages and a larger town with a few boats moored at its edge. That would have to do.

Leading her train to the wharf, she studied the boats. Two were sturdy enough to make sea voyages, so were probably headed in the wrong direction. But there were three broader vessels, clearly river craft. She looped Tennell's reins over a post, told Bodro and Pek to stay with the horses and wandered along the boats.

The first she came to was in the process of unloading, her crew carrying heavy bales down the planks. The second was quiet and empty with four men lounging on the deck.

"Good day," she called out. "Where are you headed?"

"Who wants to know?" came the reply.

"I do."

A head appeared over the side and looked her up and down.

"What do you want?" he asked.

"Passage to Lonithrya."

"Do you, now?"

"Are you going to ask questions all day, or answer one of mine?"

"Steady on, girl, no harm in a bit of fun. We might be headed that way."

"Can you take me?"

"Depends how you're paying, doesn't it?" he replied, spurring ribald laughter from his crew. Yrsa walked on.

"Hey, girl," he called after her. "No need to be like that."

The last boat at the wharf was a different design from the first two, with deeper sides, and an angled mast she'd not seen before. There was no sign of life and the boat had only a little cargo.

"Anyone on board?" she called out, walking halfway up the plank. When there was no answer, she turned to leave.

"What do you want?"

Turning back, she saw a man coming from the shielded area at the stern, his skin much darker than her own, with tattoos covering his bare arms.

"Where are you going?" she asked.

"To the inland sea," the man replied.

"Where's that?"

"Way upriver."

"Past Lonithrya?"

She heard laughter from behind the curtain.

"Yes, lady, way past that city."

"Can you take me there?"

"That depends," he replied, stroking his chin. "How many of you?"

"Me, three horses and two dogs."

"Just you?"

"And the horses and dogs."

"You have three horses?"

"What is it with you people and your questions? Will you take me or not?"

"We're travelling only half full, so we might as well make a little extra."

They haggled over a price, and the man – introducing himself as Uri – told her he was leaving soon on the tide. Yrsa went to fetch her flock, and as she walked them past the first boat she'd asked, its crew studied her and her animals with renewed interest.

"Well," one of them called out, "we didn't know we was dealing wiv' a lady of wealth."

"Didn't ask, did you?" Yrsa called back.

When she reached her boat, she separated the horses. She was fairly sure Tennell and Lucky had been on boats before, but Brimble hadn't. The plank was always the worst. Uri and the crew were standing on the boat watching her, she hadn't expected any help. They'd be waiting for her to make a mistake. She guided Tennell to the plank, and the mare walked calmly onto the boat.

"That's a fine horse you have there, Lady," Uri said with feeling. "May I?" he asked, holding out his hand. Yrsa passed him the reins and returned for Lucky who boarded equally calmly. Uri was stroking Tennell and muttering to her. Brimble was warier but made it after a few stuttering steps part-way.

She gave two whistles, making the crew turn to look at her, and Bodro and Pek bounded up the plank and onto the deck. The crew backed away; only Uri stood his ground.

"Are you sure they're dogs?" he said calmly, studying Yrsa.

"What else could they be?" she replied.

He stared at the zeffen, then at Yrsa. "Let's get underway," he called to his crew.

Yrsa stayed out of the way as they pulled out into the main channel of the river. There was little difference between them and the seamen she'd known since childhood. Calm, capable, and efficient. But she'd never been on a boat like this. It reminded her of those she'd seen in the ports on the estuary, essentially large wooden boxes with flat bottoms. Perfect for packing as much cargo as possible, and ideal on the calm waters of the river.

This one was a lot more elaborate though, with carved and painted ornamentation. Its mast was leaning aft, held up by spars and ropes in a way she couldn't work out. But it was the sail that intrigued her. The sea-going ships she'd grown up with had square sails, which flew across the line of the ship. This craft had a triangular affair, which seemed to fly almost in line with the direction of travel.

She kept a careful eye on her animals as they set off, wondering how the horses would cope. Tennell was tall enough to see over the side and seemed to be taking in the view. Lucky could see if he stretched his neck. Brimble had nothing to look at save the wooden planking, but even she seemed unworried by this new mode of transport.

Surprisingly, it was Bodro and Pek who were unhappy. They lay by her, unmoving, except when Pek threw up over the deck. Bodro followed the example of his brother a little later.

Progress was slow, but all the time they were on the water, they were getting closer to Lonithrya without tiring the horses. She had food enough for the journey, both for them and herself, and she'd smoked a fair bit of venison at Luna's, which would keep the cubs going. They had strange appetites and didn't need to eat every day, though they would gorge themselves whenever given the opportunity.

Uri had directed her to the front of the boat, where she'd been able to tether the horses and find a place to store her baggage without it rolling around. She settled on the deck and lit her pipe, watching the bank slide slowly by fifty paces away.

As the sun fell, and moonlight filled the sky, Uri wandered towards her.

"Have you business in Lonithrya?" he asked, leaning against the side.

"Possibly," Yrsa replied.
"Fair enough, you may keep your own counsel."
"Tell me about your sail," she said. "I've not seen one like it."
"You have sailed before?"
"Many times, but always on the ocean."
"Ah, so you believe all sails to be square."
"Yes," she said, smiling at the jibe.
"Here on the river, there is less room for manoeuvre and less wind. This sail allows us to catch every last breath."
"Will you moor for the night?"
"We will sail until the tide turns, then we stop."
"There doesn't seem to be much of a tide."
"It's enough to ease our passage upriver. It's arduous work moving when it turns. If we have valuable cargo we'll haul along the bank, but not today."

They fell silent as he turned his gaze to the zeffen. She wondered if he knew what they were. Landsmen often dismissed seafarers as ignorant men, but they'd seen things most people only heard of in stories.

"It's not often I see a young woman travelling alone with such a collection of animals," he said.
"Perhaps you haven't looked hard enough."
"That may be true. Your horse," he meant Tennell, "is something I haven't seen for many years."
"Where have you seen them?" she asked.
"Mainly on the shore of the inland sea, around Caropa. May I ask how she comes to be among your followers?"
"You ask a lot of questions."
"I mean no offence."
"The truth is I know little about her. I inherited her under rather strange circumstances."
"And the dogs, were they inherited too?"
"No, I found them as orphans."
"They are unlike any animal I have ever seen."

"I don't think there are many like them."

Uri was called away and walked to the stern, where two of his crew held an animated conversation with him, looking over to Yrsa a couple of times. She wondered if they had a problem with her being on board. Her own people made nothing of it, but some seamen didn't like women on ships. She was right.

"They are superstitious," Uri said on his return. "I have told them there is no problem as you are wearing trousers."

"So, I'm an honorary man?"

"To keep them happy, yes."

Chapter 19

Deep into the night, the boat headed towards the bank. A cleared strip ran along the river to allow men or animals to haul boats, with mixed woodland beyond it on this stretch. Two of the crew jumped out, drove long iron stakes into the ground, and tied the boat fore and aft.

When they'd made it safe, they set themselves up on the bank, laying out blankets and building a small fire. A cooking pot was set up on a tripod.

"You are welcome to share our meal," Uri said. "It is meagre fare, I'm afraid, just beans. We have been away longer than expected, so have nothing else left."

"How long will we be here?" Yrsa asked.

"Until well after dawn."

"I'll get you some meat."

Uri watched as she untethered Lucky and pulled her longbow from her baggage, and added the crossbow.

"I have not met many women so heavily armed," he said, as she led the packhorse down the plank. The crew were all watching, as well. "The lady is going hunting," Uri told them and joined in their laughter.

The woodland was thin nearest the riverbank, with little wildlife, and Yrsa wondered if she'd given herself a hopeless task. At least the sky was clear and the moon bright. Deeper into the trees, she heard rustling ahead of her and tethered Lucky to a branch. Proceeding on foot, she hadn't gone fifty paces when she made out a small group of wild pigs in the distance rooting around on the forest floor.

As she moved nearer, she could see hunters were rare here. The pigs didn't seem very alert and even a couple of snapped twigs under her foot brought no more than a casual glance from one or two of the animals.

Kneeling securely on the ground, she took the bow and set three arrows by her side. The first caught an adult squarely in the neck, and it dropped. The pigs froze, and before they realised what had happened and run, she managed to hit a smaller animal in the chest. It was still on its feet, so she sent another arrow into it, bringing it down.

By the time she came out of the forest, the crew were all asleep around the dying fire. This was a safe place, and they felt no need for a watch. But they woke quickly enough as the pigs slid off Lucky's back and hit the ground. They looked at each other as she led the horse back onto the boat.

When she returned to the bank, the men were still sitting around, whispering. Uri was calmly rebuilding the fire.

"It seems you were successful," he said. She gave a little shrug, hiding the smile she felt inside, grateful for her good fortune.

Overcoming their surprise, the men quickly set about the pigs. They all had a weapon of some sort. Pirates were rare, but crews occasionally came to blows over a wharf space or, more frequently, a woman further from the water. They preferred wooden clubs or coshes on these occasions to save lives, but they had blades as well.

They were usually a mixture of poor shortswords or simply large knives. They served more time cutting bread or rope.

The smaller pig was soon butchered and stuck on iron rods over the fire. The larger one was proving more difficult; their knives evidently hadn't been honed recently. She handed one of them her szanka, and he proceeded to roughly butcher it with ease. As he returned it, Uri took it and examined it carefully, before passing it to her.

"There is more to you than the eye sees," he said.

The crew were more animated in anticipation of their unexpected roast pig. They talked and laughed, and by the time their bellies were full, their mood was the best she'd seen. There was a lot left.

"What shall we do with the rest?" one of them asked Uri, who turned to Yrsa with a questioning look.

"I have two other mouths to feed," she replied.

She went to the fire and took the hind legs of the larger animal from the spit, laying them on the ground. Two short whistles brought Bodro and Pek bounding from the boat. They halted in front of her, and lay down, a few fingers' breadth from the roast meat. The nearest crewmen edged away slightly, still unsure of these particular passengers.

The zeffen's eyes were fixed on Yrsa, who gave a gentle nod, and they attacked their meal, holding it with their paws, and ripping the flesh off. Its heat was no barrier to their appetite. The crew were silent, watching them tear through the meat as if it were soft bread.

"Do they not hunt for themselves?" Uri asked.

"I hand-reared them, and the skills their mother would have taught them, I cannot."

"It seems you have a special bond."

"Yes," she replied, as both Bodro and Pek stopped eating and looked at her. "We do."

***

It was another three days and seven tides before they approached Lonithrya. As they rounded a bend in the river, Yrsa caught her first glimpse of the city. A city larger than she had ever seen. Even from a league away, it seemed overwhelming. She could see buildings taller than any she'd known, and they spread along the bank as far as she could see.

"Do you know where you are going?" Uri asked her.

"I'm looking for someone," she replied. "But I don't know where they will be found."

"I think it best if we land you outside the city. The port area is crowded and hectic. Leading your horses through that will be difficult, particularly when you don't know your way around. There will be many who try and deceive you."

"I can look after myself."

"I believe you," he said. "All the same, you'd be better off finishing your journey by road and finding one of the city inns."

"City inns?"

"They are on all the main roads just beyond the walls. I have used them on occasion. You will find safe stabling for your animals, a place to rest, and the price is fixed by the authorities. From there you can walk into the city to find your friend."

***

As she led the horses onto the bank, the crew followed with her baggage. They'd overcome their distrust of a woman, and their nervousness of Bodro and Pek. As they returned aboard, Uri strode over.

"I hope you find who you seek," he said. "In a city like this, people are only found if they want to be."

"I can only try. Thank you for your kindness."

He bowed slightly and returned to the boat. As they pushed away from the bank, the crew waved, and Yrsa returned their farewell. She checked all her baggage was secure, tethered the horses together and headed for a path leading inland. Uri had told her it led to a main road.

She found it within two hundred paces. A wide, paved surface with shallow ditches on either side. It was early in the morning, but there were already many travellers. Carts, packhorses, and even a covered carriage or two. She turned towards the city and joined them.

There were already scattered houses and buildings on either side, and these increased as she approached Lonithrya. It was slow going; many of the carts were heavily loaded, and it wasn't possible to pass them with the horses. People on foot passed by, some laden with baskets for market, others going about whatever business brought them to the city.

She looked to either side of the road, searching for the inn. Uri had said they were marked by a sign showing the city's emblem and a horse in a stall. But she didn't know what the city's emblem looked like, and Uri's description had been vague. When she saw the city wall in the distance, she knew it had to be nearby. A woman walked past with a large basket on her head.

"Good day," Yrsa said. "Can you tell me where the city inn is?"

"Why, yes, it's on the right there, behind that long wall."

The wall appeared at the side of the road, and partway along it, a wide gateway led into an open courtyard. It was busy: horses, mules, a few carts, and people everywhere. Standing for a moment, she worked out most of them were leaving, having spent the night in the inn.

As the courtyard cleared, she got her bearings. The place was impressive. There was a building in the centre which seemed to house the office, and two longer ones on either side which appeared to be stables. She tethered the horses to a post, told

Bodro and Pek to stay with them, and headed to a door that was the centre of activity.

The short queue she joined inside moved quickly, and arriving at a small booth, she found herself facing a man with an immense moustache, wearing some sort of uniform.

"Yes?" he asked brusquely.

"I want stabling and a place to stay."

"I didn't think you wanted a basket of fish," he replied. "How many?"

"Myself, three horses and two dogs."

"Sleep above the horses, or do you want a bed?"

"Err, I'll sleep with the horses."

"A solen a day for each horse. No charge for the dogs provided you feed them."

It was a lot of money, but she had no choice, at least for a few days.

"How many nights?" the man asked.

"I don't know."

"Well, do you know someone who does? Other people are waiting."

"Can I extend it if I need to?"

"Of course."

"Three days, then."

After she counted nine solens into his outstretched hand, he gave her a bunch of tally sticks and moved to the next person in line. A little dazed, she returned to the yard and her horses. The tallies had writing on them, but as she couldn't read, it didn't help much.

The stables were impressive. Built of brick, with high roofs, and huge doors, they seemed to go on forever. She noticed a sign above each doorway, one of which matched the letters on her tally sticks, so she led her team towards it. As she reached the door, a man in a simple tunic met her.

"Your tokens, please?"

She handed them over, and he checked them against her animals.

"Three horses, three days." Then he saw Bodro and Pek, and his eyes widened. "I hope you have control of those ... things."

"I do."

"If they frighten any horses, they go. Follow me."

He led her into the stables, and as they walked along the central aisle, Yrsa looked around. On either side were stall after stall of varying sizes. Each had a water trough, and iron containers on the wall full of hay. The floors in the empty ones were spotless and covered with fresh straw. They had wooden partitions which rose higher towards the wall, with a loft above.

"In here," the man said, interrupting her inspection, and handing her the tally sticks.

"What do I do with these?" she asked.

He led her to the front of the stall, where there were several hooks.

"One tally per horse per day," he said, and took three from her, hanging them up.

"Thank you," she said as he strode off, still not fully understanding, but unwilling to appear too much of a provincial idiot.

Turning to the stall, she was content. It was a large space, more than enough for all of them. She set about unloading and leading the horses to the water and hay. As she wondered if it was possible to buy grain, a lad appeared with a sack.

"Greetings, lady," he said with a cheeky grin and walked to large wooden buckets attached to the wall, which he proceeded to fill with oats. "If you need anything else, just ask."

The horses were happy, now for her own comfort. She climbed the ladder and found a large clean space which she filled with her panniers and baggage. She silently thanked Uri; this was far better than she would have found on her own and well worth the price.

It was time to tend the horses, find her way around, and plan her next move.

Chapter 20

Yrsa was brushing the horses when she sensed eyes watching her. Turning, she spotted a lad of about fifteen in the loft of the stall next to hers, who slid behind the partition when he knew he'd been seen.

"Good day," she called, turning back to her task.

"Good day," the reply came after a short delay.

"Are you a regular visitor?"

"We come every moon."

"We?"

"My master and me."

"Your master?"

"Annalphus. I'm his apprentice."

"What's your name?"

"Phren."

"Well, Phren, I'm Yrsa and I've never been here before. Can you show me around?"

"I could ..."

"How much?" she replied.

"Oh, it's not that." He paused. "It would be an honour." Although she had her back to him, she knew he was blushing. "Annalphus is due to return from the city, and I daren't be away when he arrives."

"Did he not take you with him?" she asked. "I thought apprentices were taught everything."

"This wasn't business. He spent the night in the city with ... a friend."

His grin told her all she needed to know about Annalphus's friend.

"I see. Well, I doubt it will take long. If he returns before we get back, you can blame me."

He thought for a moment before jumping down from his loft. He was a skinny lad with black hair and bright blue eyes.

"All right, but we'll have to be quick."

As she suspected, there wasn't much to the compound. Two massive stables on either side, and the central building which held the offices, dormitories for those who wanted a bed for the night, and something she'd never seen before.

"Latrines," Phren said. "You know, for pissing and ... things." She poked her head in the doorway and instantly cursed her keener sense of smell.

"There's a kitchen and eating place as well," he told her as they moved on. "But I don't use it. It's awfully expensive."

"So where do you eat?"

"There are always a range of stalls between here and the city gate selling food. You can get almost anything there for a few kels. And Annalphus sometimes brings me something back."

As they returned to the stable, he explained the tallies. You hung one out at night for each horse. In the morning, the stable lads cleaned the stall, filled the hay and oats, and took the tallies. It was simple. They were walking along the central aisle when a man appeared from what looked like Yrsa's stall.

"My master," Phren gasped and ran towards him.

"There you are," the man said. "Where have you been? I don't pay you to run off every time you're needed."

"I'm sorry," Yrsa said, arriving at the scene. "Your apprentice was kind enough to show me around the inn. I haven't been here before."

Annalphus was a big man, clearly used to an excess of food or ale, or both. He was wearing a style of clothing not known to Yrsa, but it was made of fine cloth, dyed in rich colours.

"I'm glad he has time for such diversions," he replied.

"If I have delayed you, I apologise," she said.

"Yes, well. It would be better if your employer had shown you around."

"I have no employer."

"Your husband, then."

"I am not married."

He looked at her, frowning, letting his eyes take in her clothes, and surveying her horses.

"Whose horse is that, then?" he asked, pointing to Tennell.

"That horse – those horses – are mine."

She suddenly realised Bodro and Pek were missing. They weren't in the stall with the horses. Her mind raced, wondering where they'd gone.

"It's a fine horse," Annalphus replied, grudgingly. "Where'd you get it?"

"Do I ask where your horses are from?"

He mumbled something inaudible and turned to Phren.

"Come on. We have work to do."

Phren loaded two flat bales onto one of their horses and followed his master as they walked up the aisle. When they'd gone twenty paces or so, she returned to her problem.

"Where are you?" she asked herself and rapidly scanned the stable. Then looked up, straight into the zeffen's eyes, watching her from the loft. It was well over a man's height from the ground and the only access was a row of iron bars fixed to the partition which acted as a ladder. "How did you get up there?"

They showed her by effortlessly jumping down to the floor of the stall to welcome her.

* * *

As she walked from the inn, Yrsa's excitement rose. Lonithrya was the largest settlement she'd ever entered. One or two of the ports she'd visited with her father had been impressive compared to the Valleys' towns, but nothing like this.

She stopped at one of the food stalls Phren had mentioned, bought a pie, the contents of which she couldn't immediately identify, and ate it while watching the constant stream of traffic.

After finishing her snack, she joined it. There were armed guards on either side of the huge gates, but they were there to watch for any trouble, not control the columns of people. Inside the wall, she stopped and looked around her. She'd never seen so much brick and stone. There were no houses of wood or thatched roofs. A curse or two from people passing reminded her not to stand in the middle of the road, and she moved on, trying not to look too much like an outsider.

She had no plan. Today was all about finding her way around, and she spent the afternoon exploring the city. The houses gave way to shops and workshops, every side street a hive of activity and commerce. There were larger buildings, three or four stories high, which she thought might be houses of the rich, and as she approached the centre, she passed structures she guessed were temples of some kind.

On one side of the central square was a huge building, many stories high, with flags flying from its front. On the other three sides were more shops, spilling out onto the street, with stalls and carts filling the space in between. Her head was buzzing, and she realised how difficult her task was. To find one man in all of this.

Luna had given her some clues. Her kinsman went by the name of Pacleidius, though his real name was Rald. She thought he would be making a living either telling people their future or performing sleight-of-hand tricks; possibly both. He had a bad eye, the result of an accident many years ago, which left it cloudy and dull.

"It doesn't stop him, though," Luna had said. "He'll still spot a good-looking woman at a hundred paces."

There was nothing Yrsa could do, other than start asking people. She stopped passers-by and inquired where she might find a future teller. Nobody ventured an answer, and the rest of the day was fruitless. She wasn't surprised, asking herself how she'd ever hoped to find Rald. But the city was fascinating, and several times she was caught staring at people and things she'd never seen before.

As evening approached, she headed back to the inn, stopping at the food stalls to buy a few things to eat. Seeing some hams hanging up, she asked how much they were. The stallholder thought she was joking, as her usual offering was one slice served with bread. But when she realised Yrsa meant it, they haggled over a price for two, and the woman was left in a delighted daze, clutching more money than she'd made all day.

Arriving at her stall in the stable, she saw Phren grooming his two horses next door.

"All alone again?" she asked him.

"Annalphus is spending the night in the city," he replied.

"Would this be a lady?"

He looked furtively around.

"It is, and he has a wife at home." He spotted the two hams as she laid them on the floor, and his eyes widened. "What are they for?"

"For my dogs."

"I haven't seen any dogs."

She was pleased Bodro and Pek had stayed out of sight, then had a mild panic, wondering if they were still in the loft. She gave two soft whistles, their heads appeared, and they jumped effortlessly down. She made a fuss of them, even though they'd spotted the meat.

"What sort of dogs are they?" Phren asked over the partition, his voice full of awe.

"Hunting dogs," Yrsa replied. "Come and meet them."

He walked hesitantly around the stall partition and stood a couple of paces from them.

"This is Phren," Yrsa said to the zeffen. "Be nice to him."

They slowly approached him, and he held out his hands, which they sniffed. Then licked. He put his hands on their heads and gradually summoned the courage to ruffle their coat, at which point, he had two new friends.

Yrsa gave them the hams, and they lay down to devour them. Phren watched them silently, clearly amazed at these creatures new to him. It suddenly struck Yrsa the lad's gaze might be more than amazement.

"Have you eaten?" she asked him.

"Oh," he said uncertainly. "I had a meal earlier."

"Nothing since?"

"I can't leave the inn. I'm fine."

"Here, let's share."

They sat on the floor, and she placed the food she'd bought on a cloth and split it between them. After some hesitation, he began to eat. He was clearly hungry.

"Does Annalphus not feed you?" she asked.

"He's a good man, but when he's focused on his work, he thinks of nothing else. Sometimes, I get forgotten."

"What does he do?"

"He trades parchment and paper."

"What's paper?"

"It's something to write on instead of parchment."

"I don't read, so it means nothing to me."

"I didn't until I became an apprentice."

"Did Annalphus teach you?"

"Partly," he replied through a full mouth, "but also his wife."

"What do you read?"

"All sorts of things. They have a large library."

"Library?"

"It's a collection of books, they've got dozens."

"What about?"

"Everything you can imagine. Stories about the world and things that happened in the past. Books about famous and learned men. Then there are ones about strange people and monsters and dragons. I love those. They've got some in other languages which I can't read yet, but I've learned so much."

Phren's enthusiasm was obvious. She'd seen few books in her life. Some in the ports she'd visited, and Luna had a few. But they were useless to Yrsa, who saw only meaningless characters on their pages.

"I envy you," she said.

"It's not difficult," he replied. "You need someone to teach you."

That was unlikely. She'd set off on her own and had no idea where she would eventually go. She couldn't imagine anyone she'd be likely to meet would have the time or desire to teach her to read.

They talked about Annalphus's work and Phren's part in it. He turned out to be a well-travelled lad, accompanying his master on long journeys to acquire the best quality skins to make parchment. And she learned paper came from places far to the south and the east. As he recounted his travels, she made a mental note of the places he mentioned. She could but hope to visit one or two someday.

The following day was almost as frustrating as the first. She wandered around the city, taking in the sights and smells of the shops she passed. Many were trades she knew, but some were a mystery. She asked anyone she met if they knew of a seer with a bad eye. Nobody did. She was beginning to tire when a stallholder called her over.

"If you want your future told," she said, "try the street of herbalists. There used to be one or two fire readers there."

Yrsa thanked the woman and followed the directions she'd been given. She smelt the street before she came to it. That intoxicating mix of sweet and acrid aromas which reminded her of Luna's house. The street was lined with open fronts, each hung with bunches of herbs, sacks of ground powders, dried animals, and a variety of things it was best not to examine too closely.

She reached the other end without seeing anything helpful in her search. Retracing her steps, she saw a man and a woman leaning against a wall, presuming them to be neighbouring traders, talking the day away.

"Good day," she said, walking up to them.

"Good day, missy," the woman said. "How can we help?"

"With a need and an answer, I hope. Do you have anything called temkin?" They looked blankly at her. "I think it's also called sleepy top."

"Ah," the man said. "You mean a little mushroom, grows on dead oaks in the west."

"That's it."

"We call it oaksoul here. I think I have some."

He wandered into his store, leaving Yrsa with the woman.

"I'm also looking for someone," she said. "Do you know anyone named Pacleidius?"

"Oh, we all know Pacleidius."

"Where might I find him?"

"He has a little booth at that end." She pointed down the street.

"Thank you," Yrsa said. "I'll go and find him."

"Not yet, you won't," the man said, returning with a sack. "It's far too early for him. He's still sleeping off the effects of last night."

"Or sleeping with whichever silly girl he talked into his bed," the woman added, cackling. "You'll have to come back later."

"Now," the man said. "How much of this oaksoul do you want?"

* * *

Yrsa returned to the city after dark. Luna had assured her Pacleidius was harmless enough, and the two herbalists had painted a similar picture of her quarry. Nevertheless, she wanted to check him out before making herself known to him. If he was working as a future teller, she could play a seeker of truth.

She made her way back to the street of herbalists. Most shops were still open; did this city never sleep? She looked for Pacleidius's booth. As the shop owner had said, there was a small doorway on the corner, with a smoking brazier outside, along with a board covered in strange symbols.

She crossed to the opposite corner and leaned against the wall. Looking along the adjoining lane, she saw the unmistakable signs of drinking halls and spotted one sign with a naked female form on it. She could guess easily enough what went on there.

A little into her watch, a woman approached and dipped into the booth. A curtain came down over the doorway, not opening again for some time, when the woman left. It was time to meet the man she'd come here to see.

Chapter 21

Yrsa ducked under a low beam and entered the small space.

"Ah, welcome young lady," a voice said. "Come, come, sit down."

The room was in darkness, except for a small open brazier on a wooden table, with glowing coals in it. She could make out an empty chair and dropped onto it.

"You seek news," the voice continued. "Good news, distressing news, it is all here. For the fates do not discriminate. Be you the grandest lady in the land, your life may be filled with pain. Be you the lowest whore, your destiny may be full of riches."

The voice was rich and melodious, with an accent that wavered, and the words were designed to draw the believing. Which she certainly wasn't.

"How can the Great Pacleidius help you today?"

The Great Pacleidius? She couldn't speak for a few moments, for fear of revealing her humour. Luna had said he was something of a charlatan; here was the truth. Her eyes were growing accustomed to the dark, and with her heightened senses, she could see more than her host realised.

"I have no specific questions," she replied, cursing herself for her lack of preparation. "But I am curious to know if I will ever find happiness with a husband and children." That would be a good test, she thought.

"I will seek the answer in the fire," the voice replied. "But, alas, the fire needs fuel, and the Great Pacleidius needs to eat, like any man. A silver coin will suffice."

She laid one on the table and a hand shot out to retrieve it. She could see the man clearly enough to know he was who she sought. His right eye reflected the fire in the brazier, but the left did not, it was almost white.

She pulled back as the fire flared up, and colours danced within it. She knew there were minerals you could throw into a fire to produce coloured flame, but couldn't see how he was doing it.

He appeared in a trance, waving his arms, mumbling, and humming. A real performance. She'd seen such antics in the Valleys when travelling future tellers arrived. They found enough believers to make a living.

"Lady, you have come from far away," he intoned. "Far away. I see a journey bringing you to this place. You seek something … or someone. Yes, someone. A man to ease your life. A man to look after you. Someone to bless you with children. These things will come. Be patient. They will come."

After a few more vague promises and predictions, the fire suddenly died down, and he slumped dramatically in his chair. After a few moments, he sat up, as if coming out of his trance.

"Did you hear your answers, lady?" he asked.

"Indeed I did, Pacleidius, and I thank you."

She left the booth and set herself for the second job of the evening. Wrapping her cloak around her, and pulling her hood over her head, she went back to her watching place and waited, glad she'd brought her pipe. She was surprised by the steady stream

Yrsa and the Zeffen Hunter

of visitors, and it was well into the night when Pacleidius pulled the board into the booth, along with the dying brazier.

Moments later, he shut and bolted the door, and headed along the street of drinking houses. As Luna would have predicted, he turned in under the sign of the naked woman. But he wasn't there long, coming out again accompanied by someone covered in a cloak and carrying a large stone flagon.

Yrsa followed them carefully as they headed into the night. There were still people about, and it wasn't difficult to keep pace with them. She could hear them talking and laughing as they walked, although not what was being said, but by the woman's reaction, they weren't discussing the finer points of city politics.

Eventually, they turned into an alleyway, and Yrsa watched from the entrance as they disappeared from view at the end of a leaning building. After a few moments, she followed and found a set of steps to a single door. She soon heard laughing and a few amiable shrieks. Smiling to herself, she set off back to the inn.

She was surprised to find three wooden poles across the front of her stall, and ducked under them, looking around. Everything was as she'd left it, the horses were dozing, and she greeted each of them. The zeffen jumped down and gave her their usual enthusiastic welcome. This woke Phren.

"Your black mare had a suitor," he said. "A stallion broke loose and tried his luck."

Yrsa went over to Tennell, who seemed unconcerned.

"What happened?"

"She wasn't interested," the lad replied, grinning. "I've never heard a horse as loud as her." Yrsa was stroking the big mare's neck. "She screamed and gave him an almighty kick. The lads had to come to his rescue."

Yrsa laughed.

"Was he all right?"

"When they led him back, he had blood on his face."

She stopped laughing.

"Where is he?"

Phren led her a little way along the aisle to a stall holding the horse in question. He was looking sorry for himself, and the side of his head was covered in some sort of thick salve.

"Yes?"

The voice startled her. Looking up, she saw a man and woman in the stall's loft.

"Oh, I'm sorry," Yrsa replied. "I believe one of my horses kicked yours."

"She's yours, is she?" the man replied. "A beautiful animal."

"I hope he's not badly injured."

"Just a gash, but I expect it hurts."

"Silly beast," the woman said. "How he thought he had any chance with such a mare is beyond me. But they never learn, do they?"

Yrsa returned to her stall and stroked Tennell.

"So, girl," she said, almost to herself. "You're choosy, too."

The sound of activity woke her in the morning. Her stall was being cleaned out and she watched, admiring the efficiency. Two lads led the horses to the opposite side of the aisle and tied them to rails, raked out the old straw, tipping it into large, wheeled boxes. Then they emptied the water trough onto the ground before scrubbing it clean.

They moved on, and two more came along with fresh straw, spreading it out. They refilled the water trough, added fresh hay, and filled the buckets with oats before leading the horses back in. The whole thing was over in moments. She rose and stretched. As usual, Bodro and Pek copied her. It always made her smile. She gave them some dried meat, and climbed down from the loft, chewing a piece of stale bread.

A quick check of the horses revealed they were more interested in eating than her attention, so she walked to the injured stallion's stall to check on him, but it was empty.

"They left early," Phren said as she returned.

"Was the horse all right?"

"He seemed fine. He won't try that again."

The lad may have learnt a lot from his books, but clearly understood little about stallions.

She made her way to the alley Pacleidius called home and quietly climbed the stairs. Given what the two shopkeepers had said, it was likely he was still in bed. The door was slightly ajar, but it was half-rotten and probably didn't close properly anyway.

Her ears picked up an unmistakable sound. He may be in bed, but he wasn't asleep. She composed herself, pushed the door, and stepped into the room.

"Good day, Pacleidius," she said, before the scene in front of her had time to break her voice. A naked woman on her hands and knees, with him kneeling behind her, their motion frozen by this unexpected interruption. They were both staring at her, the woman's face a picture of embarrassed horror, his, a study in irritated frustration.

"I do apologise," Yrsa said, before stepping out again, leaving the door wide open. There was no sound for a few moments.

"What do you want?" he called out.

"I'd like a word with you," Yrsa replied.

"What about?"

"The telling you did for me last night."

"I don't return payment." Yrsa didn't reply, waiting for him to think, and the result was a surprised tone in his voice. "How did you find me?"

"I know a lot about you." She let it sink in. "I'll come back shortly."

She went down the stairs and hid in a doorway. After a brief time, the woman appeared, fully dressed, and left. Yrsa climbed the stairs again, to find him pulling his long gown on, his back to her.

"The Great Pacleidius," she said, "caught in action."

"What do you want?" he replied, turning to her with a small knife in his hand, his voice more threatening. Yrsa swung her cloak open, and he saw the weapons on her belt. "I haven't time for this," he muttered, throwing his own on the bed.

"I need to speak to you. I need your help."

"A fine way to ask for it. Barging in on … well, barging in and scaring a poor young woman."

"Probably richer this morning."

A flash of anger crossed his face before a shrug of acceptance replaced it.

"So what?" he said.

"So, we may be able to help each other."

"What are you talking about, girl? You make no sense." His confidence – or his act – was returning. "The Great Pacleidius-"

"I'm not looking for the Great Pacleidius, I'm looking for Rald."

He froze, his mouth open, staring at her. His good eye bored into her, trying to understand.

"Who are you?" he asked, the act gone, his voice betraying his curiosity.

"Let's go and find something to eat, and I'll tell you."

* * *

"Well, well," he said. "Old Luna. I haven't seen her for years." They were sitting on a wall overlooking the market, eating some meat patties. "How is my kinswoman?"

"She's well. She advised me to search you out."

"Why?"

"I need your help."

"Yes, yes, you've already told me. But why?"

"I need you to train me." He looked puzzled and studied her face.

"Girl, if I'm reading you correctly, you didn't believe anything I told you last night."

"Not a word. Nice performance, though."

"Thanks, I like to give the full experience. But there's nothing to train. I make it all up."

"Rald, I don't want you to teach me future telling. I need your guidance with vaying."

He'd been about to put the last of a patty in his mouth, but his hand paused in mid-air, and he screwed his face up before letting it fall to his lap.

"Not a chance," he said. "I gave that up years ago." Yrsa sat quietly, leaving him to think. "Are you … can you …"

"Yes," she replied. "At least, I think so."

He stared out over the market, staying silent for some time.

"You haven't told me your name," he said.

"Yrsa."

"Well, Yrsa, I hope it brings you more fortune than it brought me."

"Why? What happened?"

"I don't have time to go back over all that."

"Expected by the council, perhaps?"

"I don't want to, then."

"Please, Rald. I want to know."

Silence fell again, as she let him think. It was clearly a difficult subject for him, and that wasn't something she'd anticipated. Was there something about vaying or spirit melding Luna hadn't told her? It made her keener than ever to hear his story. After a long wait, he took a deep breath.

"All right, young lady. I'll tell you why I gave up vaying, then you can leave me in peace."

Chapter 22

"I'm not telling you the whole story," Rald said. "It would take too long and bring back too many memories." They'd returned to his room, Yrsa taking the only chair while he sat on the bed. "When I discovered I could vay, I revelled in my new skills, telling anyone who would listen. Did they believe me? Of course not. Why would they? They thought I was mad, that the Gods had cursed me."

He shook his head heavily before continuing.

"I couldn't understand it. I couldn't work out why I'd been chosen. What was I to do with this ability? I'm not like Luna. She spent years learning everything she knows, years of study and toil. She's happy with her life, but that wasn't for me. I wanted everything there and then; I wanted fame and fortune. So, I found a way to use my skill to my advantage."

His face broke into a sly grin.

"I set myself up as a future teller, but not like I am now. I visited people in their homes and told them I could see their future through their animals. It was so easy. They were amazed when I told them about past events, things I couldn't possibly know. All gleaned from their dog, or their goat, or their horse."

"But their animals couldn't tell you the future," Yrsa said.

"Of course not, but they were hooked. Once I gained their confidence, it didn't matter. I could tell them anything about their future, and they'd believe it."

"What happened when none of it came true?"

"I didn't wait to find out. I moved from town to town, city to city, never lingering long."

"What went wrong?"

He gave a rueful smile.

"My greed and my lust." He saw her puzzled look. "What did Luna tell you about me?"

"She said you were a charlatan, a drunkard and a lecherous old fool."

"Ha! She knows me too well. I sometimes plied my trade for the great and the good. And they often had secrets; embarrassing secrets I drew from their animals and used to my advantage."

"You blackmailed them?"

"It worked for a while. But one or two were keener to see me beaten up in some back alley than pay me. I had some narrow escapes."

"Where does lust come into it?"

"Some of my customers were wealthy women, bored by their lives and their husbands."

"So, you …"

"Exactly."

"And their husbands …"

"Didn't like it."

"Why did you stop?"

"I moved to a city with too many secrets. Shortly before I arrived, a councillor had been murdered and his killer couldn't be found. But I found him."

"Through an animal?"

"His dog. His dog told me. And I didn't do anything about it."

"So?"

"Weeks later, they hanged an innocent man, some wretch who was tortured into confessing. I felt responsible for that man's death. I knew he was innocent, knew the real killer was safe. It gnawed away at me, and I vowed never to use my skill again."

"So, you continued with just the second half of your act, making things up."

"People are stupid," he replied, shrugging. "They'll hear what they want to hear."

"It was some performance last night."

"Give them some magic and mysticism, add a little truth and sprinkle it with the obvious."

"I'm a young woman, so I'll go on to marry and have children."

"Exactly."

"Except I'm barren."

He laughed but stopped himself quickly.

"I'm sorry," he said. "I wasn't laughing at your misfortune."

They sat in silence for a while. Yrsa wasn't sure how to continue. She needed this man to help her but now understood his reluctance.

"Did you have someone to help you when you first had the skill?" she finally asked.

"An old woman who has long passed. But I didn't stay around long enough to learn properly. I know that now."

"Do you know of any other vayers?"

"Only one," he replied.

"The woman Luna won't name?" He nodded and she was surprised to see a brief shiver run through him. "What am I to do, then?"

They studied each other in silence. He looked around forty years, though if he was blessed with long life, he could be any age. A face of character, rather than good-looking, and lean and wiry. She suspected he found it difficult to be Rald now, preferring the cover and anonymity of the Great Pacleidius.

"What is it you need?" he finally asked.

"I'm overwhelmed by it all. Since I melded with the spirits, my senses are heightened. Most I can cope with, but when I go into the forest, the noise is overwhelming. I can hear so much, I can't tell one sound from another."

"I didn't experience that," he replied. "But I've heard of it. Does it happen in crowds of people?"

She thought about it.

"Not as much, no."

"You're learning to screen out what's not important. You'll do the same with natural sounds and tune your senses to your needs."

"I hope you're right, but it's vaying I really need help with. When I came back from the melding, my dogs told me their names. I was overjoyed. But since then, I've only picked up vague things from them. It may even be my imagination willing me to believe it. And nothing from any other creature."

"You need to focus on an animal's thoughts, to let them in. It doesn't just happen; you need to search it out."

"How?" He fell silent again. "Rald, please. You're the only person who can help."

"Why would I?" he snapped. "Why would I pass on something which has cost me so much? My greed led to the death of an innocent man. Why would I help you, not knowing if you'll use the skill for good or ill?"

"If a man trains a warrior to use a sword, is he responsible for every life that warrior takes?" Rald shrugged. "Luna taught me about herbs to relieve pain. If I give too much and it kills the patient, who is responsible for that death? Me, not Luna. And if I never heal anyone again, that's not Luna's fault, either."

"All that is true."

"So, you will help me?"

"I cannot help you in the city, and my life is here."

"Your life? I think not. Your income is here, and your ale and your whores. They can be found anywhere." He smiled, acknowledging the truth in her words. "I'll pay you, if that's what

you want. Pay you to accompany me on the next part of my journey, and you can teach me on the way."
"Where are you going?"
"Towards Caropatia."
"Why would you be going there?"
"That's mine to know, for the moment."
"I don't have a horse."
"I have one spare."
"You seem to have an answer for everything."
"No, I don't. That's why I need your help."
He thought for a while.
"How much are you paying?"

When they left Rald's attic, he had all his possessions in a small sack over his shoulder.
"That's it?" Yrsa asked. "That's all you're taking with you?"
"It's all I have," he replied.
As they walked through the city, Yrsa remembered her other task.
"Are there moneylenders here?" she asked.
"You need to borrow what you're paying me?"
"I need to change gold into silver."
His eyes brightened, and he led her in a new direction.
"Are they trustworthy?" she asked as they arrived.
"As honest as moneylenders ever are," Rald replied, heading for the first booth they came to, but Yrsa wandered along the whole street. He followed her, increasingly amused, as she visited each one to get the most silver for Hilda's ingot. But he didn't complain, and whistled quietly when they were out of earshot of the chosen moneylender.
"Well, girl," he said. "I don't know where you come from, but with two hundred silver solens in your purse, I'll follow you for a while."
Yrsa stopped and turned to him.

"Listen, Rald. I have a reason for leaving where I came from, and for going where I'm going. I'm grateful you're coming part of the way, and I'll lend you a horse and feed you. But I will not be paying for your ale or your whores. I'll pay you what we agreed. What you do with it is your affair." She made a move forward but spun back again. "And don't call me girl."

He stood smiling, then hurried to catch up with the mysterious woman striding away from him.

* * *

"Do you know the way to Caropatia?" Rald asked as they walked to the inn.

"I plan to ride east. From what I do know, you can't miss it. I'm sure someone will point us in the right direction."

"It would be quicker to go by river."

"True. But then how would you train me?"

"Yrsa, I don't know if I can. I've never tried to pass my skills to anyone."

"I know, but travelling through the countryside will give us more time, and more opportunities."

When they arrived at her stall, Rald let out a long whistle through his teeth.

"That beauty is yours?" he said.

"She is. Tennell is her name."

"And the others?"

"This is Brimble, an old friend, and this is Lucky. He'll be your mount."

Rald gently greeted Brimble and Lucky, before going to Tennell and nuzzling her nose.

"Are you from Caropatia?" he asked Yrsa.

"I've never been near the place," she replied. "Why?"

"I'd be prepared to bet this animal has."

Yrsa didn't reply but suspected his words were true.

"You said you had dogs," he said, emerging from between the horses. She whistled twice, and Rald gave a choked screech as Bodro and Pek appeared in front of him, seemingly from nowhere. Yrsa stood, amused, saying nothing.

"What in the names of the Gods are those?" he said quietly.

"Rald, meet my boys, Bodro and Pek. Boys, this is Rald. He'll be travelling with us."

She bent down and greeted the zeffen, who responded with their usual enthusiasm, before turning their attention to Rald, who was still hesitant.

"They're harmless," she said, "I would have thought someone with your abilities wouldn't be frightened by a couple of dogs."

"Where did these two come from?"

"I found them as cubs," she replied.

"These are the two who gave you their names?"

"Yes."

Rald had composed himself and held out his hands. They sniffed them, before pushing up to him and he stroked their coats. She knew what he was trying.

"I'm not sure this is going to work," he said. "I've not used my skills in years, and I'm not getting anything from them at all."

"I'm glad about that," she replied. "They are under strict instructions not to tell you anything. All my animals are. Anything you learn about me will come from me, not them."

"Smart girl. Sorry, woman."

"I'm paying, I make the rules."

It was mid-afternoon, and it seemed pointless travelling a short distance before they had to find somewhere to stay. Yrsa had paid for the third night at the inn anyway and doubted the office would give her the fee back. Instead, they went shopping, stocking up on some fresh food to last a few days, a couple of sacks of oats, and three new water skins, as well as some meat for the zeffen.

"Do they eat a lot?" Rald asked.

"Enough," Yrsa replied. He'd soon see.

She invested in a second-hand light saddle for Lucky. Rald told her he was happy without one, but although he said he could ride, she suspected he wasn't used to it. She knew from experience riding bareback day after day wasn't comfortable and could cause some nasty sores. That reminded her of another problem.

"You need to get some new clothes for riding," she said.

"I can hitch my robe up."

"I saw enough of you this morning. I don't want to be reminded of it every time you mount your horse."

He wandered off, grinning, to get something more suitable. By the evening, they had all they needed. Yrsa unpacked everything, checked it, and repacked as tightly as she could. With Rald riding Lucky, they didn't have as much carrying capacity, but it would have to do.

* * *

They hadn't gone far the next morning when Yrsa saw Rald's riding ability was even less than she'd estimated. Lucky was a placid horse, more in Brimble's mould than Tennell's. But Rald didn't look comfortable, and Lucky knew it, taking the occasional liberty to give him a fright.

Yrsa dropped back and leaned into Lucky's ear.

"If I were you, I'd behave," she said quietly. "Otherwise, someone might not get his oats tonight."

Lucky shook his head and flapped his lips.

"I'm not sure that will work," Rald said, grinning.

"We'll see."

They stopped for something to eat by a river, and the horses ambled in to drink.

"How long have you had those three?" Rald asked as they sat watching them, eating two halves of a pie.

"I've had Brimble since she was a foal. The other two I've only had about five moons."

"Really? They have a strong bond with you."

"How can you tell?"

"Yrsa, vaying is about more than a few words or phrases. Oh, yes, we can hear what some animals are thinking, or saying, however you want to describe it. But it allows us to feel their spirits; that's its essence. Those animals will follow you anywhere. Well, Brimble and Tennell will. Lucky, I'm not so sure about, though he stopped playing up after your little talk."

"He had a traumatic experience, and I suspect his previous life wasn't easy. But he's coming round."

"The wound on his rump?"

"Yes, and his previous owner wasn't kind."

"Where did you get them?"

"That I may tell you in time."

"You don't trust me?"

"Would you?"

He thought about the question and broke into a smile.

"Probably not."

They rode on at a steady pace. Well, Brimble's pace as usual, though Yrsa wasn't worried. She had a feeling if they went much faster, Rald would start falling off. He wasn't relaxed on horseback, his body stiff and tense.

"You haven't ridden much, have you?" she asked.

"Is it that obvious?" he replied. "We didn't have horses when I was young. A few mules we used to ride sometimes. Since then, I've spent most of my time in towns and cities, never needing a horse. Besides, they're expensive and need a lot of looking after."

"You'll be looking after Lucky on this journey."

He gave her a sour look before breaking into a grin.

Chapter 23

The main road east passed through a settled landscape. Farms and cultivated land as far as they could see, the river occasionally visible in the distance. Villages and small towns came and went, and it was easy to pick up fresh food.

They were one group of travellers among many. Yrsa marvelled at the variety of people and goods they passed and found herself glad of Rald's company. He was a mine of information, telling her the origin of many of those they met. Whether he was always right, she didn't know.

They managed to find an inn to rest in every night. The first produced their one altercation. Rald tried his luck, attempting to put his arm around Yrsa during the night.

"Try that once more, and your good eye will match your bad," she said, without moving.

He didn't, and it was never mentioned again. Yrsa got used to Rald disappearing for an hour or two in larger towns.

They reached Eldona, large enough to call itself a city, where three great roads met. After they'd eaten in the evening at the small inn they'd found, Rald nudged Yrsa.

"That man over there is from Flengara," he whispered. "If he came by land, he would have had to come through Caropatia. He'll tell us the best way to get there."

They went over to the table, and introduced themselves, the visitor naming himself as Ignatian. They bought him a drink.

"Have you come by road?" Rald asked.

"Mainly by water."

"Oh, pity. We're heading to Caropatia and aren't sure of the best way to go."

"I wouldn't go there."

"Why's that?" Yrsa asked.

"It's an unfriendly place; not like it used to be. Doing business there is difficult. Bribes, extra tolls; it's not worth it." He looked around and lowered his voice. "They say the king's lost his mind."

"If you did want to go," Yrsa said, "how would you get there?"

"Follow the east road as far as the Great Basin, then take a boat."

"Is there no road?"

"I believe there is, but I've never used it."

They continued plying Ignatian with drink, and he told them all he knew.

* * *

"Still going to Caropatia?" Rald asked as they set off in the morning.

"I want to know more," Yrsa replied. "What Ignatian told us was mostly rumour."

"Rumour is usually built on truth."

"Let's get to the Great Basin. We'll learn more there."

Traffic on the road was thinning, and people were warier. Yrsa noticed Tennell drew glances, and Bodro and Pek were given a wide berth, even though they trotted close to the black mare.

She'd pushed Rald several times to talk about vaying, but each time he'd avoided it.

"It's time you talked," she said as they rode along an exposed ridge.

"Yrsa, I'm not sure how to begin, I haven't used the skill in years. I'm trying to bring it back, but it doesn't seem to be working."

"Can it leave you?"

"I don't know. I don't think anyone knows. There are so few of us, I doubt it's ever been written down."

"That wouldn't be any good to me, I can't read."

"You should learn."

"Who's going to teach me?"

"I could."

She brought Tennell to a halt and turned in her saddle.

"Rald, I only want one thing from you. Your help to understand my new skills. Don't try to avoid it." For once, he looked a little crestfallen. "Unless, of course, you were lying about that as well."

She nudged Tennell forward again.

"I wasn't lying," he said. "I have the skill; had it, anyway. I just need to find it again."

Yrsa pondered the situation. She knew such a skill wasn't straightforward, Luna had told her as much.

"I don't know if it can be taught," the healer had said. "Perhaps you have to work it out for yourself."

She was travelling with the only other vayer she knew, who seemed unable to use his own skill, let alone teach her.

The road was getting rougher, only paved through towns and villages, and those were further apart. The land was only cultivated in places, trees and scrubland filling the gaps between farms. To the north, they could see mountains, rising high into the sky.

For the first time, they had to camp and found a good spot a little off the road.

"Are you used to sleeping in the open?" Yrsa asked.

"Oh, yes," Rald replied. "When I moved from town to town, if I couldn't go by boat, I walked. No horse, remember? I'd sleep anywhere."

"If you couldn't find some woman to take you to her bed."

"That wasn't unknown," he conceded.

As they sat around the fire, Yrsa studied Rald. He was apparently successful with women. From some of his tales, it was clear he only paid when he had to. But she couldn't see what his attraction was. He was fair enough but had no special features, nothing which lit anything in her. She needed him for his knowledge, though. His experience of vaying.

"Could I have lost it already?" she asked.

"What?" he replied, snatched from his half-sleep state.

"Vaying. Have I lost it already? Perhaps I never had it in the first place."

"You have it. You use it. You just don't recognise it."

"What do you mean?"

"You talk to your animals."

"Everyone does."

"But have you not noticed they understand you."

"They're just well trained."

"Yrsa, you can speak to them. I've been watching how they react to you. They listen to everything you say. Think of Lucky on the first day."

She looked at Bodro and Pek, who were staring back at her. Even Tennell was watching her when she turned towards the horses. Perhaps there was truth in his words. She'd always been close to her animals, but she'd almost taken for granted how cooperative her current companions were.

"But they're not vaying to me," she said.
"How do you know? Listen to them."
"I've tried. I've tried so hard."
"That is your mistake."
"What?"
"Don't try. They hear you because you use your voice to them. Anyone can hear you. But they have to let you in to vay. They decide whether they want to be your dumb animals or vayers, and they won't do it lightly. Even when my skills were at their height, I could only vay with animals who chose to let me in. It's the same with you, you must let them in. Don't reach out for them, let them reach out to you."
"I don't understand. How do I do that?"
"That I can't explain, it's something I cannot put into words."
"I'm beginning to wish the spirits had chosen someone else."
"They don't choose you. They see something that's already there."
"I think they may have been wrong."

As she covered herself in her cloak, she felt more frustration than she could remember. She was so close to the goal, but something was getting in the way. Rald was right about her animals, though. She did talk to them, and they did seem to understand. She hadn't even seen it. But how could she understand them?

* * *

Yrsa woke up screaming in the first light of dawn. Bodro and Pek shot up, looking around for the danger. The horses were restless, and Rald was on his feet.
"What is it?" he hissed. "What's wrong?"
Her eyes were bleary, she was drenched in sweat and had a pounding headache. She slowly sat up and looked around, recognising Rald, the zeffen, the horses and the place they'd bedded down the night before.

It must have been a dream. A dream like the night in the glade. Swirling light and mist. Wonder and joy. Then pain. Agony, really. The tendrils of light piercing her head, twisting and turning, exploring her mind, while she tried to overcome them, control them.

"I ... I don't know," she replied. "It must have been a dream. Sorry."

"Are you all right?" Rald asked.

"Water, please."

He brought a skin over.

"Your ears," he gasped.

"What about them?"

"They're bleeding."

She put a finger in her ear and examined it. Blood. The other one, too.

"No wonder I have a headache."

The spirits, Bodro.

I think so, Pek.

She froze.

"What is it?" Rald asked, alarmed by the huge grin spreading over her face. "What's wrong?"

"Was it the spirits?"

"Yrsa," Rald said. "You're not making sense."

"Not to you, perhaps."

Of course.

"Was that you?" she said to the zeffen. "Can I hear you?"

It appears you can, at last.

"Who?" Rald said. "Hear who?"

She laughed, and her head hurt, but she crawled over to Bodro and Pek and hugged them while they licked her. A few moments later she turned around to see Rald standing there, clearly wondering if he was in the middle of nowhere with a madwoman.

"Rald," she said. "I can hear them. I can hear them."

Yrsa and the Zeffen Hunter

After the initial euphoria, the headache hit hard. She took a generous amount of one of Luna's potions and carefully cleaned her ears while it took effect, though they were no longer bleeding. The zeffen watched her attentively without a word.

"I'm hungry," she said.

They sat quietly and ate, Yrsa looking at the zeffen every so often, still not believing what had happened.

"They've stopped," she suddenly said to Rald in a panic. "Why have they stopped?"

"They'll vay when they want to," he replied. "They're like us. There are things going on in your head, most of which you never tell anyone else. It's the same for them. They won't always obey you either, they're not your puppets."

'What's a puppet?'

Yrsa burst out laughing, to Rald's amusement.

"What now?" he said.

"They want to know what a puppet is."

"That's another thing, they only know what you've taught them and what they've experienced. You told me you were unable to have children. Well, you've got two now, and something tells me they're going to be worse than any human child."

"Well, boys," she said softly. "I'm not your mother. I can't teach you everything she would have taught you. I'm not even sure what you need to know, but I'll do my best."

"What about the horses?" Rald asked when they'd eaten. Yrsa hadn't even considered it and went over to them.

"Brimble first," she whispered, remembering the life they'd shared. "Morning, girl," she said, hesitantly.

'I'd like some oats.'

"I'll get them soon," she replied, hugging Brimble's neck.

Lucky proved less talkative. Nothing at all, even after several tries, but she half-expected it. Then she moved on to Tennell.

"Good morning," Yrsa said, stroking the black mare's neck, before continuing in a whisper. "Will you vay with me, girl?"

'Is it worth it?'

"I hope so."

'You hear me?'

"I do. Yes, I do."

'About time. I've been waiting long enough.'

Yrsa felt elated as she poured out oats for the horses and returned to Rald and the zeffen.

"What happened last night?" he asked.

"I had a dream. Well, it may not have been a dream. It was like my melding in the glade."

"The spirits don't usually meld with anyone twice. Most people can't stand it."

As they rode, Yrsa bombarded Rald with questions. How would she know which animals would vay? Could they vay with each other? Would other people know?

"Yrsa," he replied. "Slow down. Live with this gift, experience it, enjoy it. You never know, these delightful creatures may find you boring and decide you're not worth the trouble."

She turned a worried face to look at him and called him a bastard when she saw his grin.

"No, truly," he said. "We are all different. My experiences will not be yours. Something easy for me may be hard for you. Don't force anything. Your horses are smart animals, and those two are more intelligent than any dog should be. Let them guide you."

She knew instinctively he was right, but it was hard to suppress her excitement. She wished she could tell Luna; tell her she could do it. She hoped the healer would know somehow. Her headache melted away and their ride was easy and happy. When they stopped for a rest at midday, it was beside a huge water meadow.

After they'd eaten, Yrsa went over to Tennell.

"Want a run, girl?"

Yrsa and the Zeffen Hunter

'I do.'
"May I ride you for part of it?"
'Of course. I'm your mount.'
Rald watched as Yrsa rode around the meadow, the big black mare cantering and galloping at her command, the rider laughing from pure joy. She trotted back to him before dismounting and letting Tennell have her head, and they watched her tear around until she came back panting and sweating. They had to wait until she cooled down before continuing their journey.

Chapter 24

As they travelled, Yrsa began to understand her four-legged companions, really understand them. Brimble made her laugh. She should have guessed her faithful old mare wouldn't be the most talkative of animals. She asked when she wanted something, which was rare as Yrsa knew her needs, but apart from that, she didn't vay much.

Tennell was more communicative, and Yrsa learnt a little about the mare's past.

"You understood Amluss?"

'Yes.'

"Could he understand you?"

'Not as you can.'

"Did he have you long?"

'He bred me and trained me.'

"He did a good job."

'If you say so. I only know this way of being.'

"There are few horses with your power and skill."

The mare's only reply was a little jig and a whinny. Yrsa remembered that; a little praise went a long way.

Lucky still didn't communicate. He was calm and obliging, but nothing came.

"Is Lucky all right?" Yrsa asked Tennell.

'Well enough. He's happy without his old master. Give him time.'

But the real joy was working with Bodro and Pek. They chattered all the time. She wondered how much they talked to each other; things they didn't let her hear. But as they travelled through the countryside, the zeffen bombarded her with questions. As Rald had said, they were a lot like human children.

They had an insatiable curiosity about the world and everything in it. Much of it was basic stuff. The names of things in the forest, where they were going, who the passing people were. But their intelligence astonished her. They seemed able to consider quite complex issues. It sometimes took them a while to reach conclusions, and those conclusions could be wildly wrong, but they got there in the end.

"You'll have to watch those two," Rald said one evening when they'd set up camp, and the zeffen roamed off into the woodland. "I only get to hear your side of the conversation, but it seems to me they'll soon be smarter than us."

"It has crossed my mind."

"Doesn't that worry you? Dogs can be cunning, you know."

She considered her response for a moment.

"They're not dogs," she replied.

"What are they, then?"

"Zeffen."

She watched Rald consider this information, and his changing expression told her he was struggling with it. Several times he went to say something, but no words came.

"As in mythical, old men's tales, tear you to bits kind of zeffen?" he finally said.

She nodded, and a moment or two later, he burst out laughing.

"How in the names of the Gods did a young girl, sorry, woman, come to hand rear two of their kind?"

She told him the basics of the story, and he listened intently, without saying a word.

"I didn't think they existed," he said when she finished. "But seeing them I doubt it no longer. Are they fully grown?"

"I only saw their mother as she lay dying, so it was difficult to judge her true size. But they're nothing like as large as her yet and being male, they may grow bigger."

"Gods, we'll be able to ride them."

She smiled, having thought the same on more than one occasion. At that moment, Bodro and Pek emerged from the undergrowth.

"Have you been listening?" Yrsa asked.

'We have.'

'And you left something out.'

"Which was?"

'The pact you made with our birth mother.'

"You knew of that?"

'Of course. She wouldn't have let you take us otherwise.'

'She told us to go with you. You would look after us.'

'You would save us.'

"What are they saying?" Rald asked.

"That I've left something out."

Yrsa told him about the spiritual bond she felt with their mother before her death.

"I see why the spirits wanted you," he said. "They saw what their mother saw."

"Anyone would have done what I did."

"That's nonsense, and you know it, Yrsa. Most people would have finished their mother off and killed these two."

She knew it was true.

'Why?'

"Because people are frightened of you," she replied.

'The people we pass don't seem scared.'

"No, because they don't know what you are. They believe you're dogs."

The zeffen were quiet for a moment, and she knew they were thinking. She also knew this was important for them; their lives might depend on it one day.

'So they're frightened by our name, but not us?'

"Humans fear the unknown. When we don't understand something, we make up stories about it or pretend it's not real. Most people don't even believe you exist."

'Why not?'

"You come from a land people don't know. There are many tales about you, but nobody's ever seen you. People are superstitious, and over time you've become something terrifying to frighten children with."

'What's superstitious?'

"When people believe something that's not true to make it easier for them to deal with their fears."

'Like these Gods you talk about.'

She gave them a wry look and laughed.

"You're right, Rald," she said. "They're getting too clever. They've told me our Gods are all superstition."

"They're probably right."

"Do you not believe in the Gods?"

"I've travelled to many lands, and each has its own Gods. How is that possible? I do believe there's something out there. The spirits, if you like. I don't know what they are, but I feel them."

"You talked about the spirits," she said to the zeffen. "Do you … feel them?"

'All the time.'

"Do you see them?"

'No, they're part of us.'

'And everything around us.'

* * *

They came to the Great Basin. The woodland ended, and the road continued on a raised ridge, swampy ground on either side, before it too vanished, washed away by shifting tides. The view in front of them was remarkable. The Great River flowed to the sea far to the west from this point. But here it began at the juncture of three smaller rivers, although they were invisible from where they stood.

All they could see was water and marshland, except to the north, where the ground rose gently, covered in forest before rising more sharply. Taller peaks were visible in the distance.

"I'm surprised there aren't more towns here," Yrsa said. "With all the rivers meeting."

"There have been in the past," Rald replied. "But the rivers move over this wet land; slowly, but they move. There are tales of ancient cities buried under the silt."

"Well, there are some buildings over there. Let's see if we can reach them by nightfall."

Another raised track, lined with lengths of wood, led towards the settlement, which they found was built above the marshy ground, held up by a myriad of tree trunks, driven into the mud.

Two hundred paces from it, a firmer mound held a couple of large wooden buildings and a fenced area, currently occupied by one lonely horse. As they reached it, a man came out of one of the buildings.

"If you're going into the city, leave your animals here," he said without any introduction.

"Oh, why?" Yrsa replied.

"Too heavy." He wasn't the talkative type.

Yrsa looked at Rald, who shrugged, and they led the horses to the buildings. Finding a free stall without the attendant's help – he'd disappeared again – they unloaded them and found hay and water. Yrsa told Bodro and Pek to stay with the horses to protect them and their baggage. She and Rald headed for the track to the town.

As soon as it left the area of firmer ground, it became a causeway, wooden planks on piles over the marshes and pools.

"I can see why they wouldn't want horses using this all the time," Rald said.

"Yes," Yrsa replied. "But calling it a city was optimistic."

They soon reached the first buildings, all made of wood with reed thatched roofs. The lanes between them were narrow and winding, and passing the other people they encountered wasn't always easy. The lanes widened a little as they pressed on, until they came to an open area which they assumed was the centre. They could see masts over the single-storey houses and headed towards them.

At the water's edge, several boats were tied up, all small craft for local transport rather than cargo. This place wasn't set up to handle anything in quantity, there wasn't the space.

"I'm not sure we're going to find out much here," Rald said.

"Depends what you want to know," a voice behind them replied.

They turned to find an old man leaning against a wall, pipe in hand.

"I want to get to Caropatia," Yrsa said. There wasn't much point in hiding their need.

"Caropatia?" the man replied. "Not much call for passage there recently. Best way would be a boat from here to the other side of the Basin, then find someone going through the inland sea to Caropa."

"What if I wanted to get to Demburan?"

He gave Yrsa a frown.

"You could go the same way, and travel up country. There is an old route through the hills," he pointed vaguely towards the mountains. "But nobody uses it these days."

"Why's that?"

"Because nobody goes to Demburan these days. Mind, nobody much travels to Caropa now, either."

She shared a brief look with Rald.

"Why not?"

"Buy me a flagon and I'll tell you."

He led them to a small drinking house, empty apart from the woman running it, and they bought ale, which was almost undrinkable, and listened to the man's tale.

* * *

"Was any of that true?" Rald asked as they walked back over the causeway.

"I don't know," Yrsa replied. "But it tied in with what Ignatian told us."

They fell silent until they reached the stables, as rain started to fall. The attendant was just leaving.

"Can we spend the night here?" Yrsa asked.

"You can please yourself," the man replied. "There's no food to be had." With that, he set off over the causeway.

"Do you think they chose him for the job based on his endearing charm?" Rald asked.

"Who cares?" Yrsa replied. "At least we've got some shelter. The weather's getting worse."

The rain had increased, coming in off the water, and the wind swirled it around. The stables were open at each end, but the roof at least kept them dry. They checked on the horses, who had been joined by the lonely fellow who'd been there when they arrived. Yrsa found fresh water, along with some sacks of oats.

"They're a bit stale," she said, sniffing them. "But I'd rather use these and keep our own for later."

She, Rald and the zeffen moved into the stall next to the horses and settled on the floor. There were only a couple of loose bars forming a partition.

"Don't these people have horses?" Rald said. "There are none here, well, one, and it's a long walk to the nearest town."

"Looks to me like they use the water to travel anywhere. My people used to be the same. Even now, only some of us have horses."

"How come you ride so naturally?"

"Used to it, I suppose. The first time I got on a horse, I loved it."

"Not Brimble, surely?"

"No," Yrsa replied. "Brimble never liked being ridden. I used to ride one of my brother's horses before Father bought me Gusta."

"Gusta?"

"A rather finicky stallion. They said I'd never ride him; I think Father got him cheap because of it."

"I suppose you proved them wrong."

"Yes. Though he could be a handful."

"I guess that's why Brimble is here, and he's not."

"She's dependable, tough and loyal. You can take her anywhere."

She felt a nudge at her shoulder and found it was Brimble.

'Do I deserve some more oats?'

The rain and wind blew in from the Basin, making the open stables creak and groan. They ate some of the food they'd brought with them but couldn't make a fire inside. Yrsa filled her pipe and leaned against one of the poles, savouring the different flavour of the leaf she'd bought in Lonithrya.

"I'm going to Demburan," she said eventually, her mind settled.

"Why?" Rald replied.

"Why not?"

"Come on, Yrsa. I'm no fool. Everyone we've spoken to has told us there's some sort of trouble in Caropatia, rumour and gossip making people avoid the place. Yet you want to go there.

But do you want to go to the capital, easily accessible by water? Oh, no.

"You want to go to some isolated town in the hills which you can only reach along a route nobody uses anymore. And you say you have no connection with the place." He looked briefly at Tennell. "Well, not much connection. What's the attraction?"

"You don't have to go, Rald. You've done what I asked of you."

"I've done nothing," he spat back. "I can't even vay anymore. I've not got a thing from any of your animals. I've lost the skill."

"Oh, I never told them to let you in, did I?" He gave her a hard stare. "I'd forgotten about that," she said, laughing. "You can let him in, boys and girls. Be nice to him. Anyway, you have helped."

"You've worked it all out yourself."

"Give yourself some credit, you've guided me to this point. So, if you want me to pay you, you can return to Lonithrya."

"I'm done there, time to move on."

"Where next?"

"No idea," he replied, shrugging.

"You just wander?"

"Wherever the road or the next boat takes me."

"Ever been to Caropatia?"

"No, why would I go there?" He looked at her mystified. "Why are you going there?"

Yrsa refilled her pipe and told him.

Chapter 25

As they set off the next morning, there was a sense of purpose. Yrsa had taken the risk of telling Rald all of Amluss's tale. Her doubts about him had gone. He'd proved a good companion, was intelligent, and his worldliness could be an asset.

The surprise had been the zeffen's response to the story. They seemed to understand their part in it, or at least, their mother's.

'He wanted to kill her for her blood?'

"Yes."

'Not because he hated her?'

"No."

They were quiet for some time.

'Yet you liked him.'

"I suppose I did," she said. "At least, I understand his motives." She waited anxiously for their reaction.

'Are you going to kill us for our blood?'

"No," she replied, ruffling their coats. "I have raised you. I'm not letting anyone harm you."

They began the gentle climb into the hills, away from the marshland. Trees appeared again and thickened as they climbed. The track was easy to follow, though its covering of grass showed the old man had been right; little traffic passed this way. As the track turned into the trees, they took a final look back.

From this height, they could see almost the entire basin. A huge body of water, the Great River flowing out on their right-hand side. Three rivers flowed in, widely spaced, with open expanses of marshland between them. Two came from the hills, while the third, hardly visible, came from the inland sea.

"Quite a sight," Rald said. "I've sailed across it, but never seen it like this."

"Where were you going?"

As they rode along, Rald told Yrsa a few of his adventures in the lands beyond the basin. How much of it was true, she still wasn't sure, but they filled most of the day.

They found a place to camp before it grew dark, and built a fire. The forest was different from those Yrsa had grown up with. Many of the trees were unfamiliar to her, and she heard animals and birds she couldn't recognise. The zeffen disappeared, searching out new experiences.

"Do you believe in sorcery?" Rald asked after they'd eaten.

"It was part of children's stories on winter evenings," she replied. "I never met anyone who thought it was real, but Amluss certainly did."

"Oh, it's real."

She studied him; his face was serious.

"You've seen it?" she asked.

"I have."

"Tell me."

"There are scores of people able to do conjuring tricks to fool the gullible. They can be found in every city. Gods, I've done them myself."

"Creating colours in a fire, for instance?"

"Yes," he replied, "and more. But I've seen people with real powers. People who could inflict pain and suffering, even death. People who could alter the state of things and destroy objects utterly in front of my eyes. It's not something to be taken lightly."

"We'll be careful."

"I'm not sure Amluss understood what he was trying to do."

"Nor do I."

"Then why are you doing it? You owe Amluss nothing, nor this nephew of his."

"That may be true, but until this is resolved, Bodro and Pek will never be safe."

"Why ever not?"

"Amluss failed. Who's to say someone else won't take his place and try again."

"Send them home, send them north. No one will follow them there."

"I've thought of that, and they may decide that's what they want to do. But do you think they would be accepted by their own kind?"

"That's a fair question."

"I haven't been able to teach them the skills they would need. Besides, I don't want to lose them. I raised them, and-"

She stopped abruptly and turned around.

"What is it?" Rald whispered, peering into the darkness.

"… and I'm getting better at this," she replied, laughing. "You can come out, boys."

Bodro and Pek emerged from the bushes, trotted over, and made a fuss of their adoptive mother.

* * *

The old man in the town had told them the journey was around fifty leagues, but the path seemed never to go in a straight line and was overgrown in places. It also rose steadily higher, and as it did so, day after day, the forest got thicker.

They encountered streams coming from the mountains, so water for the horses was never a problem, but their fresh food was running out.

"It's time we did some hunting," Yrsa said. "We'll stay here for two nights. I can set some traps and take my bow and see if there's any game."

"I've not heard much," Rald said.

"There's life out there; we might get lucky."

Yrsa left Rald with the horses and set off with Bodro and Pek. She laid several snare traps near their camp, then went deeper into the forest. As they went, she saw many trails through the undergrowth which must be animals, as they'd seen no sign of human activity.

'How would our mother have hunted?'

"I don't know, I never saw her do it."

It was the one skill she'd failed to teach them. Her methods were so different from any wild predator, she wasn't sure how to begin. She'd tried a few times to creep up on something, but once the zeffen spotted it, they ran at it from distance, and even with their speed, it was long gone before they got anywhere near. But perhaps it would be different now she could explain it to them.

"Sit, boys." She leaned against a tree with the zeffen in front of her. "It's all about stealth. First, you must find the prey. When you have, stay out of sight, and plan your next move. For me, that's how to get the best shot with an arrow. But for you, it's about getting as close to the animal as quietly as possible."

'What then?'

"You pounce, overpower it and bring it down."

The zeffen looked at each other, as if discussing the idea.

'Then kill it?'

"Yes."

'Shall we try?'

Yrsa and the Zeffen Hunter

"We can if we find anything to kill."

There were signs of life all around them; tracks, droppings, and the odd broken branch where something had forced its way through, but they'd seen nothing. They came across a small stream, with a worn track running across it.

"We'll hide here and wait."

Yrsa didn't hold out much hope, but it was a lovely day, and she was in a beautiful forest with Bodro and Pek. There were far worse ways to pass the time.

They'd nearly fallen asleep when they all heard a noise at the same time. She laid a hand on the zeffen to stop them from moving and cautiously looked around. About twenty paces away, a small deer of a kind she hadn't seen before was hesitantly approaching the stream. It would have been easy to bring it down with the bow, but she'd let Bodro and Pek have a go.

"Work around her," she whispered. "Slowly."

She watched them crawl away on their bellies, following each other. She was angry with herself for not telling them to split up. They disappeared into the undergrowth. All she could do was wait. The drinking deer raised its head every so often to listen and look around. She doubted any human hunters came here, so the deer's caution told her there must be predators of some kind in this land.

It seemed as if the zeffen would miss their target. They were taking too long, and the deer would be off as soon as it had its fill. Just as she was relaxing, they appeared in a blur leaping high in the air. Bodro was first, and he landed heavily on the deer which went down under his weight. But he still lacked the killer instinct and hadn't extended his claws, so the deer managed to scramble up and make a run for it.

Pek was after it like a shot, Bodro following on. Yrsa raced after them, but there was no way she could keep up. A scrabbling sound told her the deer must be down again, and as she came around a group of trees, she found them. The poor animal was on the ground, legs kicking, making a frightful noise, as Pek lay half over it, Bodro standing watching.

"Kill it," she said.

'How?'

That gave her pause. How would their kind kill its prey? She wasn't sure, but this time, she'd put the deer out of its misery. She slit its throat and its struggling quickly ceased.

"Good boys," she said, ruffling their heads. "First catch."

Bodro and Pek took it in turns dragging the deer through the forest, but it was hard work, constantly snagging on branches and bushes.

"I'd better carry it," Yrsa said.

'I will.'

They walked the rest of the way with the deer balanced on Bodro's back, Yrsa steadying it. He seemed not to notice the weight. As they emerged into the small clearing where they'd camped, Rald saw the hunters return.

"You found something," he said.

"And these two caught it."

She dragged the deer from Bodro's back, and the zeffen stood by it, looking pleased with themselves.

'We didn't kill it.'

"I don't know how your kind kill their prey."

"I expect it's like big cats I've seen," Rald said. "They throttle it or rip its throat open."

"There you are boys, understand?"

'We'll do it next time.'

Rald fed the fire as Yrsa cut up the deer. It would give them a good meal that night, with enough to keep them going as they travelled the next day.

"Do these two always eat their meat cooked?" Rald asked.

"Most of the time," Yrsa replied. "When I found them, they were only partly weaned, and Luna showed me how to chew cooked meat in my mouth and pass it to them. So they grew up on it, but they do eat some raw, particularly the innards."

Saying this, she pulled out the liver, kidneys, and heart, and threw them to Bodro and Pek, who were watching her intently. They stared at the meat in front of them for a few moments, before looking up at Yrsa.

"Eat," she said, and the organs were gone in a few gulps.

"Do you prefer it raw?" she asked.

'Don't mind. Cooked is easier to eat.'

"You would only eat it raw if you were wild."

'We're not wild.'

"Do you regret that?"

They considered for a while.

'We wouldn't be here if we were.'

'Where would we be?'

"You'd be far to the north, in a land of snow and ice."

'Can we go there one day?'

"You're free to go any time you wish."

'You would come with us?'

"Humans aren't designed to live in such lands."

They were quiet again.

'We'll stay with you.'

By the time they ate, it was dark. They sat around the fire quietly, satisfying their appetites. As usual, Bodro and Pek got the largest share, before lying out on their sides, their bellies swollen with meat.

"I think I've lost the skill," Rald said quietly.

"Are you still not getting anything?"

"A little, here and there. I don't think it's that they're not letting me in."

"Perhaps it will take time."

"I'm not worried, to be honest. It's something I've got used to being without. What would I use it for?"

"For the sheer pleasure of it."

"You and I are different there."

"You don't need anything which doesn't bring in money."

"It's not that," he said, laughing. "You have an affinity with nature. I never did. I had this gift, but never really enjoyed it."

The sounds of a forest at night drifted around their camp as they let the venison go down. At one point, Bodro rolled over, and his belly gurgled loudly.

"I wish I could tell those two apart when they vay," Yrsa said. "The horses have different voices; I can identify them. But I can't separate Bodro and Pek."

"Oh, that will come. They're brothers, they think alike. Vayed voices are like ours, they are all different. But those differences tend to be more subtle, and it will take time to learn their individual tone. It may be easier when you can vay without speaking."

She turned sharply to Rald.

"Can I do that?"

"Of course."

"How? Show me."

"Yrsa, slow down. It will come. Did you think when I got information from my client's animals, I asked out loud?"

"I hadn't thought of that."

"It will happen naturally. The only suggestion I have is every time you talk to them, pause, and think your words before saying them. You may find in time you will no longer need to say them out loud."

Chapter 26

Every three or four days, they found somewhere comfortable to camp for a couple of nights, and Yrsa and the zeffen hunted for food. She was delighted how quickly they picked up her poor efforts at teaching them. They learned how to split up and approach their prey from different angles, giving them more chance of success.

They practised crawling, though it was difficult for such large animals, and they found another way of approaching prey on their own. They stalked fully upright, holding their bodies motionless, their rear paws landing on the same spot as their front ones as they slowly edged forward. Yrsa watched them practice and found it mesmerising to see these huge creatures have such precise control of their movements.

She began to notice differences between them. Bodro was the bolder of the two, happy to rely on his size and strength to achieve his goal. Pek was more thoughtful, holding back and planning his actions.

She set them tests, and the zeffen loved these games. Sending them into the forest, their task was to find her and get as close as possible without her knowing. Even with her heightened senses, it got more difficult as they practiced, and on one memorable occasion, she felt Pek's breath on the back of her neck before she even knew either of them was anywhere near.

"I don't think I've ever eaten so well," Rald said one afternoon. It was a rest day and Bodro and Pek had gone off exploring. Yrsa and the zeffen had hunted in the morning and found a pig almost at once. They were far uglier than the ones she was used to, but they tasted much the same.

"You seemed to make a decent amount future telling," Yrsa replied.

"Oh, I never starved. But food wasn't my priority."

"Let me guess. Ale and women, then food."

"Or it could have been women and ale," he replied, chuckling.

"Have you never been tempted to settle down with anyone?"

"I've come close to it once or twice. But when they start talking about children and me learning a steady trade …"

"You've run away." He shrugged. "You've probably got a line of children from here to the Gods know where."

Yrsa stiffened as they heard noises some way off. A few furious bellows, some growls, and a pinched scream. She stood, picking up the crossbow, and looked cautiously towards the sound.

"What is it?" Rald asked.

"Something killing something," she replied.

"That's not very informative."

"I'm not the seer here."

Within moments, she heard another noise, tensing again, before relaxing. It was the zeffen coming back to camp. They weren't exactly quiet when they were moving about normally. When they came trotting in, both their heads were red, their fur matted with blood.

"Are you two all right?"

'We can't carry it.'

"What?"

'A deer. It's too big.'

Yrsa untethered Lucky, grabbed a couple of ropes, and went to follow the zeffen.

"Coming?" she asked Rald. "Sounds like we might need some extra strength."

When they reached the scene of the hunt, Yrsa laughed with delight. Lying at one end of a small clearing was a huge stag, with the zeffen standing proudly on either side of their kill.

She went over to Bodro and Pek and made a fuss of them. They'd killed it at the throat, though their technique needed honing, because from its gruesome appearance she couldn't tell if they'd ripped its throat after suffocating it or the other way around.

They'd certainly had something of a feast. Its belly was ripped open, and from the blood all over them, they seemed to have dived in to pull out the fresh juicy parts inside.

"I'm surprised there's anything left," she said, looking at the zeffen.

'Should we have waited?'

"No, it's your kill. You get to eat what you want."

They tried to move the stag, but it was heavy, and there was no way of loading it onto Lucky, even if he could bear the weight. Yrsa set about cutting it into pieces, while Rald roped the best bits together, and hung them over Lucky's back. They left the head and the remainder for the forest scavengers.

* * *

The stag lasted them three days, so they kept moving. The forest had less undergrowth as they climbed, and the path began to take detours around craggy outcrops. The ground was rougher too, and Yrsa had to check the studs in Lucky and Brimble's hooves every night. She wished she'd brought some spares, but they weren't needed for now.

One afternoon, as they looked for somewhere to spend the night, the path narrowed as it passed a large wall of rock on one side. The ground was jagged and unstable, so they dismounted and led the horses. The zeffen were nowhere to be seen, as usual. Yrsa led the way and was coming to the end of the exposed rock when Tennell stopped. She turned to see her mare sniffing the air.

"What is it, girl?"

'Something close.'

Yrsa looked around, only to see a brown blur drop from the rock above, and panic set into the column. Lucky roared and bolted, knocking Rald over, and whacking into Tennell as he fled along the path in front of them. The blur's momentum carried it into the undergrowth on the other side of the path. Yrsa followed the sound as it collected itself and rushed back.

It emerged between Tennell and Brimble, where Rald was still recovering on the ground. A large wild cat, something Yrsa had never seen before; powerful and furious. By Rald's side were the two sacks holding the remaining deer meat, which had been hanging over Lucky's rump.

Yrsa gave two loud whistles and reached for the crossbow hanging from Tennell's caparison. The whistles attracted the cat's attention, and it was momentarily torn between Yrsa, their source, and Rald and the aromatic meat. That pause enabled her to load the crossbow and point it at the cat.

Her aim wasn't good, and the bolt hit the ground by its feet. It recoiled from the impact, but recovered quickly enough, turning its attention back to Rald and the enticing sacks.

As the wild cat moved forward again, two grey shadows flew from the forest, their weight knocking it off its feet and all three tumbled across the track. There was a brief, furious battle; deep growls and a desperate hissing echoed from the rock face, but it didn't last long. As the dust settled, Yrsa walked past Tennell to survey the scene.

The zeffen had torn the wildcat apart. It was covered in deep slashes, its back and neck were broken, and blood was pooling from a long gash in its throat. Bodro and Pek were standing over it, panting, both dripping blood.

"Are you all right?" she asked them.

'Yes.'

She went over to Rald, who was sitting up, still looking a bit dazed, blood trickling from his forehead.

"And what about you?" she asked, checking the wound on his scalp. It wasn't bad.

"I … I think so," he replied. "A bit dizzy."

"Stay there."

She went to Brimble, who hadn't panicked, hadn't run, hadn't moved. She was standing where she'd come to a halt while the mayhem had gone on around her.

"All right, girl?"

'Where's Lucky?'

"He was scared and ran off."

'I'll find him.'

Yrsa was so surprised, she only just remembered to take two water skins from Brimble's back before the little horse ambled off along the path. She handed one skin to Rald and knelt by the zeffen with the other, pouring it over their muzzles.

Their wounds were slight. Pek had a scratch on his nose, and Bodro had lost a small patch of hair on his shoulder which was weeping a little. But all the blood on them was from the wildcat, lying lifeless at their feet. Rald was looking at the remains of their attacker.

"Gods," he said. "That was close."

"It would have been if it hadn't been for these two."

He reached over and laid a hand on each of them.

"Thank you," he said, bowing his head.

Tennell gave a little whinny, and Yrsa looked up to see Brimble heading towards them, with Lucky behind her. She greeted Brimble and gave her a hug, before going over to Lucky and checking him out. He had a cut on the opposite leg to his old wound. Yrsa poured water over it. It wasn't serious but needed a stitch or two.

"Well, old lad, you'll be all right. We'll find somewhere to camp, and I'll deal with it."

She began to walk to the others.

Why is it always me?' She turned back to the packhorse who was looking straight at her. *First their mother, now this.*'

"It's chance, Lucky. You'll be fine. Can you walk a bit further?"

I'll have to.'

Yrsa managed not to laugh at the animal's morose first words to her and returned to gather the column together.

When they'd settled in camp, Yrsa washed Lucky's wound and put four stitches in it.

"There you go, try not to pull it."

Thank you.'

"You're welcome. Found your voice, have you?"

Didn't have anything worth vaying.'

"You could have let me know you understood me."

Why did you save them?'

"Bodro and Pek? You don't like them?"

Their mother tried to kill me.'

"Your master tried to kill her. She was trying to save herself."

Amluss wasn't my master.'

"No, Hagrat was." Lucky visibly shivered at the name. "You won't see him again."

Thank you.'

When she turned, Bodro and Pek were sitting a little distance away, listening. Back at the fire, she watched as they went over to Lucky and sat in front of him. They stayed there for some time, then astonished her by each touching noses with the horse and trotting back to the fire.

'We understand each other.'

***

Bodro and Pek were supplying the meat on their own now. They even came back with some smaller prey; coney and the plump birds she thought were a type of partridge. She wasn't sure how they managed it, because such small animals were far more agile than the massive zeffen.

'Most of them get away,' was their answer when she asked.

A week later, the path crested a hill, and they were surprised by the view. They'd reached the path's highest point, and the forest rolled down over the crags and slopes in front of them.

"Is that it?" Yrsa asked.

"What?"

"Demburan."

"Where?

"In the far distance."

"Sight is not the best of my senses, remember?" he replied, pointing to his bad eye.

"Sorry," she mumbled, embarrassed by her slip.

"What can you see?"

"It looks like a large settlement spread out beneath a rocky outcrop. There's some sort of building on top of it."

"Probably a magical castle with your blessed prince."

"I hope the magical part is confined to Caropa."

"How far away?"

"I'd guess another week's travel."

"Do you think this road will be watched?"

"If things are as bad as we've been told, I wouldn't be surprised."

"We'll need to be careful."

"We've nothing to hide."
"Yrsa, in troubled lands, everyone has something to hide."

* * *

They met nobody in the following days, though they passed evidence of life. A few areas which had once been cultivated, occasional abandoned buildings. But no sign of recent activity, and the track, although wider and showing signs of regular maintenance in the past, betrayed no recent use.

On the fifth evening, they chose one of the empty farms to camp in. It was still intact, but the dust and cobwebs told them nobody would be disturbing them that night. Even so, they decided lighting a fire would be too much of a risk.

After eating, they discussed their next move.

"How far are we from the settlement?" Rald asked.

"Difficult to say, as we're more or less on the same level now. But I did spot the buildings on the hill earlier, so I'd say no more than half a day."

"What do we do?"

"Tomorrow, I'm going to leave you here and have a look around."

Chapter 27

Yrsa walked through the forest, wrapped in a cloak. She had thought of riding, but she couldn't use Tennell, because she suspected the mare appearing from nowhere would bring too many questions. And anyone coming from this unused road might be questioned anyway, so she settled for going on foot.

There had to be other routes into Demburan, so she set off to find one. Around midday, she saw a line of light in the forest ahead, it had to be a track or path. Edging forward, she scanned the area, ducking as someone walked by with a horse, eventually reaching the edge of a road. It was well-used, with people moving back and forth.

She stayed undercover for a while, watching them pass. She contemplated walking parallel to the road in the forest, but it would seem suspicious. Far better to walk in plain sight. The people weren't dressed very differently to her, and she hoped she wouldn't stand out. She looked both ways, and seeing nobody close, stepped out onto the road.

The forest began to thin, and farms and buildings appeared. She replied to the occasional greeting and didn't seem to cause any suspicion. A steady stream of traffic was heading for Demburan, and she studied the settlement as it drew closer.

It was large, but its size was difficult to assess. She could see the buildings were low and well spread out. The hill to one side, its back to the rocks, was visible now. It was topped by stone buildings, the central one highest of all, rising above the others, and dominating the entire settlement.

She heard horses approaching and turned to see a small group of mounted soldiers. She moved out of the way as seven men passed, dressed in quilted leather tunics, save for the leader, who wore mail. But what stood out were the horses.

Varying shades of dark grey, an unusual colour, but they were built like Tennell. Strong, proud animals, and bred for a purpose, though none were the size of Amluss's mare, and none approached the deep lustre of her black coat.

The wall of the town was a tall wooden palisade, with two wide gates on this road. One for entering, one for leaving. She watched intently, ready to change her plan, but the guards weren't stopping or questioning people. Like guards everywhere, they were just waiting for their replacements.

She was close behind a cart, and walked calmly through the gate into the city, for that's what she decided it was. It was large, with a bustling population and a fortified citadel. It warranted the name.

The traffic was slow, giving Yrsa a chance to look around. The buildings were made of wood, and thatched, but all had stone bases standing proud of the ground. There were entire stone buildings here and there, but not many.

She passed a market in full swing. There was no shortage of produce, but it appeared to be local. There were no luxuries, nothing from any distance. Certainly not the foreign wares she'd seen in Lonithrya.

The fortified hill above her was approached by a wide, gentle slope across its front. It didn't appear to be out of bounds. Each time she looked, people were going up or down. A few were soldiers, but others were dressed as she was.

She wondered if she could simply walk up and ask for the prince. It seemed unlikely. Her knowledge of princes was minimal, but they didn't seem like people who would see anyone who asked.

She bought a pie which was far better than it looked, found an inn to get some ale, and stood outside with her beaker, gazing at the hill.

"Wonder what he's doing?"

The voice startled her, and she turned to find a man next to her, also enjoying the surprisingly good ale.

"I'm sorry?" she replied.

"I wonder what Prince Varluss is doing?"

"About what?"

"The raiders, girl, what do you think?"

"I'm a visitor, I don't know what's been happening."

He gave her a long look, before sniffing contemptuously.

"Women! Never know anything. They come from the outlands over the mountains. Carry you off, that's for sure." He gave a ribald chuckle. "Varluss can't stop them."

"Who are they?"

"Some reckon it's the nomads, but no one knows for sure."

They fell into silence, Yrsa contemplating the man's words. Amluss hadn't mentioned any raids, and she wondered how they fitted into the story.

"I need to see the prince," she said. "Is that possible?"

"Some sort of princess, are you?" he replied with a laugh.

"No, just an ignorant woman who wants to petition his help."

"What for?"

"That's between my village and the prince."

"Suit yourself."

Silence fell again, but Yrsa thought it worth persevering.

"Can anyone go up there?"

"To the citadel? Yes, but you won't get far. There are guards at the top of the slope, with more at the gate. They'll stop you unless you have a good reason for going further."

"Are they open to a few coins?"

"The ordinary guards might be, but their sergeants won't. For all his problems, Varluss knows who deserves trust and who doesn't."

"Thank you, you've been most helpful."

He looked at her in surprise, uncertain he'd meant to offer his help. But what he'd said fitted Amluss's tale. The prince wasn't perfect, but he could be trusted. She just had to find a way of meeting him, and hoped the plan she'd devised would work.

As Yrsa walked up the ramp to the fortress, she tried to stay calm. The nearer she got to the first guard station, the more her plan seemed ridiculous, but it had to be tried.

"What do you want?" a guard asked brusquely.

"I have a gift for Prince Varluss."

"Want to show us?"

The leer on his face betrayed his perception of the gift.

"I'd rather not," she replied. "But I could show my appreciation in another way." She casually slid her cloak open revealing a bulging purse at her waist. "If that would be acceptable."

The guard looked over at his companion, they nodded and after handing over a few silver solens, she found herself approaching the gatehouse. Two guards were standing in front of it, and she paused, unsure where to go. One of them pointed to an alcove inside, where two more soldiers were sitting behind a table.

"Yes, girl?" one asked.

"I have a gift for Prince Varluss."

"Do you now? And I suppose you want us to let you wander into the citadel and give it to him."

"If that's how it works."

"No, girl, that's not how it works. Leave it here, and we'll see it's dealt with."

"I need to see the prince."

"Listen, leave your gift and go, unless you want trouble."

"You wouldn't dare."

The two guards looked at each other and grinned. They weren't particularly big, but she knew their type. They'd been brawling since they were children and would be tough to deal with if it got that far. She stepped back as they came around to the front of the table, flexing their shoulders.

Yrsa casually opened her cloak, revealing the szanka and two daggers at her waist. They stopped grinning; their faces wary, uncertain how to proceed. They were unarmed, their weapons lying on a bench behind the table.

"You come to the citadel armed for a fight?" one said.

"It seems a girl needs to defend herself against the prince's men in this place."

"Why, you impudent-"

"Enough!" The voice appeared before the man, who followed it from a door a short way into the gatehouse. The two guards straightened. "What is it, girl?"

"I have a gift for the prince, and I'd like to give it to him personally."

"The prince doesn't see everyone who turns up here. He's better things to do. I'll give it to him."

Yrsa debated what to do. She'd known it was unlikely she'd be able to see the prince, not to begin with. But who could she trust? This man was well dressed, his uniform expensive and it hung comfortably on him.

"I think he may want to see me when he sees it."

The captain studied her, frowning when he took in the weapons at her waist.

"Show me this gift," he said.

After a moment's hesitation, she reached behind her and pulled the bundle from under her cloak, handing it to the captain.

"What is it?" he asked.

"A gift."

"Don't play games, girl."

"I've stated my intentions. You're the one playing games."

He took a breath to calm his irritation, before beginning to unwrap the cloak. He hadn't gone far, merely revealing one end before he covered it and turned to study Yrsa again.

"You, wait here," he finally said. "You two, don't let her leave."

The two guards were still standing straight as he left, and Yrsa leaned casually against the wall.

"You can relax now," she said.

A while later, the captain returned.

"Follow me," he barked, and led her across the courtyard, up a set of steps and into the tall building backing onto the bare rock. They passed groups of people: a few soldiers, civilians rushing along, a couple of women strolling with a dog on a lead. Another set of steps up to another floor.

They came to a door guarded by two men who straightened as he approached.

"In here."

She went through the door and found herself in a large room with windows on either side. A man was sitting behind a large table, with others standing around it. Two were soldiers, the three others in civilian clothing. On the table was Yrsa's cloak, with Amluss's sword lying on it.

"Where did you get this?" the seated man asked.

"If I knew who was asking," she replied, "I might be prepared to answer."

One or two of the men bristled at her boldness, but he merely smiled, before rising.

"I am Varluss, Prince of Demburan and of Caropatia."

"I am Yrsa. And these men are?"

"My captains and counsellors. All trusted men."

"You trust more easily than I do."

He sat again, sighing.

"Very well, leave us."

The group reluctantly left, one or two giving her furious looks as they passed. She fought hard to control her anxiety, but so far, the plan had worked. After they'd left, the man who brought her from the gatehouse remained.

"Darian stays," the prince said. "He is my cousin and kinsman, and responsible for my safety. I have no secrets from him." Yrsa studied Darian, who returned her gaze, unmoved. "I ask again, where did you get this?"

"You recognise it?"

"Where did you get it?"

"It's going to be a long day if all we do is ask each other questions, and answer none."

Varluss smiled, giving her a gentle nod.

"Very well, this sword belongs to a kinsman of mine." Yrsa stood silent, staring at the prince. She wanted more before she would accept Amluss's trust in the man sitting before her. He was clearly amused by the situation, eventually relenting. "He is my uncle, Prince Amluss. Is that enough for you? Will you now answer my question?"

"Amluss is dead," she replied. The prince's face gave nothing away.

"I feared as much," he said, "given his sword is with us, yet he is not. I still want to know how it comes to be in your possession."

Yrsa pulled a stool from under the table, made herself comfortable, and told the prince of Amluss's fate.

Chapter 28

"He never wavered, cousin," the prince said when Yrsa finished her tale.

"Did you ever doubt him?" Darian replied.

"No, but we haven't heard from him in two years. I feared he was already dead."

"He came so close."

"We'll have to find another way."

"I may be able to help you," Yrsa said.

"You?" Darian said scornfully. "How?"

"Have faith, cousin," the prince replied. "If Yrsa travelled all the way here, I don't believe it was just to return a sword. Nor do I think she has told us the whole story."

He was smiling at her, and she felt herself beginning to blush. She hadn't known what to expect. Amluss had told her the prince was an honourable man, an intelligent man. But he hadn't told her how attractive he was. As a man, he probably didn't notice such things, but she did.

"I have told the truth," she replied. "But I have not told you everything."

"Why not?" Darian asked.

"Because I don't know you, only what Amluss told me about you."

"You didn't trust him?"

"I hardly knew him. It might have been the ramblings of a dying man."

"Yet you travelled here anyway. Why?"

"Cousin," the prince said. "The lady will tell us what she wants to. I don't think torture would reveal any more."

"Is torture a frequent practice of yours?"

"It was a figure of speech."

"I'm glad to hear that."

"Though I am wondering why you are holding back."

"I want to hear your side of the tale. Is what Amluss told me true? What is happening in Caropa? If I believe what you tell me, I may be willing to help you."

Darian burst out laughing at her arrogance, but Varluss held up his hand.

"All right. I will tell you our story."

* * *

As Yrsa slid off the road into the forest, she took a moment to let out a long breath, all the tension coming out with it. But fog was coming down and she wanted to get back to the abandoned farm before it and the darkness of night led her to lose her way.

She smelt the farm before she saw it, the scent of smoke from damp wood filling her nostrils. She couldn't fault Rald; smoke from a fire would be lost in the fog. When she arrived, the zeffen greeted her madly.

"I was getting worried," Rald said.

"Something smells good," she replied.

"These two came back with a pig. I'm afraid I couldn't butcher it with my knife, so I'm roasting it whole. It should be ready. How did you get on?"

As they ate, Yrsa told them how she'd got into the citadel, and met the prince.

"You've got enough nerve to be a future teller," Rald said. "I thought you were checking the place out, not going in."

"It seemed the best thing to do."

"Did they believe you?"

"Amluss's sword was the proof."

"And?"

"What do you mean, 'and'?"

"Come on Yrsa, what happened when you'd told them your tale?"

"They told me the rest."

Rald waited a few moments, but Yrsa stayed silent.

"Well, are you going to tell me?"

"They confirmed what Amluss had said. He was hunting these two's mother for her blood. He'd been told it was the only way to release his brother from the queen's control."

"Wait, wait. Amluss's brother is …"

"King Ragluss of Caropatia."

"Ah. And Varluss is …"

"The king's son … and heir."

"Why can't Varluss deal with his mother?"

"The queen isn't Varluss's mother. She died when he was young. A few years later a mysterious woman appeared at the court, accompanied by three men, claiming to be an exiled princess from beyond the known lands.

"She intrigued people. Beautiful, intelligent, kind to everyone. The king let her stay and gradually fell in love with her. Even Varluss was happy his father had found a new queen, and she was popular.

"But things changed. The men who came with her were appointed to court positions, slowly becoming more powerful. The king became ill, often unable to carry out his duties. Varluss and Amluss assumed they would take on the workload, but the king told them the queen and her advisors would handle everything.

"And that's what happened. Amluss tried several times to convince the king to change his mind, until one day he was sent into exile and told never to return. That was seven years ago. Varluss was sent here."

"Out of the way."

"Yes, but perfectly legitimate. Something about a dual kingdom and Demburan being the seat of the heir. Varluss has only heard from Amluss three times since then. But in one of the letters, he claimed to have discovered the queen's identity. She was no princess, but a woman who'd been exiled from Flengara years before for unnatural practices."

"Sorcery?"

"Amluss thought so and went to Flengara to learn anything he could uncover. He spoke to people who'd known her, he searched the records, and he found an old man who told him of her power, which he believed was considerable. It was this man who told him the only way to resist it was zeffen blood."

"So he set off to find some."

"The rest you know."

"Except for the important question."

"Which is?"

"What was the blood for? What was someone – anyone – supposed to do with it?"

"I was hoping Varluss might know, but he doesn't."

'He wanted our mother's blood but didn't know what for?'

"It seems so, yes."

* * *

The next morning, the fog had cleared, and it was a bright, sunny day.

"Are you sure this is wise?" Rald asked as he and Yrsa stood by the old track.

"I couldn't think of an alternative. He has to know everything, otherwise he won't trust me."

"Trust you? What about me?"

Rald had turned out to be a better companion than she'd dared hope. Even Luna would have been proud of him. They heard horses approaching and she held her breath until two lone riders could be seen a hundred paces away.

"Good morning, Yrsa," the prince said as they met.

"Good morning," she replied. "This is my companion Rald. Rald, Varluss and Darian."

"Sire," Rald said, bowing slightly.

"Ah," the prince replied. "You at least know how to address a prince with respect."

"We don't have princes where I come from," Yrsa said. "Respect is earned, not inherited."

"Give up, cousin," Darian said. "You can't win."

"It appears not."

Yrsa was drawn to the horses both men were riding. Large black animals, stallions both. She went to the prince's mount, and stroked its head, trying to reach out to it. The animal flapped its lips and leaned towards her.

"We will have to watch this one," the prince said to Darian. "Semlac doesn't normally take to people so easily."

"He is a beautiful animal," Yrsa replied. "As is yours, Darian."

The two men dismounted, tethered their horses to a rail and followed Yrsa and Rald towards the farmhouse.

"They are nothing compared to Amluss's pride and joy," Varluss said wistfully. "The zeffen must have been truly terrifying if that finest of all mares bolted. It is sad indeed she was lost."

"She didn't bolt," Yrsa replied. "Amluss told her to get away. And she wasn't lost." She softly called the mare's name, and the prince looked on astonished as Tennell walked from the stable, coming to a stop by her, and nuzzling her neck. The prince looked at Darian, who shrugged. Then Tennell whinnied.

"What is it, girl?"

'May I?'

Yrsa released her, and she trotted over to their visitor's horses, heading straight for Semlac. A quick sniff, and they both launched into a bout of whinnying.

"Do they know each other?" Yrsa asked.

"I should hope so. Semlac is her son."

They watched the reunion for a few moments until Varluss turned to Yrsa.

"Good though it is to know Tennell is safe, I cannot believe you brought us out here just for this reunion."

"I wanted you to meet my boys."

Two soft whistles brought Bodro and Pek trotting out of the house towards them. The prince and his cousin froze, their eyes glued to the zeffen brothers, who took up station on either side of Yrsa.

"Meet Bodro and Pek," she said. "Boys, meet Varluss and Darian."

"Are ... are they what I think they are?" the prince asked, trying – and failing – to flatten his voice. Both men's hands were on their sword hilts.

"They are zeffen," she replied.

"One of them killed Amluss?"

"Their mother did."

"Their mother?"

"Let them sniff you. Perhaps then you will relax, and I will tell you their story."

She watched, hiding her smile as these two proud men nervously let the zeffen sniff them and lick their hands. She led the party into the house, the prince and his cousin warily eyeing the huge creatures walking by their side.

* * *

"What made you take them on?" the prince asked when Yrsa finished. "Most people would have left them to die."
"Or killed them," Darian added.
"I told you I like a challenge," she replied.
"But you knew their reputation?"
"They were used to frighten us as children."
"And that didn't put you off?"
"They were orphans, I couldn't leave them."
"And Amluss?" Darian asked. "What happened to his body?"
"I had to leave it. I'm sorry. At that stage, I didn't know their mother was mortally wounded, she could have returned. I had at least two broken fingers and a horse with a gaping wound that needed attention. I had nothing to dig with, and couldn't risk a funeral pyre, even if I could have built one. I had to leave."
Darian considered her reply, studying her.
"Would you have done differently, cousin?" the prince asked.
"No," he finally replied. "I would have made the same decision."
"But it wasn't Tennell who was injured?"
"No," Yrsa said, "that was Lucky. You haven't met him. He belonged to Amluss's companion."
"The man in the inn."
"His name was Hagrat."
"He seems an unlikely friend for Amluss," Darian said to the prince.
"He probably served a purpose."
"He wasn't a friend," Yrsa said, "he was a bondsman. Besides, don't princes need someone to do their dirty work?"
"I wonder if he survived his injury?" Darian asked.

"He did," Yrsa said quietly. They turned to her with puzzled looks, as did Rald, as she hadn't told him that part of the story. "He and an accomplice tracked me down."

"What happened?" the prince asked.

"I killed him. Tennell killed his mate."

Silence fell on the room, as the three men considered the woman in front of them.

"Well, Yrsa," the prince finally said. "I will remember not to upset you."

"This is all well," Darian said, "but it doesn't help us. And we must return before people wonder where we are."

"That is true," Varluss replied. "You offered to help us, Yrsa, but I'm at a loss to see how."

"I have an idea," she replied. "But it's not fully formed yet."

"Return to the city with us, and we can discuss it."

"Are there spies around you?"

"I cannot discount it," Darian replied. "We've exposed one or two very easily, so there may be others better hidden."

"Then I think it safer not to parade Tennell and these two through the streets."

* * *

Yrsa and Rald led the horses through the darkness, Bodro and Pek following behind. The directions Darian had given them led them off the road a little way before the city gates and along a dry stream bed.

Eventually, this took them to the edge of the rocky hill which rose above the city, and they pushed into a narrow fissure where the water would have flowed into the stream. It was just wide enough for a horse to pass, though Lucky wasn't keen, and Yrsa had to have a gentle talk with him.

After fifty paces, the fissure opened into a cave, and Yrsa saw a light off to the left. She headed towards it and found Darian waiting for them.

"This way," he said, and led them through several small caverns, each with smooth floors.

"What are these used for?" she asked.

"They aren't, now we're at peace. But in times past, the people hid in these caves if the city was under attack."

"What about the northern raiders?"

"They're a nuisance, not a real threat. They don't come near Demburan."

They came to heavy wooden doors, Darian tapped out a signal, and they swung open. This led them into a short tunnel before the doors were closed, bolted, and barred. The process was repeated at the other end.

Moonlight poured in as the second set of doors was opened. They found themselves in a small courtyard, and Yrsa realised they were between the cliffs and the citadel. Two lads took the horses and led them to a small stable in one corner.

"They'll be looked after," Darian said. "Nobody comes here without my approval. Follow me."

He led Yrsa, Rald and the zeffen through another heavy door, and they climbed a circular stairway. She counted the doors off the stairs, and on the fifth level, Darian opened a door into a room with stone walls and some wooden furniture, including a large bed.

"You can use this as your room. It's rarely used, so you'll be undisturbed. I'll have someone come and attend to your needs. Settle in, and I'll let you know when the prince is ready to see you."

"Thank you, Darian," Yrsa replied. "Is it possible to set up another bed? I wouldn't want Rald to sleep on the floor."

Darian laughed, as Rald smiled ruefully.

Chapter 29

Later that night, Darian collected Yrsa and Rald and led them along the deserted corridors. Bodro and Pek trotted along behind.

"This is the prince's level," he said. "After dark, nobody except his staff come up here without an invitation or my agreement. Although I'm not sure I agreed to those two coming as well."

"They get bored," Yrsa replied as lightly as she could. "They won't be any bother."

She had no intention of telling her hosts she wanted the zeffen present when her ideas were discussed. Varluss was an intelligent man, but she doubted he was ready to accept Bodro and Pek understood everything they heard.

They walked through the large room where Yrsa had first met the prince and his council. Through a side door, they found him in a smaller room with a fire in the hearth. The room was lined with shelves, and she strained to see them in the low lamplight. Then she saw books, books on every shelf.

"Good evening," the prince said. "Are you here to see me or my library?"

"I'm sorry," she replied. "I've never seen one before."

"A prince or a library?"

"Neither until yesterday."

Darian closed the door, and the prince pointed to some chairs. They all sat, while Bodro and Pek headed for the fire, and made themselves comfortable on the floor.

"I guess they go where they please?" the prince said.

"No," Yrsa replied. "If you'd like them to move …"

"They're fine," he said. "I wouldn't want to be the one to move them."

"They're very obedient, but still learning."

"They aren't adults, yet?"

"No, less than a year old."

"Gods, how much more will they grow?"

"I don't know, but they're nowhere near their mother's size."

The prince looked at Darian, and they both turned their gaze on the zeffen.

"You have a plan?" the prince said.

"More a series of ideas," Yrsa replied. "But I'm not sure how we put them all together."

"Tell me."

"First of all, can you tell Rald everything you know about the queen?"

"What sort of thing?"

"Everything," Rald said. "How she arrived, how she dresses, her jewellery, who she is close to, how she speaks to people."

Rald listened intently as Varluss recounted everything he could remember, with Darian chipping in. Only Yrsa noticed the zeffen were listening, very much awake. When the prince ran out of memories, Rald was silent for a while.

"Well?" Yrsa said.

"There are two possibilities," he replied. "She may just be clever, using her charm and intelligence. A bit like you." Yrsa rolled her eyes. "Or, she could have some powers of sorcery. But you say she has never done anything in public to arouse people's suspicions?"

"Not as far as I know," the prince replied. "It's well known she patronises those who tell the future or claim mysterious skills, but I've never heard of anything else."

"Have there been any unexplained illnesses or deaths?"

"A few, particularly when she was building her power. There were rumours she may have had a hand in it, but people were thinking of poison, not sorcery. I'm not sure I believe in it myself."

"Don't doubt its existence."

"You are a sorcerer yourself, perhaps."

"I cannot claim any such powers, but I have studied the subject."

"Why?" Darian asked.

"Curiosity and profit," Rald replied.

"Profit?"

"Many things are called sorcery, and most of them aren't. Changing the colour of a flame in a fire, curdling milk, making things appear and disappear."

"The kind of thing travelling conjurors entertain the people with," the prince said.

"Exactly. I will admit, I have played that role. But I've also seen things I cannot explain, and spoken to enough learned men to know some people have a power that is more than conjuring."

"And Amluss thought the queen was exiled from Flengara for unnatural practices," Darian said.

"I think if we take it all together, we have to assume she has such power, though to what degree, we do not know."

"But even if she has," the prince said, "what can we do about it? My father is also my king. I am in no position to walk in and accuse his wife of sorcery."

"How is your father?" Rald asked.

"He's been ill for some time, a shadow of his former self, weak and feeble. He sits most of the time in a chair, seeing nobody, talking to nobody, except when the queen allows it."

"Who runs the kingdom?"

"Manitrios, Garameen and Tannaq hold most of the power. They are the men who came with her."

"Do they do it well?"

"At first glance, yes. The state functions and nothing is neglected. But dig deeper, and you see it is run mainly for their benefit. They take their cut of the profits from business deals, and visiting merchants must pay extra taxes to secure the use of the best wharves at the port.

"They set men against each other until trust is gone. They back one group for a while before turning on them. I hear people are frightened to speak out, and visitors from other lands are now rare, I gather."

"Why didn't people put up more resistance to these men taking control?" Yrsa asked. "Surely they could see what was happening?"

"It was done slowly and carefully at first. It was some time before we all realised what was happening. By then, it was too late. Amluss tried and you know his fate. For myself, it is mainly because of the dual kingdom. My father is the king, but Demburan has always had a special place in the kingdom.

"It was a separate state for generations and has always been the preserve of the heir to the throne. Where we learn to rule, if you like, and take responsibility for securing the northern border. Traditionally, the king leaves the heir alone, and we play little part in the affairs of the rest of the kingdom."

"So, it was easy for the queen to make sure you were penned up here."

"Looking back, yes, though I didn't see that when I was younger."

"We're still not getting anywhere," Darian said, tetchily.

"What about the raids from the Outlands?" Yrsa asked. "How big a problem are they?"

"They launch sporadic forays. Steal a few cattle, burn the odd barn, the occasional kidnap, though the victims are usually released a few days later. They're always long gone by the time we get there, and we've had to evacuate some of the more remote farms and villages nearest to the mountains."

"So they're a nuisance. Enough to keep you occupied, and make your people doubt you."

The prince and Darian looked at each other.

"It had crossed our minds," Varluss replied.

"Paid by the queen."

"We have no evidence."

"Do you doubt the raids will cease if you remove her?"

"But how do we do that?" Darian said, the prince giving him a concerned look.

"If it is sorcery," Rald replied, "we must find her weakness."

"Why would she have a weakness?"

"All sorcerers do, if you believe the tales."

"And Amluss thought it was zeffen blood?" the prince asked.

"He did."

"How did he know?"

"That, we will never know for sure," Yrsa said. "But if we are to try and end this, we have to work on the basis he was right."

"I am uncomfortable with this," the prince said. "We have thought many times the queen may be responsible for the woes in our land. But I would be usurping my father's authority if I try to depose him."

"But you don't need to depose him. You need to expose the queen."

"I don't see how I can do one without the other. She seems to have complete control over him."

"How often do you see him?"

"Only once a year in the last three years. Just before winter threatens to pen me in here. I'm due to travel at the next turn of the moon."

"Then we need to work fast."

"To do what?" Darian asked.

"I need to be in Caropa with these two when you are there."

Both Varluss and his cousin were mystified.

"Yrsa," the prince said. "I think perhaps your thoughts are somewhat ahead of your relating them to us."

"I need to get these two into her presence."

"To do what?"

"I'll know when we're there."

"That's not reassuring."

"Varluss, if I try this and it doesn't work, you can deny all knowledge. If I succeed, you will be there to deal with anyone who tries to support her. I assume she also controls the guard around your father?"

"We think so, but know little of their true loyalties."

"You'll need to disarm them."

Varluss looked at his cousin, who shrugged.

"It's more than we've come up with," Darian said. "It's time we did something."

"But how will you get to see the queen?" Varluss asked. "They no longer hold public audiences. When I last visited, the courtiers were present, but nobody else."

"That's a problem," Rald replied. "You can't just walk in, Yrsa."

"No," she said. "We need an invitation."

"And how are you going to get one?"

"With the help of the Great Pacleidius."

* * *

"I must be mad," Rald said as they set up a canvas tent on the edge of the marketplace.

"This will be easy for you," Yrsa replied, concealing herself in the false back. "You've been training all your life for this moment."

A future teller was rare in Demburan and soon attracted custom. Most were men, encouraged by their friends, laughing and joking about what this stranger might tell them. They listened, amused by Rald's theatrical performance.

"He says I'm going to find gold," one said coming out, as his friends laughed. "He must think I'm a fool."

But when the fool was walking home that night, the worse for drink, he noticed a purse on the road and found three gold crowns in it, carefully placed there by a trusted member of Darian's guard on Yrsa's instructions.

Another of Rald's visitors discovered her pigs had multiplied overnight, as he had predicted. Yet another couldn't believe the price he got for a cow at the cattle market, the most expensive cow in the kingdom. Exactly as the future teller had foretold.

"It seems to be working," Darian said at their evening meeting a few days later. "I'm told you're the talk of the taverns."

"But will it work in Caropa?" Rald asked.

"Are you suggesting my people here are simple?" the prince said, though he was smiling.

"Not at all," Rald added hurriedly. "But you have to admit, Caropa is a little more sophisticated."

"It is, but there is a market for future tellers there, as everywhere."

"We'll have to make sure we're more sophisticated, too," Yrsa said.

As they went to leave, Yrsa paused by the shelves to look at the books.

"Help yourself," the prince said.

"I was only looking," she replied. "I can't read."

"Perhaps I can read to you?"

Rald gave her a wink and left, followed by Darian, who closed the door behind him.

"I don't think that's an effective use of your time," Yrsa said.

"I don't work after dark."

"What do you do after work?"

"Not much, to be honest. But my library keeps me entertained."

"You're not married? Isn't that strange?"

"If my father were still in control of himself, he would have found a suitable candidate."

"But the queen is happy for you not to have an heir."

"Probably."

"You must have women keen enough."

"Oh, plenty."

"But you selflessly turn them all away."

"Not all, no."

The prince watched as Yrsa walked slowly along the bookshelves, running her fingers over their bindings.

"You're not what I imagined a prince to be," she said.

"You thought I'd spend all my time riding around, ordering the men about and ravishing the women?"

"Something like that. I might enjoy being ravished."

"I'd rather keep my balls, thank you."

She leaned against the shelves.

"That only happens if I've said no."

"What happens if you say yes?"

Yrsa replied by removing her belt and pulling the tunic over her head, before undoing the cord, and letting her trousers fall to the floor.

"Why don't we find out?" she said, walking towards him.

He surveyed her nakedness, clearly liking what he saw.

"What about these two?" he asked, gesturing to Bodro and Pek.

"What about them?"

"I'm not sure I like the idea of them watching."

"Oh, they'll sleep all the way through."

He slowly shook his head as she removed his short tunic and undid the belt at his waist.

"Are you always this forward?" he asked.

"If you don't like it …"

"No, carry on."

He lifted slightly to allow her to remove his trousers, and the expression on his face changed from amusement to pleasure as her touch began to tease him. The chair, the floor, and a padded window seat became the settings for their passion as they took each other to the peak and back.

* * *

As they recovered, she raised her head to see him smiling.

"You're not shy, are you?" he said.

"No," she replied, her breathing settling. "Never have been."

He went to move, but she pushed him down again.

"I have you where I want you. Be a good boy and stay there."

Chapter 30

By the time Yrsa left the prince's rooms the next morning, they'd reached those peaks a couple more times.

'You seem to like him.'

"I do, boys," she replied to the zeffen walking by her side along the corridor. "He'll do nicely for now."

She opened the door into their room to a familiar scene. Rald was lying on the bed, with a buxom little blonde riding him. The girl stopped but didn't try to cover them.

"Are you going to make a habit of this?" Rald asked, his voice betraying his frustration.

"Sorry," she replied. "I'll go and find something to eat."

"In the other room," he barked.

She went through the side door into the room Darian had added to their accommodation. They used it as a day room and ate their meals there. On the table was some fresh bread, cheese, and ale. On the floor, two large bowls held a variety of meat offcuts.

"Eat," she said, and Bodro and Pek attacked their morning meal, as Yrsa poured a beaker of ale and ate. However hard she tried, she couldn't block out the noises drifting in from the next room. Rald was quite vocal, his groans and moans deep in his chest. The girl's sounds were altogether different, little high-pitched squeaks. She was certainly enjoying herself.

Eventually, the door opened, and Rald came in wearing just his tunic. The girl followed shortly afterwards, still adjusting her dress.

"Will that be all?" she asked, her face still red from her exertion, but otherwise with little hint of embarrassment.

"I think so," Rald replied. "Yrsa, do you need anything else?"

She was puzzled for a moment, then realised the girl must be one of the staff in the citadel and had brought the food and ale.

"Oh, no, thank you. I have everything I need."

The girl gave the merest hint of a curtsey, smiled at Rald, and left.

"You've been busy," Yrsa said.

He turned to her sharply, then saw the smile on her face.

"Well," he replied, "she offered …"

"And it would have been rude to refuse. What's her name?"

He thought for a moment, before shrugging sheepishly.

"I have no idea."

"Who is she?"

He looked a little embarrassed.

"I asked Darian if there was anywhere in the city I could find a bit of … company. He wasn't keen on letting me out."

"I should hope not."

"But he said he knew a few of the citadel staff who might oblige, and a little later she turned up."

"She seemed keen."

"Keen? She never stopped. Did you have a good night?"

* * *

They worked on their act. During the day, Rald and Yrsa travelled to local villages, he as the Great Pacleidius, she as his assistant. Varluss gave Rald some clothes more appropriate to his role, while Yrsa borrowed a couple of dresses to better fit hers. It seemed to work, and they honed their performance.

"I see what you're doing," Darian said one evening. "But if you get invited to meet the queen, my men aren't going to be able to do what they're doing here. Whatever Rald predicts for her, how are you going to make it happen?"

"We're not," Yrsa replied.

"What are we going to do then?" Rald asked, confused.

"If we get that far, we're going to change the act."

"How?"

"Varluss, you're going to tell Rald about some well-known members of the court: their pasts, their families, their businesses. Nothing scandalous, nothing embarrassing. Just things they wouldn't dream this strange seer in front of them would know. Rald, you need to listen and take it all in."

"Thanks."

"If we get an audience, the Great Pacleidius can entertain the court by telling them all about themselves."

"How will that help?" the prince asked.

"You're also going to tell us all about your father, Amluss and especially the queen."

"Ah," he said. "When you've gripped the crowd and earned their trust, you turn your sights on her."

"Exactly. That's when we do need to know the scandalous and the embarrassing."

"I'm not sure I follow," Darian said.

"We need to make the queen angry," Yrsa replied. "It's the only way she might show who she really is."

"Oh, great," Rald said. "Nothing I like more than an angry sorcerer."

"It's the only chance we have."

"What do we do if she does reveal herself?"

"We'll work that out when it happens."

Yrsa and the Zeffen Hunter

* * *

"I'm leaving you here for a while."

Yrsa was in the small stable behind the citadel. Her horses were watching her, though Brimble was more interested in her oats.

'Where are you going?' Tennell vayed.

"To Caropa."

'To finish Amluss's task?'

"Yes," Yrsa replied, still coming to terms with the mare's intelligence.

'Can I not take you there?'

"You are too well-known here. I need to travel unseen."

'Me, well-known?'

"Yes," Yrsa replied, smiling at Tennell's streak of vanity.

'Will you come back for us?' Brimble vayed.

"I hope so, but I cannot promise. You will be well looked after if I can't."

She gave each of them a big hug, tears in her eyes.

'We will ask the spirits to protect you,' Lucky vayed.

"Thank you," she replied, surprised by his words.

Rald joined her in the small courtyard, along with Phinus and Mapian, the men who were going with them from Darian's guard. They were two of his most trusted men, had helped with the deceptions so far, and seemed to be enjoying the role.

They went out through the cave network and when they reached the end of the fissure, Darian was waiting with a horse and cart. They'd pondered how to travel. If it had been just Yrsa and Rald, they could have walked or used a couple of local horses.

But the zeffen were the problem. Although nobody seemed bothered by them, they needed to keep their existence from the eyes and ears of the queen. Darian had suggested a cart, and it was an inspired solution. Bodro and Pek could travel in the back, and Rald and Yrsa could sit up front or lead the horse. They'd look like many a travelling couple.

Phinus and Mapian, dressed in ordinary clothes, also had a cart and would travel separately, some way behind, only communicating if it was necessary.

As they set off, Yrsa tried to hold her nerves in check. She'd come up with this plan and the others were sceptical, at best. She was putting her own life at risk, that of Rald, and possibly the others as well. But something told her it was worth it, and she hoped her intuition was right.

* * *

Caropa was a hundred leagues from Demburan, but they travelled slowly, stopping each night at a convenient town, where the Great Pacleidius worked his magic, helped by the two guards. It was unlikely word of these deeds would reach Caropa before they did, but it kept them busy and helped them stay in character.

One afternoon, Yrsa brought the cart to a sudden stop in the middle of the road.

"What is it?" Rald hissed.

"Look," she replied. To the left of the road was a series of fields, carefully fenced and tended. They stood out in the middle of the forest. But it was what was in those fields that drew her.

They were full of Burans. The horses of Demburan. Varluss had told her all about the breed. They were strong, intelligent, and loyal, and Amluss had been their greatest champion and their greatest breeder. They were mostly shades of grey and used by the guard and those shown special favour by the king and royal family.

The darker they were, the more they were valued, and the real rarities were pure black. Like Tennell and Semlac. Varluss made no secret of the fact Tennell was the finest Buran anyone had ever seen, and it saddened Yrsa. Tennell was the best horse she'd ever ridden, but she knew the mare had come home. She was too valuable to be allowed to leave again.

As they reached the plains, the traffic on the road increased, and the land was all cultivated. Farms and rich estates spread out in front of them, with Caropa visible on the horizon. They would soon be there. The following day, they decided to keep going until they reached the city, even if it meant travelling in the dark.

Varluss had a palace there but owned other properties, and it was to one of those they were heading. Yrsa suspected they allowed him to entertain in private, and the thought amused her. He amused her. He certainly satisfied her and had proved a generous lover, though it had taken him a while to get used to her unashamed enjoyment of their activities.

When they reached their destination, they expected to find a house or villa and were surprised to find only an inn.

"Where is it?" Rald asked. "Are we lost?"

"I'm not sure. We followed the directions."

"Good day, friends." She turned to find Phinus striding towards her, through the people walking in the street. "Looking for a place to stay?"

"Yes, we are," she replied.

"This is the best inn in the city."

Yrsa led the horse and cart into the yard, and Phinus guided her into a stable. A big man took the reins from her, giving her a moment's panic.

"Kelix will look after the horse," Phinus said. "Follow me."

She called Bodro and Pek from the cart and they all followed him to a door at the end of the stables. He looked around before ushering them inside.

"Welcome to a little outpost of Demburan in Caropa," he said.

They were on one side of an open quadrangle surrounding an area of grass, with doors leading from it at regular intervals. They followed him until he stopped by one.

"This will be yours," he said. "I'm afraid you'll have to share; all the others are full."

Three men walked by in conversation, pausing briefly to look at the zeffen, calmly standing by Yrsa.

"Are these all guards?" she asked.

"Most of them. The inn at the front is what it seems. One of many in the city, but it's run by a retired sergeant. This section is normally quiet, but if the prince wants to visit without the queen knowing, he comes here. As does anyone on his less than official business."

"It's busy today."

"The prince heard someone may be planning something which could lead to unrest. He felt it his duty to be able to deal with it."

"The queen doesn't know about this place?"

"As far as we know, but anything's possible with her. If you need anything, ask, and we can rustle up some protection whenever you need it."

"I hope it won't come to that."

"Don't mind if it does. There's a bit of friction between us and the Caropa palace guard nowadays. Many of the lads wouldn't mind a bit of action."

After Phinus left, Yrsa and Rald settled into their room, and Kelix brought their baggage.

"I hope they don't start anything," Rald said.

"From what we've seen of Varluss's guard, they're a disciplined group. And we might need them."

"That's not very reassuring."

At Phinus's suggestion, they took their meals in the inn, two resting travellers among many, and set out the next morning to make sure Caropa knew the Great Pacleidius had arrived. On the first day, they concentrated on the poorer areas, Rald accepting a few kels for his predictions, Phinus and Mapian ensuring a few came true. On the second day, they tried a larger market.

Yrsa had expected the city to be tense and its people subdued, given all they'd been told. But at first sight, it seemed normal enough. It wasn't as vibrant as Lonithrya, and given it was also a major trading port, it should have been.

The people were friendly enough, but as she watched them, she saw a wariness when they talked, as if they feared someone might be listening or watching. The markets had plenty of produce, but it was all local; nothing imported.

Over the course of the third day, they were visited by three well-dressed men Phinus had warned them about. They were people Varluss trusted and had agreed to join the deception. Their job was to spread the word among their peers, and they played their part. Whether it would work or not, only time would tell.

* * *

By the end of the sixth day, Rald was attracting long queues, and they were tired when they returned to the inn. Going through the rear door, Yrsa was taken aback when she saw the zeffen lying on the grass, a group of guards making a fuss of them.

"Well," she said to Rald. "I leave for a few hours, and do they miss me?"

Bodro and Pek heard her voice, jumped up and ran over to greet her.

'We did miss you.'
'We were making friends.'

She was glad they were. The men had been wary of the zeffen. She understood. They'd grown considerably since they'd left Lonithrya and would make any man question his courage. When they stood beside her, their heads were level with her chest, and she was as tall as most men.

The group greeted her and moved off, as she and Rald went to their room. She was about to go and get something for the zeffen to eat when she paused.

"Have they been feeding you?" she asked.

'They're very generous.'

'We've had three meals today.'
"Are you still hungry?"

Their look confirmed her immediate realisation it was a stupid question, and she went off to the kitchen. The brimming bowls she came back with disappeared as quickly as usual.

"Are they ever full?" Rald asked.

"I've seen it a few times, but not often."

"I'm hungry as well."

"Let's go and get something." Rald went to follow her. "Your gown."

"Ridiculous thing," he replied, slipping it on again.

The inn was a popular place with the locals; clean and well-run, and there hadn't been a hint of trouble. The food was surprisingly good, too. As they were finishing their meal, a man entered in palace livery.

"Play the part," she hissed to Rald, who looked at her puzzled until he saw the landlord pointing the new arrival in their direction. The man approached their table.

"The Great Pacleidius?" he asked.

"I am, sir."

"I have a message from the palace."

"Indeed?"

"An invitation to attend their majesties."

"I would be honoured, my good man."

The messenger handed over a letter, bowed, and walked out of the inn. Rald put it on the table and carried on eating. Yrsa could hardly contain her impatience; she knew a few people were watching them.

"Well?" she said quietly.

"I think we can wait a little longer," he replied softly. "Don't want to seem too keen."

After what seemed like an age, they calmly rose from the table, walked to the yard, into the stable, through the door and raced to their room, Rald opening the letter as they ran. He scanned its contents.

"I am commanded to attend their majesties … the day after tomorrow at midday … where I am to perform my telling before the whole court … for their entertainment."

The last words were said with a shake of the head.

"Perhaps they know you, after all," Yrsa said, trying to relieve the tension they both felt.

"It's real," Rald said, not hearing her.

"Time for your greatest performance."

Chapter 31

Yrsa and Rald went over their plan, but given how much they didn't know, it was more a series of options. They both knew if the queen had the power of sorcery, the unexpected was more than possible.

Darian appeared in the afternoon.

"Are you sure you know what you're doing?" he asked.

"We know the risks," Yrsa replied, "if that's what you mean."

"And you know the prince might not be able to help you?"

"I'm not naïve."

"He will if he can; we all will. But if you fail, the kingdom still needs an heir. I won't let him get himself killed if the queen is still in control."

After he left, Yrsa turned to the zeffen.

"You've heard all this," she said. "Am I being reckless?"

'We don't understand humans very well.'

'If she's so powerful, how can you defeat her?'

"That's where you come in."

'You've told us that, but you haven't told us how.'

"Amluss believed your blood would oppose her powers. If he knew how, he didn't tell me or Varluss."

"But from what I've learned over the years," Rald said, "she will have some sort of channel for her power."

'Channel?'

"An object she uses to focus it, to direct it."

"So," Yrsa said, "we need to try and identify it."

"We think you are both immune from her power."

"Or won't be seriously hurt by it," Yrsa said. "But you could still be in danger."

She waited as they absorbed the information. They'd been at most of the meetings over the last few weeks, quietly taking in what was said, unknown to Varluss and Darian. They would have been thinking about what they'd heard.

"If you wish to help, we'll be grateful," she said. "But I'm not forcing you. This is your choice."

'As far as we can see, this queen is the one responsible for our mother's death. Without her, Amluss wouldn't have hunted and killed her.'

"I suppose that's true, yes."

The zeffen looked at each other briefly; it was in these moments Yrsa wished she could hear their thoughts.

'We'll help. What can we do?'

"I'll need you when we go to the palace, and I'll explain that later. But first I'm afraid I need to fill these."

She took the two crystal phials from the table.

'What with?'

"Some of your blood."

* * *

As they set out for the palace, Yrsa and Rald had prepared as well as they could. They'd watched the guards slip out of the inn in ones and twos, armed but covered in cloaks. They didn't tell her where they were going, or what exactly they had planned, but

Darian had told her they'd be nearby if they were needed, and if it was possible to use them.

The city felt the same as the other days they'd walked around. It was their own anxiety that made them feel different. The palace was prominent on a low hill overlooking the harbour, so they headed towards it. It was a grand building, but not as elaborate as Yrsa expected. It was old and hadn't been updated as styles changed. Its symbolism was what mattered.

"Ready?" Yrsa asked Rald, as they entered the square.

"I never thought I'd end my days in a palace."

She turned to him and saw a grim face under the hood of his cloak.

"The Great Pacleidius never dies," she replied.

There was a steady stream of people coming and going and they were ignored as they climbed the steps to the huge open doors. They went unchallenged as they entered, and found themselves in a waiting area, with smaller doors at the other end. Yrsa could see the audience chamber beyond, people inside milling around and talking.

She looked for someone who might know what they needed to do. Spying a young man in livery crossing the room, she stopped him.

"Excuse me, we have an invitation. Who do we make ourselves known to?"

He inspected the letter she showed him.

"The Chamberlain," he replied. "Follow me." He led them to the next set of doors and looked around. "That's him," he said, pointing across the room. "The tall man with the gold staff."

As they headed towards the Chamberlain, nobody paid them much attention, which surprised Yrsa at first. After all, Rald had gone the full Great Pacleidius, with a rich robe and cloak Varluss had had made for him, with spiritual symbols embroidered all over it.

It would have stood out anywhere else, but as she looked around at the courtiers dressed in their finery, she realised he didn't look particularly out of place. They walked slowly, as Rald would play his role as someone wearied by his age and the weight of his gifts. They'd even used some ash to add grey to his hair. It would allow Yrsa to play the role of his assistant, free to intervene in any conversations.

The Chamberlain was talking to a large man in a rich, quilted tunic which was a size or two too small. She couldn't hear their conversation, but the man looked eager to get away. An opportunity he took when he spotted Yrsa and Rald waiting.

"My dear Chamberlain," he said. "I will leave you to those awaiting your attention."

He waddled away as fast as he could, while the Chamberlain turned to them.

"Yes?"

"Sir," Yrsa said, as humbly as she could, holding out the summons. "May I introduce the Great Pacleidius?"

"Ah," he replied, his eyes taking in the two newcomers quickly. "The mysterious future teller." He waved the letter away. "You'll be called when their majesties are ready for you."

"Yes, sir," Yrsa replied, giving a brief nod, and leading Rald away. She headed towards some tall windows on one side of the room. They were unglazed and didn't appear to have shutters. This huge space must be cold in the winter, she thought.

They looked out over the harbour and bay, exactly as Varluss had said. It was a beautiful sight, the blue sea calm on this autumn day. There were ships in the harbour, but not many, given its size. The talk of people avoiding the city was true.

There were similar windows on the opposite wall which looked out over the gardens, and she was tempted to cross to them. Phinus and Mapian had been the last to leave the inn that morning, and they'd taken their cart to the prince's palace which was on the other side of the garden. In the cart were Bodro and Pek.

Resisting the temptation, she took the opportunity to look around the room. There were only four guards. Two at the door they'd entered, and one on either side of the dais on which the thrones sat. Though they held long halberds as well as their swords, they seemed more for show than a threat.

As for the courtiers, they were a mixed group. Some in rich, fine clothes, intended to impress; others dressed well but in darker, more workmanlike shades. Some talking animatedly, others standing mute. There was no laughter, everyone seemed on their best behaviour.

A loud gong interrupted her thoughts, and the court quieted, turning to the dais. From behind a curtain to one side, the chamberlain appeared, swinging his staff theatrically, followed by the king in a chair, carried between two poles. The queen walked by his side. Yrsa's breath caught as she saw Varluss walking behind, followed by two more guards.

The king's chair was placed by the throne, and the two bearers helped him transfer from one to the other. They were some distance away, but she studied him. Varluss had told her he was in his fifty-fifth year, yet he might have been eighty. Bent, shaking, and frail, slumping into the throne as the bearers made him comfortable.

When he was seated, the queen took her place beside him. Varluss knelt in front of his father, kissed his hand, and rose. Giving a perfunctory bow to the queen, he descended the two steps and took his seat to the side of the dais.

"Ragluss the King is present," the chamberlain declared in a loud voice, and everyone in the hall gave a half-bow. He turned to the dais, Yrsa saw the queen give a formal nod, and the business of the day began. This audience was an opportunity for the great and the good to make their obeisance to the throne. A few disputes were brought for judgement, and a couple of foreign visitors were introduced.

Throughout the whole thing, the king said nothing. The queen did all the talking. She made a play of consulting her husband, but the decisions were hers, the favours were hers. Yrsa watched the woman she had come to expose.

She was an elegant figure, tall and slim, with dark hair, wound up under her crown. It was hard to judge her age, but there was a severe beauty about her. Yrsa knew the spirits were able to prolong life; she didn't doubt sorcery was able to perform a similar feat.

Varluss looked unimpressed with the whole procedure. He was sitting in his chair, legs crossed, his arms resting on the sides. Darian was standing a few paces behind him and had already spotted Yrsa and Rald.

"She's wearing a lot of jewellery," Rald said.

"A ring on nearly every finger."

"It could be any of them."

"How will we know?"

"I really-"

"The Great Pacleidius." The Chamberlain's summons echoed around the room.

Yrsa gave Rald a wink, though she was probably more nervous than him, and led him towards the dais. There were whispers and a couple of contemptuous sniggers. Several paces in front of the steps to the thrones was a line on the floor, where she stopped. Rald bowed, and Yrsa did her best to curtsey, a movement alien to her.

"So, you are the Great Pacleidius," the queen said, studying him. "We have frequently heard your name of late."

"Majesty," Rald replied. "I hope it was associated with good fortune."

"It seems good fortune follows you."

"Indeed, Majesty. But the future holds good and bad for us all. To hear one, it is necessary to hear the other."

"I am no stranger to future tellers," the queen said. "Nor to those who would pretend to possess their skills."

"There are those who would use trickery and theatre to lure the common people. But I think it would be less easy to fool you, or those good citizens present today."

"Well, Pacleidius, if your skills match your silky words, they must be great indeed."

A ripple of dutiful laughter filled the air.

"And who is this?" the queen asked.

"This, Majesty, is my assistant."

"She is learning your profession, perhaps?"

"She possesses no such skill. I grow old, and my eyes are not what they were. The girl helps me get around and supports me, and there are times when my strength fails, and she is able to speak for me."

"I see. Well, we should see your skills. Perhaps you may tell me something of my future?"

"I would be honoured, Majesty. But if you are a student of future telling, you will know it is impossible in front of so many people. Their thoughts, their future would cloud your own."

"Indeed."

Yrsa leaned in to Rald as if to whisper to him.

"What are you saying?" the queen demanded.

"Majesty," Yrsa said. "I merely suggested before conducting a private telling for you, the Great Pacleidius might demonstrate his other skills for the entertainment of your guests."

"What other skills?"

"I read people," Rald said.

"What do you mean?"

"I will show you, with your permission?"

She frowned for a moment, before waving a hand.

"Yes, yes, go on."

Rald straightened slightly, his head rising, and held his hand in front of him. Yrsa wondered if he was going a bit far.

"Balison," he said. "Is there a Balison here?" Yrsa heard some whispers from one corner. "Is there someone named Balison?"

"Yes," a voice replied hesitantly. "I'm Balison."

"An honourable name for an honourable man. A good man." Yrsa turned to see a large figure, well-dressed, looking slightly nervous. "A man who likes his food." There was a ripple of laughter, and Balison smiled, rubbing his large belly. "In fact, likes all the pleasures of life. He has a wife who shares those pleasures so much, she has given him twelve children."

"Thirteen," Balison shouted above the amusement.

"Thirteen," Rald replied. "I couldn't see one in the crowd."

More gentle laughter. Yrsa looked around, the audience was warming to this strange character before them. Even the queen seemed to be enjoying it. Only the king remained unchanged.

As Rald moved on to the next courtier Varluss had given him information about, she watched the prince's father. He didn't move, just stared straight ahead, his eyes lifeless. One hand was laid on the arm of the throne, but it was the other which caught her eye.

It was clamped around a walking cane, made of twisted wood with a top which appeared to be a small orb of crystal. She could see it shaking as his trembling ran through it. But his hand wasn't on the top, it was gripping two-thirds of the way up. That was no way to use a cane, and he hadn't walked in, anyway. Then she noticed that every so often, the queen grasped the orb, rubbing her hand over it.

Rald was still telling the courtiers about themselves, and they were enjoying it. Enough to astonish them, with enough humour to make them laugh, without risking offence. He was slowly lowering his voice as if becoming hoarse, and Yrsa took her cue.

"Majesty," she said, laying her hand on Rald's arm. "Pacleidius grows tired. But I'm sure he is happy to continue if I may be his voice."

"Yes," she replied. "I am enjoying hearing of the court's vices."

Yrsa leaned down, as if to listen to Rald, then stood tall, looking around the room.

"Is there a Paloquira here?
Yrsa tried to control her breathing as she bent by Rald again. "The walking cane," she whispered. "The cane between them."
She rose again and turned to the room.
"Paloquira," she said, "is there no Paloquira here?"

Chapter 32

The courtiers looked around, waiting for someone to claim the name, clearly unfamiliar with it.

Yrsa walked in a small circle around Rald, seeking this mystery woman in the audience.

"Paloquira, you're here somewhere. Don't be shy."

People shrugged and peered over their neighbours, anxious to identify the missing person. She completed the circle, allowing her eyes to pass over the thrones. The queen was no longer smiling, her face hard and cold, her hand gripping the top of the cane.

"There is no one of that name here," the queen said, her voice as cold as her look. "Pacleidius must have tired himself too much."

"No, Majesty," Yrsa said. "There is a Paloquira here. A woman who was expelled from Flengara for unnatural practices." Her voice grew in strength as she spoke, still circling, talking to the courtiers who were listening intently. "A woman who sought refuge in a nearby kingdom claiming to be a princess from a far-off land.

"A woman who used her sinister power to ingratiate herself with the king, who took her as his wife. A woman who continues to use that power to weaken him and make him a shadow of his former self. A woman who-"

"Enough!" The word filled the room. The courtiers seemed to shrink from it.

The queen stood, her face evidence of the struggle within her. Torn between showing her power and laughing it off. Yrsa waited, knowing the next moments could determine life or death.

The stillness was almost painful, two hundred people or more afraid even to breathe. It went on for what seemed a lifetime. Eventually, the queen's body relaxed, and an obviously false smile appeared.

"Pacleidius has a wonderful imagination," she said. "But he needs a rest."

"Pacleidius was not the source of that information, Majesty," Yrsa said, looking straight at her.

"Then who was, girl?"

"Prince Amluss."

The queen visibly blanched, as all around her, people gasped and whispered, and a thud suggested someone had fainted.

"Amluss?" the queen hissed. "Amluss was sent into exile for his treason. He's probably sitting in some alehouse somewhere, telling his false tales to anyone who will listen. Including you, by the sound of it."

"Amluss is dead."

There were more whispers, followed by silence again. Yrsa noticed Darian slip away from his position behind Varluss.

"Oh, I am sorry," the queen sneered. "A drunken brawl, perhaps."

"No. A zeffen ripped him apart."

Yrsa hardly heard the gasps, the shrieks, the renewed whispering. All she saw was the look on the queen's face. A moment of fear, then a cold appraisal of the woman in front of her, challenging her position.

"Dear girl," the queen said derisively. "They are mythical creatures. Whatever makes you believe he encountered something from the realms of fantasy?"

"I saw his wounds. And I saw the zeffen."

"Then you are living in a fantasy too. We will listen to no more of this."

Yrsa threw off her cloak, exposing the weapons at her waist. She unhooked the sword and slid it along the floor towards the dais. The queen studied it for a moment.

"So, you have Amluss's sword," she said. "It proves nothing. What happened to the zeffen?"

"It died of its wounds," Yrsa replied.

A brief flash of victory crossed the queen's face before she laughed.

"How convenient," she said, addressing the room now, aware the courtiers were wavering. "You come here with a traitor's sword and a ridiculous tale of his death. You claim he was killed by a mythical beast; better, you saw this beast yourself. Yet I see no proof."

"You would like proof, Majesty?"

"There is none, girl," she spat.

Yrsa gave two loud whistles, and shrieks erupted from the garden side of the room as Bodro and Pek leapt through the windows, and trotted towards Yrsa, standing on either side of her. The courtiers were backing away, horrified, some already fleeing towards the doors.

"You know what these are, don't you, Majesty?" Yrsa said. "Or should I call you Paloquira? Allow me to introduce Bodro and Pek. They are zeffen." A few plaintive cries echoed around the room, and at least one more heavy thud was heard. "You know they are real, and you fear them. It was their mother who killed Amluss, and you know why he was hunting her. Because your power can only be broken by one thing. Zeffen blood."

The look on Paloquira's face told Yrsa that Amluss had been right. She was staring at the zeffen, her face distorted with fear. But it didn't last long. She took a deep breath, straightened, and her expression changed as she pulled the cane from the king's hand, leaving him to slump forward.

As she slowly raised it, the doors to the audience chamber swung shut, a scream coming from an unfortunate courtier whose leg was crushed as they slammed together. The other members of the court, finding their exit blocked, frantically looked around for another escape route. Some were throwing themselves through the windows into the garden.

"Seize that girl," the queen demanded, her voice brittle but strong. "And kill those monsters."

The guards by the dais stepped forward hesitantly, clearly wishing they were somewhere else. Those standing behind moved to back up their comrades. They lowered their halberds and advanced towards Yrsa.

The zeffen moved in front of her, snarling, and Bodro launched himself at the first guard, who shrieked as this huge animal landed on him, knocking him to the ground. He raised a paw, his claws extended, and swiped it across the guard's shoulders.

"Bodro!" Yrsa called after hearing the guard's screams. "Enough!"

He heard, and the zeffen retreated and resumed their stance in front of Yrsa. But the sight of their mutilated comrade was enough to make the others falter, and they came to a stop between her and the queen, uncertain of their next move.

It was decided for them when a disturbance broke out at the back of the room, as the doors were forced open again, and Varluss's men poured in, with more jumping through the windows from the garden. A brief fight, hidden by the milling courtiers, vanquished the guards by the door.

Darian and some of his men appeared between the zeffen and the dais guards, who decided they preferred fighting men to mythical beasts. Another brief skirmish saw two or three fall to the ground before the others yielded and laid down their weapons.

The queen saw it was over, but that made her dangerous. She now had little to lose.

"So, girl," she said. "What are you going to do now?"

"You cannot kill these two. They are immune to your powers."

"Maybe, but I can destroy you." She raised the cane in her hand and without warning, Yrsa was thrown back ten paces, landing in a heap on the floor, the queen laughing. "Did you think that old fool knew what he was doing? Amluss tried to kill one for its blood and failed. These two are alive, so unless you're going to kill them for theirs, you have failed, too. For as I cannot harm them, they cannot harm me. Our power is in balance."

She walked down the steps of the dais, raising her cane again, and Yrsa was thrown back once more, hitting the floor hard, winded. She tried to sit up and saw Pek approach the queen, but it was as if an invisible barrier came from her outstretched hand, holding him back. He could not reach her. Bodro joined him, pushing against this unseen force, and getting angrier, snarling deep in his chest.

Yrsa reached into her tunic, pulling out the crystal phial, full of Pek's blood. The sight of it made Paloquira pause.

"I already have their blood," Yrsa said, trying to get her breath back. "You cannot kill me, either." She slumped to the floor again.

"Perhaps, but it won't save others."

The queen turned to Darian's guards, and one after another, they were thrown backwards, slamming into the furniture, the walls or the floor. Rald let out a loud cry and advanced on her. Yrsa saw a malicious grin on the queen's face as she lifted her cane towards him, and he flew across the room, crashing into the wall above head height, before landing on the floor.

They'd hoped the phials would protect them from the queen's power, but they hadn't thought about physical injuries incurred along the way. Rald was lying lifeless and still, but Yrsa had no time to help him.

The courtiers were fleeing, running from the room, screams filling the air. The queen turned her attention towards the king, and Varluss jumped up and stood in front of his father. Yrsa's heart sank, he stood no chance.

'*The cane,*' she thought, trying to fill her mind with the word, trying to vay to the zeffen. '*The cane.*'

As the queen focussed on the king, she failed to spot a grey blur leap towards her, and she cried out as Bodro slammed his jaws onto the cane, snatching it from her hand. As he flew through the air, he ground his teeth into the wood with all his strength.

A terrible cracking echoed around the room like thunder, and the cane emitted a sound that pierced the air, accompanied by a cry from deep within the zeffen's chest. He landed in a heap, the cane spilling from his mouth. He was horribly still.

Paloquira laughed; a menacing, cackling laugh.

"Was that your best?" she sneered at Yrsa. "It seems your faith in these brutes was misplaced."

Yrsa looked over to the prostrate Bodro and saw blood seeping onto the floor from his mouth. Pek was standing by him, guarding his brother, and snarling at the queen.

Paloquira went to retrieve her cane, but several paces from it, she stopped abruptly and let out the shrillest cry Yrsa had ever heard. The cane was smoking; whisps rising delicately, increasing all the time as the blood from Bodro's wounded mouth penetrated the surface.

Tiny flames erupted from it, growing, engulfing the shaft, and as the orb fell from its mount to the floor, it shattered, filling the room with a flash of brilliant light. All that was left were shards of crystal and a line of ash on the floor.

Paloquira fell to her knees, head in hands, wailing. Her power was now unchanneled. Useless. Gone.

Before Yrsa knew it, Pek flew at the kneeling figure.

"Pek!" Yrsa tried to shout. "No!"
It was too late. He tore the queen's throat out.

Silence filled the room, all present stunned by what had happened, as Pek returned to his lifeless brother. Yrsa crawled over to them. Bodro was still alive.

'Will he live?'

"I don't know, Pek. I don't know."

She remembered Rald and looked over to see his chest moving, so he was at least alive. Phinus and Mapian were kneeling by him. A few guards were still on the floor, being helped by their unharmed comrades. Varluss appeared by Bodro's prone form.

"Is he …"

"He's alive. Can I borrow a couple of your men?"

"Help her," he told two guards. "I must get my father away from here."

"Find something to carry him on," she said to the men, who disappeared and returned with what looked like the top of a table. Together, they rolled Bodro onto it as Darian arrived.

"Follow me," he said, and they tried to lift Bodro, but he was too heavy. Darian called another two guards, and the four of them lifted him and followed their captain. Yrsa saw Phinus and Mapian carrying Rald and fell in behind them.

They went through the garden and into the prince's residence. Darian directed Yrsa into one room, and Rald another. She found herself in a bare bedroom, but the bed was all she was interested in, and the guards slid Bodro onto it from the tabletop. He was still unconscious.

"I've sent for someone to look after Rald," Darian said from the doorway. "I think he was just knocked out; he'll live. What do you need?"

"Is there a herbalist nearby?"

"I've no idea. I'll find out."

As he left, she cursed herself for not bringing her supplies from Demburan. She knew what drugs she needed, but their names seemed to change in almost every city.

Pek was sitting on the floor by his brother's head, as Yrsa checked Bodro over. His breathing was shallow but regular, and he had no other obvious injuries. But his mouth was a mess. His lip was torn open, he'd lost several teeth, the inside of his mouth was blistered and burnt, and she suspected his jaw was broken.

"Excuse me, lady?" A young woman stood at the door, nervously eyeing Pek. "You need a herbalist?"

"Is there one near?"

"Yes. My family own it."

Yrsa gave a silent thanks to the spirits.

"What's your name?"

"Farona, lady."

"I'm no lady. Call me Yrsa. I need several things, but I'm not sure if they have the same names here." They spent a few moments identifying what she needed, finally understanding each other. "And can you find me a steel needle and some fine gut?"

While Farona was gone, she went to Rald's room. Darian was right; he was still unconscious as well or in a very deep sleep. But his breathing was normal, his heartbeat regular, and a guard was watching over him. She instructed the man to call her if Rald came around and returned to Bodro.

She asked for hot water and bathed his mouth and jaw, thankful that removing the blood revealed no new injuries.

'Why is he still asleep?'

"I hope it's the shock, Pek."

'Could it be that woman's power?'

"I hope not."

They sat quietly by Bodro, Yrsa stroking his shoulder.

'Was I wrong to kill her?'

"Yes, Pek," she replied, ruffling his head. "But I understand why you did, and I won't let anyone blame you for it."

'What would have happened to her?'

"She would have faced judgement from the king or a court. But I suspect you've saved them from some tough decisions."

'Then why was it wrong?'

"You know how people fear your name. When they hear you killed someone, it might increase that fear."

He thought for a while.

'I understand. I am sorry.'

"There's no need. She deserved it."

'I still don't understand humans. You say it was wrong, but also that she deserved it.'

"I'm afraid we are not consistent in our thinking. But it's best not to kill anyone else for the moment."

They both turned to Bodro when he coughed deep in his chest, his body spasming a few times. Yrsa feared the worst, but it settled, and his eyes opened a little.

"Bodro?"

Nothing came. She looked at Pek.

'He is in pain.'

"I'm waiting for something I can give him to help."

When Farona returned, she hovered near the door with a basket.

"Will you help me?" Yrsa asked.

"If I can," the girl replied nervously.

"Are you afraid of them?"

"I heard they're zeffen."

"They are."

"And they killed someone," she said, looking at Pek. Word gets around quickly, Yrsa thought.

"Pek did," she replied, "but he was defending his brother here."

"They say it was the queen."

"It was."

The girl thought for a moment, then came to the bed, watching Pek nervously all the time.

"What can I do?" she asked.

Together, they mixed something for the pain, Yrsa gently sliding it down Bodro's throat. Then a salve which she applied to the burns in his mouth.

"That should ease the pain," she whispered to him. "Farona, I need you to hold his head."

The girl hesitantly grasped Bodro's skull.

"This will hurt," Yrsa told him. "I need to stitch your lip together."

'Do it,' came back faintly.

As Yrsa set to work with the needle, Farona began to relax.

"Their fur is so soft," she said.

"They're big softies, really."

It took eleven stitches, and Bodro only flinched once.

"Sorry," Yrsa muttered.

"It's funny, isn't it?" Farona said. "How we talk to animals as if they understand us."

Yrsa and Pek shared a knowing look.

When Yrsa paid Farona for the things she'd brought, the girl asked if they needed anything else.

"Can you find some water for Pek? And something for him to eat?"

"What does he eat?" Farona replied, her face betraying a little of her earlier fear.

"Any meat, raw or cooked."

"I'll see what I can find."

She returned with a jug of water, and a bowl of meat scraps. Pek drank and ate a little, but he had no appetite.

"I've done all I can for now," Yrsa said to him after Farona left. "All we can do is wait. You stay with him. I'm going to see how Rald is, I'll only be in the next room."

Chapter 33

Yrsa tapped on Rald's door and went in; she was unlikely to find him in a compromising position on this occasion. So she was surprised to find the little blond from Demburan sitting on a stool next to the bed. The girl rose quickly and gave a flustered curtsey.
"What are you doing here?" Yrsa asked.
"Darian thought I might like to come."
Yrsa hid her smile at the girl's blushes.
"Has he been awake?" she asked.
"Yes, sort of. He seemed ... a bit odd."
"He was knocked out; it can do funny things to you."
The blood had been washed from his head, revealing a raw patch of skin where the hair had been ripped out. Although it looked horrible, it would heal if kept clean. But she worried about the impact. He'd hit the wall hard, and if his head had taken the full force, it may have driven out his wits.
"Did you clean him up?" she asked.
"Yes, lady. Did I do wrong?"
"No. And I'm Yrsa. What's your name?"
"Chlea."

"Well, Chlea. We need to check him for other injuries. Can you help me?"

Between them, they stripped Rald, and Yrsa was relieved when she found broken skin on his shoulder. The area around it was already showing signs of bruising. At least that may have taken the brunt of the impact rather than his head.

"Keep him as comfortable as possible. I don't want to do anything until he wakes. Will you come and find me when he does?"

"Yes, lady. Sorry, Yrsa."

She returned to her room, to find the two zeffen on the bed. Bodro was where she'd left him, but Pek was curled behind him, his front leg laid protectively over his brother. They were both asleep, so Yrsa quietly went to the chair and joined them.

She was amazed when the next morning, Bodro was wide awake, wanting to get up. But she insisted he rested, other than an assisted walk to the garden for relief. He was still in pain, but her remedies kept him comfortable. He was also hungry, and that proved more of a problem. She still thought he'd broken his jaw, but it was so swollen she couldn't be sure.

Playing mother again, she chewed some meat, handing it to him as a soft mess. It had been easy when they were small, but now he needed a lot of food, and it took a long time.

Rald was recovering as well. When Chlea fetched her, Yrsa found him awake, and he seemed sane enough. But he had a terrible headache, and every time he tried to get up, his balance went, and he fell over.

"Chlea," Yrsa said. "He must stay in bed and rest. You have my permission to tie him down if he tries to get up."

"Is this how Luna taught you to treat your patients?" Rald asked.

"No. This is all my own style."

"Yrsa," he said more quietly. "What happened?"

Yrsa and the Zeffen Hunter

She sat by his side and told him everything that occurred after he was thrown across the room. Chlea listened intently.

"You did it," he said when she finished.

"Bodro and Pek did it. It wasn't quite how we planned."

"Come on, we hadn't planned that far at all. Is Bodro all right?"

"He's not good, but a bit better this morning. As long as he has no injury I've not found, I think he'll live." She rose and made her way to the door. "By the way," she added, turning back. "When I said you must stay in bed, that means alone. No vigorous activity."

Rald laughed, and Chlea went a deep red.

* * *

Yrsa had only seen Varluss briefly since the events in the audience chamber. The queen had been running things for years, and with her gone, he had to take over, at least temporarily. One evening, he appeared at her door.

"How is he?" he asked of Bodro.

"Getting better every day, thank you. I'm amazed at how well he's doing. How's your father?"

The prince slumped in a chair.

"He's no different," he replied. "I thought with that woman gone, he'd get better."

"So did I."

"Is there nothing we can do?"

"Let's talk to Rald."

They walked to his room, and Yrsa knocked. Chlea opened the door, and seeing the prince, did a deep curtsey.

"Sire," Rald said. "Forgive me for not getting up, but when I do, I either vomit or fall over."

The prince asked after his health, smiled when he was told Chlea was caring for his every need, thanked her, and asked if she would leave them for a private conversation.

"I don't know what to do," the prince said after explaining the situation. "His healers are baffled, but I don't trust them anyway. If the king cannot be cured, I will need to formalise my position."

"What happened to the queen's advisers?" Yrsa asked.

"Manitrios and Tannaq have been seized and locked up, but Garameen has disappeared. A few of their cronies have been dismissed and I've replaced them with people I can trust."

"And the palace guard?"

"They don't seem to be a threat. Darian's going through them, and we'll have to move or dismiss the captain and one or two sergeants, but the men themselves seem happy to support whoever pays them."

"Like soldiers everywhere," Rald said, laughing until he remembered laughing hurt.

"Rald," Yrsa said. "Why didn't the queen's death release the king from her power?"

"Perhaps his body and mind have been dulled for so long they will not recover."

After the prince left, Yrsa returned to her room. Bodro was up and about, even managing to eat for himself if someone cut the meat into tiny pieces. And this evening, Farona was sitting by the bed, feeding him while Pek lay at her side. She'd overcome her fears and become a favourite of theirs.

"How do you find yourself working in the prince's residence?" Yrsa asked. "You didn't want to work in your family's business?"

"I did," Farona said bitterly. "But it didn't work out. My father just wanted me to fetch and carry."

"And you didn't want to do that."

"I wanted to learn his skills, but he wouldn't teach me. You're a healer, how did you learn?"

"I'm no healer," Yrsa replied. "But I spent a few moons assisting one, so I've learnt some of the simpler treatments."

"I wish I knew even that much," Farona said.

Later that evening, Varluss visited Yrsa and Rald again. They were official visits, a prince at work, and he was in serious mood. Three of his guards had died in the showdown with the queen, along with seven of her men, and it had been the day of their funerals. And the king had not recovered, so he was having to assume many of his father's duties.

After Varluss left, Yrsa considered the situation. Why had the queen's power evaporated, save for her effect on the king? What had they missed? When she had almost fallen asleep, it hit her. She jumped up, opened the door, and bumped straight into Chlea.

"Sorry, Yrsa," the girl said. "But Rald asks if you will visit him."

He was sitting up in bed, grinning inanely.

"I've been thinking …" he said.

"The king?" she replied.

"Zeffen blood," they said together.

* * *

Varluss and Darian led them into the palace, Rald leaning on Yrsa, as his balance still wasn't good. They'd sent the king's healers away and told his personal staff to leave. In his room, the king was in bed, propped up against a pile of cushions. His expression was the same as it had been on the throne.

"Will it work?" Varluss asked.

"We don't know," Yrsa said. "But the blood protected Rald and me from the worst of Paloquira's power, and it destroyed the cane. It should have the power to release the king."

"What do we do with it?" Darian asked.

"We've been thinking about that," Rald said. "The king must drink it."

The prince's expression was everything Yrsa had expected.

"Drink it?" he said, his voice filled with horror.

"Yes," she replied. "Unless you can think of another way to get it into his body."

He shared a look with Darian, who gave his familiar shrug.

"Presumably your father can drink?" she asked.

"If someone holds it for him."

She went over to the table by the bed, picked up a fine glass, and emptied the contents. Taking the crystal phial from around her neck, she opened the top and poured out the blood it held.

"Will that be enough?" she asked Rald.

"Try two for luck," he replied, handing his over.

She offered the glass to Varluss, who visibly withdrew from it. Then to Darian, who stared at it blankly.

"Call yourselves men," she said dismissively, and went over to the bed, sitting by the king's side.

"Majesty," she said quietly. "Time for a drink."

She held the glass to his lips, which he opened a little. Tipping it, she let a small amount enter his mouth before removing the glass. She watched until she saw him swallow, and repeated the process until the glass was empty. It was painfully slow.

There was no instant response, no smoke or fire, as with the cane. Yrsa's hopes waned. Perhaps they'd thought too literally. Then she noticed a spasm in the king's chest. And another. More followed, weak at first, but getting stronger.

"A bowl," she shouted. "Quickly."

Someone passed her a comfort bucket, and she placed it just in time as the king began to vomit. And vomit, and vomit. The bucket filled as his body was racked with involuntary contractions. Blood, yellow bile, green bile, and the Gods knew what else. The stench was overpowering.

Eventually, the king slowed, his body having emptied itself. Varluss was standing at the end of the bed, his look a mixture of disgust, horror, and hope. Darian was standing by the window, trying to avoid the smell. Rald was watching with fascination from a chair he'd managed to find.

Finally, the king slumped down, and Yrsa froze until she saw him breathing normally. She removed the bucket, placing it on the floor.

"Water," she said, and the prince filled a glass and handed it to her. She put it to the king's lips, and he surprised them by raising a trembling arm and taking it from her, before emptying it, nearly starting the retching again.

Yrsa got up and moved away, motioning to the prince, who took her place. He took his father's hand and the king turned slowly towards him, blinking. He studied the man sitting on his bed, seemingly wracking his brain to identify him.

"Varluss?" he whispered eventually. "I've had some terrible dreams."

"You're safe, Father."

"That's good. Where is the queen? And where is my brother?"

* * *

"He remembers little of recent years," Varluss said. "We're keeping him isolated at the moment, with Darian controlling access, and telling him things a bit at a time."

Yrsa hadn't seen the prince for three days. He'd been constantly at his father's side, though he'd sent updates through Darian.

"How is he?" she asked.

"Weak, but he can shuffle around and he's talking normally. He wants to meet you."

"Is that wise?"

"I need you to tell him of Amluss's demise. It will help him believe."

The next day, Yrsa went to meet the king. She saw the difference at once. He was sitting upright in a richly embroidered cross chair, Darian standing discreetly in the corner.

"Majesty," she said, bowing her head.

"Come closer," he replied. "My eyes are still cloudy." He studied her for a moment. "I gather I owe my recovery to you, young lady."

"I have played only a small part, Sire."

"Then my son lies?"

"No, Majesty, I meant-"

He chuckled, and she saw where his son had acquired his good humour.

"Now," he said. "I want to hear your story. I want to hear of my poor, dear brother, and I want to hear of these beasts you have tamed. Sit."

Varluss brought a stool, she collected herself and told him everything.

The king listened intently to the whole story, visibly moved at the fate of Amluss.

"They will tell tales of your efforts," he said at the end.

"I am too young to become a legend, Sire. I'm simply happy you are recovered."

"Not yet," he replied. "But hearing how I have been these last years, it appears I am more like my old self." He took a drink, his throat still adjusting to speaking again. "Now, I wish to meet these creatures who have given their blood to save me and my kingdom."

Yrsa rose and went to the door. Bodro and Pek were lying outside.

"Come in," she said quietly, "and meet the king."

They walked forward, stopping before him.

"By the Gods," he said. "They are magnificent animals."

Lie down,' Yrsa thought. To her delight, they dropped. The king reached out and gave Pek's head a stroke, then Bodro's.

"I wish I could make you understand how grateful I am," he told them. "And how sad that my foolishness in falling for that woman led my brother to kill your mother. If I could take it all back, I would."

"They understand, Sire," Yrsa replied.

"And you, Yrsa. How can I thank you?"

"I seek no reward, Majesty."

"And yet you wear two of my brother's weapons at your waist."

"I am sorry," she replied. She'd given no thought to the daggers which she'd taken to wearing and went to unclip them from her belt.

"I did not mean that," he said. "I know Amluss, and he would have been more grateful than you know for staying with him to the end. I believe he also bequeathed you this." Darian passed him Amluss's sword. "It would be a shame to break up such an illustrious set," he said, handing it to her. For once, Yrsa was surprised into silence.

"Thank you, Majesty," was all she managed after a few moments.

"Do you know the story of those weapons?"

"No, Sire."

"Varluss will tell you sometime. Now, we need to consider the future."

"The future?"

"I am a king, and kings need to make difficult decisions." Yrsa was puzzled. What was he saying? "Your actions have given me my life back, given my people their king back, and for that, I will be eternally grateful. But they have also caused consternation and bewilderment, particularly in this city.

"No doubt, rumours have already spread across the land. I need to bring normality and stability back again." Yrsa felt her heart sink. "I ask you to leave Caropa. At least for a time. It may seem harsh and ungrateful, but that is the burden of kingship."

"You're quiet," Darian said, as they walked back to the prince's residence, Bodro and Pek at their side. They'd left Varluss with his father.

"Just working out what I need to do," Yrsa replied. "I'll have to travel back to Demburan to pick up my horses and baggage before I move on."

"His Majesty didn't ask that. All he asked was you leave Caropa, not Caropatia."

"But …"

"Return to Demburan. Varluss will join you when he can."

Chapter 34

The small convoy set out for Demburan. Rald was in a cart with Chlea to look after him. He could walk well but was still getting headaches, and his balance hadn't fully recovered. Another cart had supplies, as well as a place where Bodro could rest.

His recovery had amazed Yrsa. He had broken his jaw, but it didn't seem to bother him too much, and she'd made a discovery. Zeffen regrew their teeth. Those he'd lost were already being replaced, little tips coming through his gums. But he'd not eaten properly for some time, and his energy wasn't back to normal.

They were accompanied by Phinus and Mapian and several of their comrades. The journey wasn't rushed. There was no hurry, and there were stopping places arranged for each night. By the time they reached Demburan, events in Caropa seemed a long way away. When they arrived, Phinus led them to their old room.

"The prince thought you and Chlea might use these quarters," he said to Rald, who gave a bow.

"What about me?" Yrsa asked.

"He thought you might make use of his rooms," he replied, trying not to smile as he left them. Rald felt no such restraint, laughing until his head hurt.

"I'll leave you two," she said. "But remember, be careful of vigorous activity, your head isn't right."

She managed to close the door before the thrown beaker reached her and it clattered harmlessly against the wood.

Once she'd taken her baggage to the prince's chambers, she headed down the spiral staircase, keen to see her horses. When she arrived at the little stable, it was empty.

"Where are my horses?" she asked the guard by the gate who stared back blankly. "The horses that were here?"

"Oh, I think they were taken to the prince's stable."

"Where is that?"

"I'm not at liberty to say."

Running up the stairs, she headed to the main level and looked for someone she knew. She spotted Mapian.

"Where are the prince's stables?" she asked him. "They've taken my horses there."

"Right-hand side of the courtyard, middle gate."

She hurried down, suddenly anxious. Her horses had been safe where they were, hidden. But as she walked, she relaxed, accepting it made sense to move them somewhere larger. The need for concealment was over.

Through the gate, she found a hive of activity. Stable blocks on three sides of a square, beautifully constructed, and as clean as the citadel. All around were Burans, being groomed, walked, and trained.

The fourth side opened out onto fenced paddocks, with open pasture beyond, running along the base of the cliff. Clearly, the city wasn't allowed to encroach on this space.

"Can I help you?" a voice asked, and she turned to find one of the guards standing by her.

"I'm looking for my horses. A black Buran, a scarred packhorse and a large pony."

"The huge mare? She's yours?"

"Yes." For now, she thought.

"Come this way."

He led her to the end of one of the blocks and through the door. There were two black Burans in adjoining stalls, along with an empty space. Somehow, she knew that was Semlac's home and this must be the prince's personal stable. Beyond that, three stalls had been opened into one. It was empty, the doors leading out were open.

"They'll be outside," the man said.

She walked across the stall, and out through the open doors. In front of her was a fenced grazing area, and there were Tennell, Lucky and Brimble. She stood watching them for a few moments and was surprised by her tears.

"Hello," she said softly.

All three turned, saw her, and trotted over, whinnying. It took some time for all the greetings to be completed, the hugs to be given and the news to be relayed. She spent the evening grooming them, checking them over, spending time with them, and realised how much she'd missed all three of them.

The next day, she went back to give Tennell some exercise.

"Have they been riding you?" she asked.

'No.'

"Fancy a run out?"

'Yes, please.'

Once she'd kitted the mare out, she led her from the stable and mounted. Several men were watching her.

"Excuse me," she said. "Is there anywhere I can give her a good run?"

"There's an open area at the far end," one replied.

As they passed the paddocks, she took in the horses grazing, and those being exercised and trained. Almost everyone stopped to watch her.

When she reached the end of the fencing, she came to a huge open meadow. Her face broke into a grin, she tapped Tennell on and into a trot. Then a canter, followed by a gallop, giving her her head for a while, thrilling at the power under her.

Tennell was in her element, and they began to play, Yrsa tapping from time to time and the mare responding instantly. Turning, changing speed, weaving around invisible obstacles.

As she pulled her mount up for a rest, she looked over to the stables and was surprised to see a crowd of people watching. She wasn't sure she liked being the centre of attention, she'd had enough of that in Caropa. But she couldn't stay out in the meadow all day, so headed back.

"Do you want a run on your own?"

'Yes, please.'

When she was a few paces from the crowd, she saw they were all smiling and felt a sense of pride. But it waned slightly when she realised it was Tennell with the skills, not her. She dismounted and unstrapped the saddle.

"Go."

Tennell gave a little whinny, turned, and trotted off.

"Did you train her?" one of the men asked.

"I can't take that credit. Amluss did."

"Amluss? The king's brother? Then is that Tennell?"

"It is."

"I told you it was," he said, slapping another on the back. "She's some horse."

And she was proving it, thundering around the meadow, bringing gasps and laughter from the group. Then causing some apprehension when she galloped towards them at full speed, coming to a rapid halt a pace or two in front of Yrsa.

'*Show off,*' she vayed, as she led the mare through her new admirers.

* * *

"Have you decided when you're going?" Yrsa asked Rald. They were walking around the courtyard of the citadel. His head had almost healed, and the headaches were fewer and less severe, but his balance was still troubling him at times.

"I want to leave before winter settles here," he replied. "I gather this city can be snowed in for weeks."

"I've heard the same."

"What are you going to do?"

"You haven't answered my question," she said.

"I might travel to Flengara."

"Future telling?"

"I wonder if that particular part of my life might be over."

"What would you do?"

"I'm not sure, but we could find something."

She stopped and turned to him.

"We?"

He smiled sheepishly.

"Chlea is going to ask the prince if she can leave with me."

"What's it got to do with him?"

"The prince's household took her in when she was six. She feels she needs his agreement. What about you?"

"I feel it's time to move on as well."

"What are you going to do?"

"Travel, see other lands." She stopped walking. "Oh, Rald. That sounds so childish, doesn't it? I don't know what I'm doing. More has happened since I left home than I could ever have imagined. I could become a healer, but I don't think that's my destiny. And what about the spirits? They picked me, but what for?"

"They don't have a reason. They aren't going to choose your life for you. That's for you to decide."

* * *

The prince and the rest of his household returned three weeks later, during a light snowstorm. There had been several. Few had settled, but winter was making itself felt. He held a council session to tell them of events in Caropa and then sent for Yrsa and Rald. As usual, Bodro and Pek tagged along.

"While I am undertaking official business," Varluss said, "I will deal with the two of you."

Yrsa and Rald looked at each other, surprised by his formal tone.

"My father, the king, wishes me to formally thank both of you for everything you have done. Money alone cannot make up for your wounds and experiences, but he hopes these gifts will be welcome." He placed two leather purses on the table and Yrsa and Rald offered surprised thanks.

"As for our four-legged friends," the prince continued, "he cannot think coin will be of much use. So he has sent them these." He laid two intricate collars on the table. "Somehow, I think they may not take to them as permanent adornments, but I hope they may understand what they signify."

Yrsa had thought about collars before, if only to show people they were not wild animals. But she hadn't yet discussed it with the brothers.

"Sire," Rald said. "If you are still discussing business, I have something to ask."

"Yes?"

"Will you excuse me? I'll be back as soon as I can."

He turned and hurried from the room. The prince gave Yrsa a puzzled look, before turning to Darian. Both were smiling.

"What have I missed?" he asked.

"I think it better if Rald tells you himself," Darian said.

Yrsa picked up one of the collars and turned to Bodro. "This is for your bravery," she said and gently laid it around his neck, securing the buckle, and twisting it until it seemed comfortable. "And yours," as she fastened Pek's. "Say thank you."

The prince frowned again as they went around and licked his face until he started laughing.

"Sometimes I could swear they understand what you say to them," he said.

Rald reappeared with Chlea, who was as flustered as Yrsa had expected.

"Sire," Rald said, standing straight. "I intend to leave your city shortly, now I have recovered. Chlea and I have formed a friendship ..." Darian stifled a laugh. "And we wish to ask if she can accompany me."

"Why ask me?" the prince replied, though with a smile. "Chlea is free to make her own choices."

"Sire," Chlea said hesitantly. "I came into your household as an orphan and everything I have I owe to you. I thought it right to seek your permission."

He stood and came around the table.

"You do not need my permission, but if you wish to accompany Rald on his travels, you have my blessing."

He kissed her forehead, and she gave a blushing curtsey. Rald took his purse from the table, took Chlea's hand and they left the room.

"Come on boys," Yrsa said, collecting her purse and heading for the door.

"Yrsa," the prince said. "I would like to see you when I've completed business here."

"As I'm sleeping in your bed, I think that's quite likely."

She could still hear Darian laughing halfway down the corridor.

It wasn't long before Varluss was free, and Yrsa was waiting for him in his bed. The hours which followed were ones of lust, passion, forcefulness, and tenderness. They'd not been alone together since she'd left Demburan, and they made up for it. Little was said, their bodies doing the talking until they were both exhausted and sated. They fell asleep in each other's arms.

* * *

They said goodbye to Rald and Chlea. Varluss had given them a small cart and a horse to pull it and loaded it with supplies. He and Darian wished them both well and returned to the citadel. Yrsa gave Chlea a hug.

"Look after him," she said. "But don't let him boss you around."

"Don't worry," Chlea replied. "I know how to deal with him."

She turned to Rald, and they embraced.

"Thank you," she whispered. "Thank you for everything."

"I didn't do much," he replied. "Just let you work things out for yourself."

"Perhaps, but I couldn't have done it alone."

He pulled away, hands still on her shoulders, and his one good eye focused on her.

"One last piece of advice," he said. "Be careful who you tell about your gifts from the spirits. Better to keep it to yourself."

Chlea mounted the cart, and Rald led the horse out of the courtyard. They waved one last time, and Yrsa stood, wondering if they'd ever meet again.

* * *

Yrsa got out of bed and went to the window. Snow was falling; it was time to decide. There was a knock at the door, and she turned to Varluss who waved his hand, reminding her of her nakedness.

"Come in," she called, and the prince's valet entered, stopping when he saw her. "Don't mind me," she said. He brought in some hot water and left it on the side, laid out some clothes for his master, going about his duties as if she wasn't there.

"That wasn't fair on the poor lad," Varluss said when he'd gone.

"He's never seen a naked woman in this room before?"

"One or two, perhaps," he replied, shrugging. "Then it's not the actions of a lady."

"I never claimed to be a lady."

"You could be. You might marry a prince."

"And what would your father say?" she replied, turning to face him.

"I don't think he's in a position to judge anyone's choice of wife."

She turned again to the view from the window.

"You know my answer," she said. "Besides, you must marry someone who can provide you with an heir."

"So, you're leaving?"

"I didn't say that." An idea had come to her a few days before. "I'm offering you a deal. I'll stay until spring, and over the winter you can teach me to use a sword and to read."

"It seems to me," he said with an amused frown, "you're getting more out of that arrangement than I am."

"If you don't think I'm worth it, I could always ask Darian."

"He is a better swordsman than me."

"Can he read?" Varluss nodded. "Sounds tempting. Is he a better lover, as well?"

"That, I don't know. You'd have to ask his wife."

"Oh, he's married? Then it seems I'll have to make do with you."

"I can't win, can I?"

"That's why you want me, but I'll let you win sometimes. Not right now, though," she said, climbing onto the bed. "I have you right where I want you. Be a good boy and stay there."

* * * * * * * * *

Yrsa's adventures continue in **'Yrsa and the Wakers'**.

Acknowledgements & Notes

Many people have helped me bring this story to the page. Some have been with me from the beginning, while others have come aboard for my foray into fantasy.

First of all, I'd like to thank my writing partner, Keldi Hale, who has the misfortune of being the first person to read nearly all my work. Over the years, she has provided me with much-needed advice, support and encouragement.

Then there are those who have read the manuscript at various stages of its development. Davida de la Harpe, Martha Chargot, and Susan Collins provided many valuable and insightful thoughts. Samantha, Chloe, Keira and Bethany did the same for early versions when the story wasn't fully formed.

All have helped immeasurably to improve each new version of the story, and I will be eternally grateful to all of them. Its final state is, of course, wholly my responsibility.

And finally, a huge thank you to Melissa Nash who created the wonderful map of Yrsa's world from a terrible sketch of mine and a few notes. Her work is simply stunning.

If you've enjoyed this book, please think about leaving a review, either on the marketplace where you bought it or on one of the book review sites, such as Goodreads. Reviews are so helpful for other readers (and authors, as well!).

Yrsa still has much to discover about herself and her world, and I hope you will join her on her future adventures.

You can keep in touch with all my writing by visiting my website where you can also subscribe to my newsletter, or connect with me on social media.

Website: www.alexjmarkson.com
Twitter: @alexjmarkson
Facebook: Alex J Markson
Goodreads: Alex J Markson

Alex J Markson
August 2023

Printed in Great Britain
by Amazon